JUST ONE DRINK . . .

He looked at her with fear in his eyes. "Will it be very painful?" he asked.

She smiled and shook her head. "No. I'm going to use some psychic commands to make you relax."

He gave a weak grin. "Like mental Xanax?"

"Why don't you take off your shirt and lie on the bed?" she said.

He lay back and closed his eyes. She stood next to the bed and concentrated, commanding him to relax and feel no fear.

His face became soft and peaceful, and he smiled slightly. "Um, this is nice," he mumbled. "Kinda like the gas the dentist gives."

She eased down on the bed next to him and turned his face away slightly so she could get to his neck. She felt herself begin to change as she lowered her face and gently bared her growing fangs.

When she bit into the skin over his jugular vein, he moaned softly and stiffened slightly, then he went limp as her mental commands caused him to relax once again.

As his warm, salty blood flowed into her mouth, she drank, feeling her face coarsen and begin to coalesce into her Vampyre persona.

Within minutes, her skin began to feel hot, then it burned and itched under the influence of the hormones that the feeding released into her bloodstream. Her breasts swelled and her nipples became hard. Her arms went around his shoulders and she pulled his neck tighter against her mouth. She felt him become hard as he pushed his pelvis against hers, his eyes blank and staring as he panted in desire. . . .

BOOK YOUR PLACE ON OUR WEBSITE AND MAKE THE READING CONNECTION!

We've created a customized website just for our very special readers, where you can get the inside scoop on everything that's going on with Zebra, Pinnacle and Kensington books.

When you come online, you'll have the exciting opportunity to:

- View covers of upcoming books
- Read sample chapters
- Learn about our future publishing schedule (listed by publication month *and author*)
- Find out when your favorite authors will be visiting a city near you
- Search for and order backlist books from our online catalog
- Check out author bios and background information
- Send e-mail to your favorite authors
- Meet the Kensington staff online
- Join us in weekly chats with authors, readers and other guests
- Get writing guidelines
- AND MUCH MORE!

**Visit our website at
http://www.kensingtonbooks.com**

DARK BLOOD

James M. Thompson

PINNACLE BOOKS
Kensington Publishing Corp.
http://www.kensingtonbooks.com

This book is dedicated to Terri and the "boys"—
Brock, Brent, Travis, Donovan, Darren, and Hunter.
They make it all worthwhile.

One

The body drifted deeper into the inky black waters of the Houston Ship Channel, arms and legs moving slowly in the sluggish current as if in a macabre underwater dance of death. Lights from searching ships passed close but never touched it as the grotesque shape settled slowly into the foul chemical-tainted mud of the channel's floor.

The skin and tissues on the edges of the nearly severed neck, pushed together by the body's position on the channel floor, slowly began to knit together. Microscopic cells, under the direction of the DNA-controlling plasmids coursing through the blood, began to migrate and reattach themselves while capillaries and blood vessels reformed and established new blood paths to supply the new tissue with life-giving sustenance.

As blood flowed into the brain, which had shut down under the onslaught of dozens of 9mm bullets, neural cells began to fire and discharge. Murky thoughts were generated, bringing to consciousness memories of the preceding few hours.

Elijah Pike, born in the early 1800s, began to wake. Flashes of barely remembered scenes flickered into being, like images from an old kinescope film being played back.

Pike dimly remembered a group of men, dressed in black SWAT-team uniforms, daring to invade his lair in the dead of night, drifting through the full moon's shadows like ghosts as they boarded his ship.

His body jerked under the water at the recalled fury of this invasion, and his teeth gritted and gnashed at images of him slashing the interlopers with his claws and fangs, killing them and flinging their lifeless bodies aside like empty husks.

Dank water caressed his bloodless lips; they curled in a grin of satisfaction at the memory of the black man who was their leader and how his face contorted in agony and surprise when Pike ran him through with his *katana*, the Japanese long sword he'd had for over a hundred years.

Pike remembered standing over the last of the invaders, his blade pointed down at the man's heart, when he heard the voice of a friend scream, "No-o-o!"

As he slowly drifted toward the surface of the frigid water, Pike recalled hesitating and glancing at his friend and colleague, Matt Carter, who was walking through the rain toward him, arms outstretched.

"Roger, how much is your life worth?" Matt had shouted. "Just how much carnage can you endure just to go on living?"

Pike had lowered his sword and turned to lean on the rail of his ship, wondering the same thing. *How much would I give to let go, let them kill me, and perhaps become human again, even if only in death?* he'd thought.

The last thing he remembered was the sound of an automatic weapon as streams of bullets stitched across his back and neck, almost severing his head from his body before he tumbled over the rail and into the ship channel.

Pike came fully awake in the water, his body screaming for oxygen, his arms flailing and his legs kicking to drive him upward. As his face broke the surface, he gasped and grabbed a stanchion on the pier. Unmindful of the razor-sharp barnacles piercing his arms, he hung there in the water, rain still coursing down from darkened skies as he let his body finish its healing.

He floated, swaying on the current, immobile for four hours until the process was complete. The rain was lessening and the ships that had been searching for his body had long since given up and gone back to shore.

Elijah Pike, now fully alive, grabbed hold of the rotting, barnacle-encrusted timbers on the wharf and laboriously climbed to the top of the dock. The creature recalled that he was known as Roger Niemann, doctor of medicine, and was a member of the Vampyre race. He rolled onto his back on the damp concrete, coughed and choked as he inhaled dank, sulfurous air drifting inland from over the channel, and wondered not for the first time in his two hundred years if he should be glad to still be alive.

Niemann slowly looked around, checking to see if the area was clear of the numerous policemen who'd tried to kill him scant hours before.

The area seemed completely deserted, so, with a grunt of exertion and pain, Niemann rolled over onto his hands and knees, his head hanging down, still too fatigued from his ordeal to get to his feet.

He gingerly felt the still-ragged edges of his neck wound, his mind filled once again with wonder at the recuperative abilities of his Vampyre body.

After he caught his breath, still unable to stand, he scrabbled on hands and knees across the wharf until he was in the shadows of the warehouses across the street.

Keeping his back to the wall, ever watchful for guards or policemen who might have remained on the scene, he moved toward his own warehouse fifty yards away.

As he inched his way through the darkness, he glanced back across the street. His converted freighter, the *Night Runner,* was still moored there, seemingly deserted, festooned with yellow crime-scene tape as if decorated for some obscene celebration.

When he got to the door of his warehouse, he found it heavily bolted and chained, with more of the yellow tape stretched across it. Thankfully, the police must have thought him dead, for there was no guard left to prevent his access.

Grunting, he grabbed the padlock in his right hand and twisted. The tortured metal screamed as it parted under the force of his grip, and he sucked in his breath, worried the sound might bring unwanted visitors to his former lair.

The night remained silent except for the throaty gurgle of the ship channel, the creaking and groaning of his nearby ship as it shifted slightly on the current, and the mournful cry of a distant foghorn.

Niemann opened the door and slipped inside, his eyes seeing clearly in the almost total darkness of what had once been his only refuge.

He moved silently down the corridor, stopping once to look at the chalked outlines of the bodies he'd left behind during the final assault on his domain by the police.

He felt a momentary disgust at what he'd done, but it soon passed as he did a quick inventory and found that most of his precious possessions, acquired over two centuries of living as a Vampyre, remained untouched.

Weak from his rejuvenation, he needed to feed, but there was no time. Moving as quickly as he could manage, he gathered as many of his things as he could and began to move them across the street onto his ship.

Dawn was only a couple of hours away and he planned to be at sea before the sun came up. He needed to put as much distance as he could between Houston and himself before the authorities discovered that his ship and possessions were gone.

He chuckled to himself as he carried another load up the gangplank. "The fools will never believe I survived," he whispered aloud, a habit he'd acquired after many years of solitary existence. "They'll just put it down to common thievery along the docks, a not unusual occurrence in this area of high crime."

Soon he had everything he needed, including his hoard of gold and jewels and cash he would need to set up a new life somewhere else, where the Normals still didn't believe in the existence of his race.

After disengaging the *Night Runner* from the dock, he stood at the helm as he eased it down the channel toward the Gulf of Mexico and freedom. Once on the open sea, he would paint over the name and change it to something else to avoid detection by the Coast Guard once the alarm was raised.

He took a deep breath of the salty sea breeze and smiled at the cloud-covered moon, wondering what new adventures awaited him on his journey.

Two

Steve "Shooter" Kowolski, homicide detective on the Houston Police Department, finished packing the picnic supplies in the trunk of his '66 Mustang convertible. Shooter, known for outlandish combinations of colors in his clothing, was dressed today in plaid madras shorts, a bright-yellow tank top, and leather sandals for a picnic trip to Herman Park. He heard a door slam and looked up as his girlfriend, TJ O'Reilly, came down the walk.

As always, the sight of her quickened Shooter's heart rate and caused a fluttery feeling in his stomach. A confirmed womanizer and bachelor until he'd met TJ, Shooter had fallen deeply in love with the young woman; he was now entertaining thoughts of marriage and children and a life with her by his side.

TJ, a resident in internal medicine at Baylor College of Medicine, stood five feet two inches and had tousled black hair that partially covered a pretty, gaminelike face. She and Shooter were scheduled to meet TJ's roommate, Samantha Scott, and her boyfriend, Dr. Matt Carter, in less than an hour.

"Come on, babe," Shooter called as he slammed the trunk lid, "we're gonna be late."

TJ, whose expression was typically open and friendly, blinked in the bright glare of Houston's summer sun and stared at Shooter for a moment as though she wasn't quite sure who he was. She searched in her purse and pulled out a large pair of sunglasses and put them on, covering her eyes and half her face. After a moment, her face cleared and she smiled slowly as if awakening from a dream. "OK, OK," she responded with a short laugh, and jogged toward the car. "Don't worry," she said as she vaulted over the door without opening it and flounced into the passenger seat. "They'll wait for us. We've got the beer and burgers."

Shooter got behind the wheel, started the car, and pulled away from the curb, wincing as the Mustang backfired a couple of times and belched oily black smoke from the muffler. He had a brief thought that the faithful chariot was long overdue for a tune-up, but the thought vanished when TJ put her hand on his thigh and leaned her head back against the seat.

As Shooter drove, he cast surreptitious glances at TJ. She seemed to have recovered from the strange episode of an hour before, but he was still worried about the way she'd looked as she sat in his kitchen, blood from the raw hamburger meat dripping down her chin, her eyes glazed and unseeing.

He decided he'd have to say something to Matt and Sam about it, but out of TJ's hearing. There was no need upsetting her since she apparently had no recollection of the event.

Since it was Saturday morning, the typically horrible Houston traffic was light, and Shooter pulled to a stop in front of Sam and TJ's apartment twenty minutes later.

When Shooter opened the door and got out of the car, TJ glanced at him. "Why don't you just honk, sweetheart? They know we're coming."

"Uh," Shooter answered, "I've got to run in and go to the bathroom. That beer is going right through me."

TJ laughed, throwing her head back and looking like the girl Shooter had fallen in love with. "I told you it was too early to start on that stuff," she said.

Shooter's heart almost broke. She was the most beautiful woman he'd ever seen, and he was afraid to think about what might be going on inside her even now.

"I'll only be a minute," he said, slamming his door and hurrying up the walk toward the apartment.

Matt Carter answered the door immediately after Shooter's knock. "Hey, pal, come on in," Matt said, turning and walking over toward a large picnic basket on the couch. "Sam's almost ready."

Matt Carter, an associate professor of emergency medicine at Baylor College of Medicine, had been Shooter's best friend since grade school. Nice-looking, with short brown hair, Matt was a little under average height and had a trim, athletic body. He was dressed more conservatively than Shooter in cut-off blue jeans and a white T-shirt that read BAYLOR RUGBY on the front.

Shooter glanced back over his shoulder to make sure TJ was still in the car before he entered the apartment and shut the door behind him.

"Matt, we gotta talk," he said, his voice serious.

Matt looked at him, still smiling. "Uh-oh. Don't tell me you forgot the beer?"

"No," Shooter answered. "It's TJ."

"TJ?" Matt asked, the smile fading from his lips when he saw Shooter's expression of concern.

Just then, Samantha Scott walked into the room, still tying her long, reddish auburn hair back into a ponytail for the ride in Shooter's convertible. Sam, as she was called by almost everyone, was a junior professor of pathology at Baylor and was every bit as pretty as TJ, though her Irish ancestry had given her fair skin and a light dusting of freckles across her cheeks to accent her almost red hair and green eyes. She had on a light summer dress that fell to just above her knees and was low cut enough to have caught Shooter's attention on any other day.

"Hey, guys, are we ready to boogie?" she asked.

Sam stopped when she noticed the serious expression on the men's faces. "What's going on?" she asked, walking over to stand next to Matt as she looked into Shooter's eyes.

"It's TJ," Shooter said. "She's . . . She's starting to act weird again."

Matt and Sam looked at each other. They'd spent many nights over the past few weeks working together in the hospital laboratory to cure TJ of the blood infection the vampire Roger Niemann had infected her with after kidnapping her. They'd been sure they'd succeeded.

"What do you mean, 'weird'?" Sam asked.

Shooter flung his hands out, his exasperation clearly showing on his face. As a homicide detective, he wasn't experienced in relating medical signs and symptoms. "Just, weird," he finally said. "Like, this morning, when we were getting the food ready for our picnic, I found her in the kitchen, sitting there with a mouthful of raw hamburger meat, and she looked like she was in a trance. When I shook her and asked her what she was doing, she kinda woke up and didn't remember anything about it."

Matt put his hand on his friend's shoulder to calm him down. "I'm sure it's nothing, Shooter. She was probably just daydreaming or something."

Sam's lips were pursed and her eyes narrowed. It was clear she was taking Shooter's concerns more seriously. "Was there anything else?" she asked.

Shooter nodded. "Wait until you see what she's wearing today for the picnic. She's covered herself from head to toe almost, and it's supposed to hit ninety degrees today."

Matt glanced at Sam and her very skimpy sundress and sandals.

"Did you ask her why?" Sam asked.

Shooter shook his head. "No, I was afraid I might upset her. You know how worried she's been about what that son of a bitch did to her."

Before Sam or Matt could answer, the door opened and TJ walked in. "Hey, are we going to go on a picnic or stand around here jawing all day?" she asked, grinning.

She was dressed in long pants, a long-sleeved man's white shirt, and had a wide-brimmed hat on with the large sunglasses covering her eyes.

Sam glanced at Matt and then back at TJ. "Jesus, girl, what're you wearing all those clothes for?" Sam asked, walking over to TJ. "You realize how hot it's gonna be out at the park today?"

TJ looked down at her clothing. "Well, you know how the sun makes my skin itch and burn. I don't want to get sunburned."

Sam took her by the arm and led her back toward her bedroom. "We've got plenty of sunscreen, TJ. Come on and let's get you in something a little cooler."

"Yeah," Shooter said, a lecherous grin on his face as he tried to make light of the situation, "how about showin' a fellow a little more skin?"

TJ glanced back over her shoulder, returning his

smile. "With your libido, you don't need any encouragement, big guy."

After the girls had left the room, Matt said hesitantly, "She looks OK to me."

Shooter's face sobered, his eyes still on TJ's bedroom door. "Well, maybe I'm overreacting, but keep your eye on her and see what you think."

"Sure," Matt said. "Now, let's get this stuff loaded up while the girls are changing or it'll be dark before we get to the park."

As Shooter helped Matt take the picnic basket and cooler out to the car, he said, "You know, Matt, I've lived here all my life and I've never been to the Houston Zoo."

Matt grinned as he replied, "Then you're in for a real treat. Just don't stand too close to the monkey cages. They tend to throw shit at people who stare at them."

The picnic started off on a good note. Even though it was a Saturday and the park was already beginning to get crowded, the two couples were able to find a spot with a barbecue pit nestled in a shady grove of oak trees off by itself. There was just enough of a breeze to make the heat of the morning bearable.

Matt spread the blanket while Shooter filled the pit with charcoal and got the fire started. TJ and Sam opened the baskets and got out the hamburger meat and fixings and began to cook the food.

Matt handed everyone beers and before long they were eating hamburgers and potato salad and listening to Shooter regale them with tales of some of the more stupid things crooks had been doing lately.

As Shooter talked, both Sam and Matt kept an eye on TJ, trying to be unobtrusive about it. Both wanted to see for themselves if there was anything in her manner to suggest their attempted cure of her recent infection with the vampire's blood had been unsuccessful.

They were soon relieved to find that TJ was acting perfectly normal and seemed to be enjoying the day as much as everyone else was.

Shooter finished his story and his hamburger at the same time. He crushed the paper plate, stuck it in the waste barrel nearby, and brushed his hands off.

"Now, let's go see this zoo I've been hearing so much about," he said. "I'd kinda like to see if the animals here are any better behaved than the ones I deal with every day down at the station."

The tour of the zoo began uneventfully, with the four friends enjoying ice-cream cones and sodas as they walked among the exhibits.

"OK," Shooter said, licking ice cream off his fingers. "Enough of the snakes and sea lions. Where are those monkeys you told me about, Matt?"

Matt leaned over to TJ and whispered, "I told Shooter he might find some relatives in the monkey house, and he's anxious to go see for himself."

Shooter put his arm around TJ's shoulders and pulled her away from Matt. "Don't be going an' tellin' her something like that about the future father of her kids."

"Hell, if that's true, then we've got to go see the monkeys. TJ needs to see the kind of gene pool she's getting involved with," Matt said.

Sam pointed to a nearby sign. "The Primate Compound is over that way."

They followed the signs and were soon standing before a row of cages containing dozens of different species of monkeys and apes.

The animals were running and playing in their

cages, climbing fake tree trunks and swinging from old tires hung from ropes, chattering and howling and squealing at each other.

TJ moved closer to the bars, pointing to a chimpanzee in a corner. "Matt, is that the one you said was related to Shooter?" she asked.

The chimp, seeing TJ's arm out, ambled over to the front of the cage, expecting a handout. When he got close, his eyes seemed to fix on TJ and his nostrils flared. He sniffed loudly and his lips curled back from his teeth in a nasty snarl, revealing fangs three inches long.

He screeched and began to jump against the bars, beating them with his fists and gnashing his teeth as he became more and more agitated.

Others in the cage, reacting to his actions, rushed up to the bars, their eyes fixed on TJ while they screamed and screeched and jumped up and down with flailing arms.

TJ's eyes widened and her hands went to her mouth as Shooter pulled her away from the cages.

"Jesus!" Matt said, taking Sam's arm and easing her back. "I've never seen them do that before."

"Me either," Sam said, her eyes moving from the monkeys to TJ, a worried, calculating expression on her face.

"I've had enough," TJ said in a hoarse voice, shaking her head and walking away from the compound.

"Yeah," Shooter agreed, glancing over his shoulder at the still-screeching monkeys as he led TJ away from the cage. "Let's head back. I think we left some beer in the cooler that has my name on it."

The two couples were silent on the drive back to the apartment shared by Sam and TJ, each absorbed with private thoughts of what had occurred at the zoo.

When Shooter pulled up in front of the apartment complex, he looked back at Matt and Sam. "I think I'll take TJ on over to my place. I've got some new movies on video and we'll just hang there for a while."

"That's a great idea," Sam said, glancing at the back of TJ's head. "Our place needs a good cleaning and I'll get Matt to stay and help."

"What?" Matt asked.

She patted his thigh. "Just kidding, sweetie," Sam said. "Maybe I'll let you beat me at a game of gin rummy instead."

Matt frowned. "Well, that wasn't exactly what I had in mind for tonight."

Sam winked at him. "OK. Come on in and we'll discuss it."

When they got to his apartment, Shooter hastily picked up various bits and pieces of clothing lying around the living room and cleared a place on the sofa in front of the TV set.

TJ, still somber after the incident at the zoo, made no comment about Shooter's notoriously poor housekeeping, but merely sat on the couch and stared at the blank TV.

Shooter, a worried frown on his face, turned the set on and said, "I'll make us some popcorn and then we can watch the movies."

TJ looked up at him, her eyes meeting his for the first time since they'd left the zoo. She patted the cushion next to her.

"Not now, Shooter. Come sit by me."

Shooter sat down next to her and put his arm around her shoulders, pulling her head down against his neck. "You OK, babe?" he asked gently.

TJ put her hand on his chest and looked up into his eyes. "I don't know, Shooter. . . . I really don't know."

Shooter couldn't resist the look of hurt and fear in her eyes. He bent his head and kissed her gently on the lips, whispering, "I love you, TJ."

Suddenly, as if a switch had been turned on, TJ reached up and put her arm around his neck and pulled him into her, opening her mouth and returning his kiss with an unaccustomed fervor.

As her tongue flicked his lips and she leaned back, pulling Shooter on top of her, Shooter responded.

He fitted his body to hers, his hand on her breast as they ground against each other. Moments later, TJ's hand was on his belt, pulling and tugging until she had it undone and his shorts unbuttoned.

Shooter wasted no time and within moments they were both naked, lying together on his couch, pressing tight. As he moved between her legs, TJ put her hands on his chest and shook her head. "Not yet . . . not yet . . . ," she murmured.

She pushed him over onto his back and moved her head down his body until her hair was brushing his groin. Shooter laid his head back and moaned as she took him in her mouth.

TJ was like a wild woman, moving and moaning and groaning as she made love to him with her lips and tongue. Briefly, Shooter wondered what was going on. TJ had never been like this before, but then his thoughts were silenced by the pleasure she was giving him and he ceased to think at all.

Just before he climaxed, he grabbed her head and pulled her up on top of him. She clamped her mouth to his as she spread her legs and took him inside her steamy wetness.

When he groaned in final release, she moved her mouth to his neck and began to suck and chew once more as her hips pumped with his.

Moments later, she almost screamed as she came with him, collapsing on top of him, her chest heaving.

Neither noticed at first the small stream of blood trickling down his neck, or the droplets staining her lips crimson.

Three

As I approached my ship, I paused to admire the new name: *Moon Chaser*. Not as poetic as *Night Runner*, perhaps, but it would do—and the police weren't looking for this one.

This space on the New Orleans docks was not as convenient as the one on the Houston Ship Channel, since I now had to walk almost four blocks to get to the warehouse I'd rented to store my possessions in and to serve as a "safe house" in case the authorities got too close again. However, if I'd learned nothing else in over two hundred years of living on the fringes of society, it was how to make do with what I had.

I entered the cabin and put the bags of groceries and supplies in the galley. The trip from Houston had used up most of the food and I liked to keep the refrigerator on the ship fully stocked in case of a hasty departure—another thing I'd learned in my years on the run.

Once I was finished with my housekeeping, I brewed a pot of tea and went out on the deck to enjoy the night. The air was fresh and smelled of incipient rain, with subtle overtones of iodine and salt and rotting fish.

I sipped my tea and took deep breaths, trying not to think of the pain of the last few days as my body had healed itself from the wounds I'd suffered. My Vampyre body's ability to heal itself comes with a price—the process is both time consuming and extremely painful.

I leaned back against the rail of the *Moon Chaser* and considered what I had yet to do. I'd already gotten the ship berthed and resupplied, and secured a warehouse and transferred all of my things there. All that was left now was to construct a new identity and find a position in the medical establishment that would enable me to carry on my research and find and track new victims who would be safe to feed upon.

The thought of feeding caused the Hunger to begin to stir within me. My body was reminding me that the human food I'd eaten wasn't enough. . . . I needed blood to fuel the repairs that had been made to my tissues, and I needed it sooner rather than later.

In order to put the thought of blood and hunting out of my mind, I went to my cabin and opened the safe, using the combination 1-8-0-1, the year of my birth.

I reached in and took out the new journal I'd bought when I found the police had taken the one I'd been working on since my Transformation into the Vampyre race. Luckily, there was nothing in the old journal to compromise my safety, other than the fact of my race's existence. Knowing how bureaucracies work, I felt sure the police department wouldn't allow themselves to believe that Vampyres actually existed. And even if they did, they would never allow the news to become public knowledge.

That was one of the strange things about the human race: for the most part, they refused to believe in the existence of the Vampyre race. At least, the more educated, higher classes didn't accept it. The peasants have always believed in me and my kind, and in fact built up an entire repertoire of talismans that would supposedly protect them from us, ranging from crosses to garlic to holy water. That these didn't work, the poor victims only found out at the moments of their deaths.

Perhaps, in the final analysis, the only thing that kept my new race from propagating and overrunning the humans was our own disgust at what we were and what we had become. It was this natural reticence to transform more humans into the horrific beings we were that kept us from taking over the world. For that, I was as thankful as the poor humans would be if they but knew the true facts.

I sat at my desk and picked up my pen. Dipping it in the India ink I used for my journal entries, I wrote in the day's date and began to write of the recent assault on my ship and the attempt on my life.

When I got to the part where the police abducted my new mate, TJ O'Reilly, I paused. The pain of the loss was still too fresh to allow me to be objective in my reporting of the event.

I put the journal away, fixed a fresh cup of tea, and went back out on the deck. I gazed at the moon, wondering if they would be able to stop the process of Transformation I'd begun by having her drink of my blood.

I doubted it, for I'd been trying to undo my own infection with the organisms that cause Vampyrism for over a hundred years, without success.

Thinking about TJ made my heart hurt. I hadn't realized just how lonely my existence was until I fell in love with her and began the process of making her my own.

Immortality didn't seem quite so bad when I could look forward to spending it with someone I could love and cherish. Someone who wouldn't age and die after a few years and leave me alone again. Now, without her, the years stretched before me like an endless black chain of desperation.

I shook my head to clear it of such thoughts. There would be plenty of time to grieve over my loss of TJ—entirely too much time. I finished my tea and went back into my study to work on the paperwork that would be necessary for me to find a new position and to continue my work to somehow reverse the disease process that had turned me into a monster.

Hours later I had my résumé ready, fake of course. Tomorrow I would approach a local clinic about a job. It shouldn't pose too much of a problem. After all, I'd had plenty of time to become adept at forging credentials, as well as using makeup to cause my face to appear to age normally.

As I prepared for bed, the Hunger began to make its presence known once again. The feeling started with a slight emptiness in my gut and was soon followed by an overwhelming urge to rend and tear and find the sustenance that my Vampyre body craved. Blood.

Full in the throes of a feeding frenzy, I tore the door to my closet open and found my hunting uniform, black jeans and shirt. All the better to blend into the night that was my friend and ally in my search for the right victim to satisfy my craving.

Since I was new in the city and had no prepared database of "safe" victims—those whose blood had tested negative for both AIDS and the "Mad Cow" prion—I would have to take my chances and feed on blood that might end up being poison to my system.

Even though the heightened healing power of my Vampyre body was remarkable, I knew from my research and the deaths of many of my kind, that it could not stand up to the ravages of the prion, which caused Creutzfeldt-Jakob disease, or CJD. Luckily, the disease was not nearly so prevalent in the United States as in the European countries, where it was still known as "Mad Cow Disease." Still, I would have to be extremely careful, if the blood lust the Hunger caused would let me.

As always, I planned to try and take my victims from the lower strata of society. . . . This was a small sop to my conscience, which still caused me to feel terrible that my need would be met at the cost of an innocent person's life.

At times, when I was on a regular feeding schedule, I could control the Hunger enough to take only what I needed to survive and leave my victims alive, albeit with their memory of my feeding clouded so they had no recollection of the event. But now, with my body fresh from the ordeal of the extreme energy needed for the healing of my recent wounds, I knew that would not be the case. I would most certainly drain every drop of the precious liquid that meant life for me, and death for my chosen sacrifice.

Still, I vowed to do my best to take only what I needed and to leave my new victim alive, to fight the almost unendurable urge, which was coursing through my body now, to rend and tear and destroy. It had been the trail of bodies that had led the Houston police to me and had cost me my freedom and almost my life in my last identity as Roger Niemann. If I could not prevent a recurrence of that pattern, I knew that I would not have enough time to complete my research—and possibly cure myself of the disease of Vampyrism—before I'd be forced to move once again.

Feeling better and filled with a new resolve to try not to kill, I left my ship and began my search.

As I strolled down Lakeside Drive along the wharf area, not having had time yet to procure another automobile for transportation, I kept my eye out for a bar or saloon that would be suitable for my quest.

I wanted one that was darkly lit, so there would be few witnesses to my appearance should the police bother to question the patrons, and yet the place had to be of sufficient quality that it would be crowded with plenty of women for me to choose from.

I don't know why I prefer women to men for my victims, though either will do to satisfy the Hunger. Perhaps it is because for me the act of feeding is at least partly sexual in nature. Certainly, the adrenaline that flows into the bloodstream of the victim when they become horrified at what is happening adds a rather piquant spice to the taste of my meal; when the act of feeding is accompanied by a sexual act, it is much more satisfying.

After all, a gourmet can survive on hamburger, but will always prefer filet mignon.

As I approached a bar with a neon sign that said SAILOR'S ROOST, a pair of young black men stepped from an alley and blocked my path.

"Hold on there, sucker!" one of them growled, affecting a tough, menacing tone to his youthful voice. They couldn't have been more than fifteen or sixteen years old.

"Where you think you're goin', honky?" his companion asked as he took a knife from his pocket and pressed a button on the side. A long blade flashed from the handle and glittered in the light of the neon sign.

I smiled, revealing teeth that glowed with eerie phosphorescence in the darkness. As a longtime denizen of the night, I was used to encounters such as this, much more so than the innocents standing before me.

"I have business in that bar over there," I replied calmly. "And if you . . . gentlemen want to survive this night, I'd suggest you pick someone else to hold up."

The two young men glanced at each other, their expressions surprised at my lack of fear. They looked around as if making sure I wasn't an undercover policeman with backup nearby. Their insolent grins returned when they saw I was alone.

"I think you the one gotta worry 'bout survivin' this night," the first boy growled, pulling a small-caliber pistol from his belt and aiming it at my stomach.

I didn't have time for this. The Hunger was raging and I knew that before long I would lose control and stealth would no longer be possible.

I looked at the door to the bar, regretful that my feeding tonight wasn't going to be as satisfying as I'd planned, and I let my Transformation begin.

The second boy opened his mouth to speak, but stopped with it hanging open as he noticed my hands becoming claws, with long, pointed nails growing from the ends of my fingers.

With an expression of horror, his eyes moved to the tissues of my face, which were melting and coalescing and changing as my lips pulled back from fangs that eased from my gums, dripping red drool.

"What the fuck?" he said, stepping back and

holding his knife out in front of him as if it were a cross that would protect him from the monster I was becoming before his eyes.

"Jesus . . . ," the other managed to whisper before I stepped forward and swiped backhanded at him. My razor-sharp claws cut through his neck muscles like so much butter and his head was nearly severed from his body.

Before he could fall to the ground, I was on his companion, my hands brushing his knife to the side as my fangs sank into the tender flesh over his carotid artery.

He stumbled back, moaning and trying to cry out as I sucked the life from him, holding him in my arms like a lover. I almost gagged at the bitter taste of the drugs coursing through his bloodstream, but my Hunger was too great to be concerned with taste. I continued to feed.

When I was done, I dropped his empty husk on the sidewalk and picked up the other body, which was still pumping blood from the stump of his neck. I managed a few quick drafts before he, too, was empty.

A body in each hand, I dragged them back into the alley from whence they'd come and threw them into a Dumpster behind the bar. I found a couple of cardboard boxes nearby and placed them over the bodies, covering the remains from sight as best I could. With any luck, they wouldn't be found until the garbage truck that emptied the Dumpster deposited them at the city landfill. I preferred not to draw any attention to the dock area if it could be helped.

Now all that was left was for me to get back to my ship without being seen. The feeding had been messier than most and my shirt was soaked with blood, though it appeared black rather than red in the moonlight.

The Hunger satisfied, for the moment, my body slowly changed back into its more human form. With a quick glance from the alley to make sure no one was about, I headed home. I was satiated but strangely unsatisfied, my loins heavy with unrequited passion and my mind filled with sorrow at two more deaths that would be added to the ledger of lives cut short by my disease.

As usual, the remorse about what I had done only hit me after my blood lust had been satisfied. The only thing that kept me from becoming morose about the night's activities was the fact that the young men I'd killed had surely deserved it as much as any I'd taken in the past.

Walking toward my ship, I fervently hoped now that the worst of my Hunger was assuaged, I would be able to control it enough to partake only of non-lethal feedings in the future. Otherwise, I would have been better off remaining at the bottom of the Houston Ship Channel for all time.

Four

Matt leaned against the wall of the doctors' lounge in the Ben Taub Hospital emergency room and rubbed his eyes. He was dog tired. He'd just finished a twelve-hour shift, from seven in the morning to seven in the evening, supervising the ER's house staff; it was all part of his duties as an associate professor of emergency medicine.

He stifled a yawn and looked at the blackened, stained coffee urn in the corner, wondering if his stomach lining could survive another cup of the potent brew. He was trying to decide two possible outcomes—getting an ulcer or falling asleep at the wheel driving home—when the door opened and Jeff Strickland, the chief surgery resident on duty, stuck his head in.

"Hey, Matt, they're paging you," Strickland said.

Matt glanced at his watch. "Damn, five more minutes and I'd be out the door."

Strickland grinned and shrugged. "Such is life as a professor, Matt. That's why they pay you the big bucks."

Matt grimaced at the humor. Everyone knew professors were paid far less than they could make in private practice. "Yeah, right," Matt groused, wondering if he should just ignore the page and pretend he'd already left for the day.

But, as usual, his conscience and almost compulsive dedication to his duty prevailed.

He stepped to the corner and picked up the phone, dialing the operator as he yawned again.

"Dr. Carter," he said when the hospital operator answered.

"You have a call from a patient up on surgery, Dr. Carter," the feminine voice said. "Would you like me to put him through?"

Matt frowned. He never received calls from patients after they were admitted to the hospital, even ones he'd treated in the ER. "Uh, sure," he said, wondering just what this was all about and who might be calling him.

After a couple of clicks, the operator said, "Go ahead, sir. Dr. Carter is on the line."

A male voice said, "Matt?"

Matt recognized the voice immediately as belonging to Damon Clark. "Damon?" he asked. "What are you doing back in the hospital?"

"Why don't you come up to my room when you get a chance and I'll tell you. Room three twenty-two."

"I'll be there in ten minutes," Matt said.

"Oh, Matt," Damon said.

"Yeah?"

"See if you can bum a couple of smokes. The bastards took mine when they admitted me."

Matt grinned, shaking his head. Damon, chief of detectives of the Houston Police Department, was an inveterate smoker. About the only thing he did that was politically incorrect.

"You know the Taub is a nonsmoking facility, Damon," Matt said.

"What are they gonna do, arrest me for smoking?" Damon said with a chuckle, quoting a line from a movie.

"I'll see what I can do," Matt said, and hung up.

A few minutes later, while riding up to the third floor in the elevator, Matt reviewed what he knew of Damon Clark. The first black man to be made chief of detectives on the Houston Police Department, Damon was independently wealthy and was a fixture in Houston society. Handsome, articulate, and extremely politically astute, he'd been the first to recognize the presence of a serial killer working the Houston streets the previous year. The killer's trademark of slashing throats and draining his victims of their blood had caused him to ask for help from the medical community. Matt and Sam and Shooter had gotten involved, eventually determining the killer was a vampire.

After a long investigation, in which the creature had killed one of Damon's female officers, Damon had finally led the assault on the killer's ship, which resulted in the death of the vampire. During the assault, the vampire had managed to skewer Damon through the abdomen with a sword, resulting in his losing almost half his small bowel and a portion of his colon. Matt hadn't heard from Damon since his release from the hospital after a series of difficult operations a few weeks back.

Matt knocked on the door to room 322 and entered. He tried to keep the look of shock off his face at Damon's appearance. The man seemed to have lost twenty pounds and his eyes were sunken in his face. He still wore his trademark gold-rimmed designer glasses, but his once-lean frame now looked gaunt and his eyes had a yellowish tint to them.

"Hey, Damon," Matt said.

Damon looked up from his hospital bed and grinned. The smile reminded Matt again that this was one of the most charismatic men he'd ever known.

"Howdy, Matt," Damon said. "Close the door and come on in."

Matt shut the door and took a seat next to the bed.

"Were you able to get what I asked for?" Damon asked, glancing at the door to make sure it was closed.

Matt pulled a wrinkled cigarette from his shirt pocket, along with a kitchen match. "Yeah. We had a homeless man in the ER needing some stitches in his head. He made me give him a dollar for the cigarette and match."

Damon reached out and took them from Matt's hand. "Worth any amount when you really need one," Damon said. He got out of the bed, opened the window a crack, and sat on the window ledge as he struck the match and took a deep puff.

"Those things'll kill you," Matt said.

Damon gave him a look, smoke trailing from his nostrils and an expression of sublime satisfaction. "Sure they will, but only if your doctor friends don't do the job first."

"Speaking of that, just why are you in here?" Matt asked.

"Adhesions," Damon said shortly. "Seems there's some scar tissue building up around where they took my guts out and they want to go back in and get rid of it before it causes an obstruction."

Matt nodded. Scar tissue as a result of massive bowel injuries was fairly common. "Well, at least it's nothing serious."

"Serious is in the eye of the beholder, Matt, my

boy," Damon said sarcastically. "Anytime they cut me open and poke around in my insides, I consider it serious business."

"When are you scheduled?"

"Tomorrow morning, first thing. That's why I wanted to talk to you."

"Anything I can do, Damon. You know that."

Damon took a final drag off the cigarette and threw the butt out the window. He grinned. "Got to get rid of the evidence or that Nazi nurse will have my hide."

Matt looked at the tray across Damon's bed. "Yeah," he said, "she might take away your bouillon as punishment."

"That wouldn't be punishment; that'd be a blessing," Damon said. He walked over to the closet and took out a leather-bound book. "This is the real reason I wanted you to come," he said, handing the book to Matt.

The book appeared to be very old, with a leather cover that was cracked and wrinkled with age and pages that appeared to be made of parchment rather than paper. The writing inside was done with India ink and was in long hand in a style that seemed . . . ancient.

Matt looked up at Damon over the book, with a questioning expression.

Damon sat on the edge of the bed. "Shooter tells me you all have been having some trouble with TJ," he said.

Matt nodded slowly, wondering what that had to do with the book. As he considered Damon's statement, he was unsure of how much he could tell Damon without breaking patient confidentiality.

Damon held up his hand. "I know. You can't talk about a patient without her consent, but I think there are some things in that journal that may be of help to you and the doctors who are treating TJ."

Damon hesitated and his eyes got a faraway look in them. "It's a hell of a read."

"Just what is this book?" Matt asked, glancing again at the old-style writing on the pages.

Damon's eyes came back into focus. "It's the journal of Roger Niemann. The man . . . or thing we killed on that ship."

"The vampire?" Matt asked, unable to keep the incredulity out of his voice.

Damon held up his hand, a half smile curling his lips. "You know the department never admitted he was anything other than a serial killer, Matt."

"But we know different, don't we, Chief?"

Damon frowned. "I don't know what to think, Matt. One of my men found that book in the ship and gave it to me after he looked through it. He didn't think it should go into the evidence room at the station. He was right. That thing is political dynamite."

"What do you want me to do with it?" Matt asked, unconsciously running his hands over the supple leather.

Damon shrugged. "Read it. Study it. There may be some things in there that will do TJ some good. I owe my life to Shooter for what he did to protect me on that ship, so this is the least I can do."

Matt got to his feet. "Thanks, Chief. I'll go through it tomorrow after I've had some sleep." He stuck out his hand. "Good luck tomorrow, Damon."

Damon shook his hand. "The doctors tell me luck has nothing to do with it."

Matt nodded, but he was thinking luck is always a part of surgery, no matter how skilled the surgeon.

Most surgeons admitted to each other they'd rather be lucky than good any day.

He told Damon he'd check in on him after his surgery the next day and left the room, cradling the ancient journal under his arm as he walked tiredly down the hall.

When Matt got to the parking garage, he tossed the journal into the passenger seat of his new Mazda Miata convertible and got behind the wheel. He'd bought the Miata with the insurance money he'd received when his '65 Vette convertible was wrecked while chasing the vampire Niemann a few months back. While not as throaty sounding as the muscle car from the sixties, the Miata at least had reliable air-conditioning, a must in Houston's ninety-plus summer heat—and it was a fun ride.

Since it was only a little past eight in the evening and the temperature was manageable, Matt put the top down and cruised home to his town house in University Place near Rice University.

Since he was heading away from the medical center, the Sunday-evening traffic was against him and he made good time, arriving home twenty minutes after he left the parking garage.

He parked in his space, took the journal, and trudged slowly up the walk to his door.

Once inside, he kicked his shoes off, headed to the bedroom, dropped the journal on his bedside table, then flopped facedown on the bed without bothering to undress. He was deep asleep within minutes.

Five

Matt woke up the next morning feeling a little hungover from his twelve-hour shift. Since it was a Monday, he had no official duties until his one o'clock class on emergency medicine with the sophomore medical students.

He climbed slowly out of bed and shuffled into the kitchen, smacking his lips. He hated falling asleep in his clothes. It made him feel rumpled and dirty until he took his shower.

In the kitchen, he put a pot of coffee to brewing and opened the freezer. He took out a can of frozen orange-juice concentrate and a package of frozen strawberries and put them on the bar to thaw while he took a shower.

Once he'd scrubbed the grime of the ER out of his skin and hair, and brushed the taste of stale coffee off his teeth, he threw on a terry cloth robe and went back into the kitchen. He put the orange juice and the strawberries in a blender and turned it on while he poured himself a cup of coffee.

Taking the morning paper off the front step, he took his coffee and fruit drink out on his porch. He sat at the table there and began the process of starting his day.

After downing his coffee and juice, he went to his bedroom to get dressed for the day. When he took his robe off and threw it on the bed, he noticed the leather journal lying on his nightstand. He'd forgotten all about it.

He put on some jeans and a short-sleeved cotton shirt and took the journal into his living room. After fixing himself another cup of coffee, he sat in his favorite chair and opened the journal. In faded but still legible India ink, the top of the page was labeled with the date June 24, 1870. Matt felt the page with his fingers. Parchment. Perhaps the book was that old after all. He settled back in his chair and began to read.

Jesus, Matt thought after he'd scanned the first few pages. This must be Niemann's diary. He glanced back at the entry of the first page. If the journal was accurate, that would have made him over two hundred years old. He opened the journal back up and continued to read, his forgotten coffee growing cold on the table next to him.

An hour and a half later, Matt slowly closed the journal and leaned back in his chair. He found he was covered with sweat and shivering. After reading the innermost thoughts of the monster he knew as Roger Niemann, he felt almost sorry for the creature. It was clear from his journal he'd struggled as best he could against his fate . . . trying his best to satisfy his fiendish cravings while doing as little damage as he could. Still, Matt thought, the man was an admitted killer of no telling how many innocent people over two hundred years.

Damon had been right—the book was dynamite. Matt knew he'd have to share its contents with his friends as soon as possible. There might just be something in the book that would shed some light on the mysterious illness that affected TJ after being forced to drink the creature's blood.

He put the journal on the side table and went to take another shower. He felt dirty just from reading about the horrors of Niemann's life.

After he finished his class that afternoon, Matt put in a call to Shooter at the police station.

"This is Detective Kowolski," Shooter said as he answered the phone.

"Hey, Shooter. It's Matt."

"Yo, Doc. What's happenin'?" Shooter asked in his typically jovial voice.

"I saw Damon yesterday in the hospital," Matt answered.

Shooter's voice sobered. Damon was a hero of his and a man he respected above all others in the Houston police bureaucracy. "How's he doing?"

"He came through his surgery all right this morning. His doc says he's gonna be just fine."

"That's a relief," Shooter said. "We need him back here as soon as possible." He lowered his voice to a conspiratorial whisper. "The lieutenant that took his place is a raving asshole—"

"Shooter," Matt interrupted, "Damon gave me something they found on Niemann's boat the night of the attack."

"Yeah? What?"

"A journal. A sort of diary he'd written about his life."

"That must be interesting reading," Shooter said sarcastically. "The ravings of a lunatic."

"Believe it or not, it's fascinating," Matt said. "In fact, I'd like to go over it with you and the girls tonight."

"I don't know, Matt," Shooter said. "I'd kinda like to put all that behind us." He paused and Matt could hear him take a deep breath. "TJ's acting strange enough without being reminded of what happened to her before."

"I think we need to do it, Shooter. For TJ, if nothing else," Matt pleaded. "There are some things in the book that may help TJ get over this."

Shooter's voice changed at Matt's mention of helping TJ. "In that case, I'll be there," he said firmly.

"How about I whip up some spaghetti and meatballs and we make a night of it?"

"Sure. I'll bring the wine."

Matt groaned. "Only if you promise not to buy that cheap Chianti you brought last time."

"OK, OK, I'll spring for a really good red, maybe some Mad Dog Twenty-Twenty this time," Shooter said, referring to the preferred drink of the winos who lived in Houston's Fifth Ward.

"Shooter . . . ," Matt said.

"All right. How about some hardy Gallo Burgundy?"

"Try some Soave and it's a deal," Matt said.

"See ya at seven," Shooter said, and hung up.

Matt then dialed Sam in the pathology office and made her the same offer.

"You gonna have real anchovies in the Caesar salad?" she asked.

"Jeez, girl, I'm offering you a home-cooked meal of my best dish and you're quibbling over fish in the salad?"

"All right," she said, chuckling. Then her voice became more serious. "Do you think TJ should be there? She's still pretty shaken about what Niemann did to her."

Matt considered it for a moment, finally answering, "Yeah, I do. After all, it's her condition we're gonna be discussing and trying to find a cure for. It's her right to know all the facts."

Sam sighed, still unsure of the wisdom of revisiting TJ's pain. After a moment, she said, "We'll be there. Can we bring anything?"

"Sure. Could you stop off at the bakery on Rice Boulevard and pick up some of their garlic French bread?"

"That's a deal," she answered, adding in a low voice, "But, Matt, I sure hope you know what you're doing."

"So do I, babe," Matt said. "So do I."

Six

Matt fussed over the meal as only a bachelor who cooked for fun rather than for nourishment could. Matt had always been popular with women, though more for his personality than for his looks. He had never seriously considered marriage—at least not until he'd met Dr. Samantha Scott a few months ago. He'd always figured his career would preclude him giving enough time to a wife and children.

Since meeting and dating Sam, however, more and more he found himself wondering just what life with her would be like. The days when he couldn't see her seemed to drag on interminably, and his last thoughts at night and his first musings in the mornings were invariably of her.

Now, with the expectation of seeing her for dinner, he hummed and sang to himself as he prepared the meal. Earlier he'd run by Moody's Meat Market in the Village near his home to procure a healthy supply of both hot and medium hot Italian sausage to mix with the ground round for his meat sauce.

He cut the sausage into inch-long, bite-size chunks and sautéed it over a low flame on his stove along with the ground round. While part of the meat cooked, he fashioned meatballs out of the remainder, adding a pinch of this and a dollop of that, as his mother had shown him when he was learning to cook for himself. The spaghetti itself he would leave until just prior to serving.

As he cooked, he went over in his mind how he would tell the story of Elijah Pike and his amazing, if somewhat distasteful, life.

Shooter, as usual, showed up a bit early. He liked to sit and watch Matt cook and then chat about the day's happenings on the rare occasions when they were able to get a night off together. They'd been friends for so long they were closer than brothers, with none of the sibling rivalry that confused relationships between blood kin.

Matt stirred the pot of meat sauce and said over his shoulder, "Why don't you open that wine and let it breathe for a while?"

Shooter grinned. "With this particular wine, it might be better to let it age a bit more first."

Matt glanced back. "When was it bottled?"

Shooter picked up one of the bottles he'd brought with him and pretended to look at the label. "About six hours ago," he replied jokingly.

Matt wiped his hands on his apron, which had KISS THE COOK written on it in large red letters, and leaned back against the stove. "Please tell me the wine at least has a cork in it and not a screw-top cap like the last bottle you brought."

"Oh, it has a cork all right," Shooter said. "Trouble is, it's made of plastic."

Matt laughed in spite of himself. "You'll never change, will you, Shooter?"

Shooter looked aghast. "I hope not! My women would be terribly disappointed if I did."

A voice from Matt's front door called out, "I hope you meant to say 'my woman.' " TJ and Sam walked in.

"Oops," Shooter said, covering his mouth. "My secret's out."

TJ placed a large tinfoil sack containing garlic French bread on the counter and stepped over to plant a kiss on Shooter's lips, her hand grabbing his throat at the same time. "Are you trying to get yourself strangled?" she asked.

"Just kidding, sweetheart," Shooter said, wrapping his arms around her and hugging her to him while winking over her shoulder at Matt and Sam.

Sam moved to stand next to Matt and looked down into the pot of simmering meat and sausage. "Mmm, that smells delicious."

"Yeah, Matt's not a bad cook, for a guy," Shooter said.

"What do you mean, 'for a guy'?" Matt asked, offended. "For a man who can't boil water, you're awfully quick to criticize."

"Hey," Shooter said, holding up his hands, "have I ever turned down a meal?"

"Speaking of meals, when do we eat?" Sam asked, giving Matt a quick kiss hello. "I'm starved."

"Put the bread in the oven and I'll start the noodles. They'll take exactly twelve minutes."

Sam opened the refrigerator while TJ readied the bread. "I see the salads are already made."

"Shooter, set the table while Sam gets the salads out and we'll be ready to chow down," Matt said.

"What wine did you get?" TJ asked as she put the bread in the oven.

"It's called Panama Red," Shooter said. "And I got a hell of a deal. . . . Two bottles for five dollars."

"What?" TJ exclaimed, turning to look at the bottles on the counter.

"Just kidding," Shooter said. "Actually, it's a Cabernet Sauvignon."

"Whoa," Sam said, "I'm impressed, Shooter. I didn't know you spoke French."

"French?" Shooter asked, a look of surprise on his face. "I thought it was an Italian wine."

Once the meal was over, everyone congratulated Matt on a job well done.

TJ looked at Sam and winked. "I think you should keep him, Sam. After all, a man who can cook and doesn't pick his nose in public is a real find nowadays."

Sam cast a speculative eye on Matt. "Well, to be perfectly honest about it, I have given some thought to making an honest man out of him."

"You mean you approved of the meal, even without the tang of formaldehyde to spice it up?" Matt asked, referring to Sam's job of doing autopsies in the morgue.

"Yes," Sam replied, getting up from the table. "In fact, it was so good, I've brought you a present."

She disappeared into the living room and reappeared moments later with a large box under her arm.

"What's that?" Shooter asked. "A cookbook for the culinary challenged?"

"No, it's an espresso machine," Sam replied. "A reward for you two men who spend your days drinking that awful liquid laughingly called coffee in the squad room and emergency room."

"Well, crank it up," Shooter said, his hand automatically reaching toward his breast pocket for the cigarettes he'd left in his Mustang. TJ refused to let him smoke in her presence and was continually after him to give up the filthy habit, as she called it. Shooter was trying, but, to be honest, wasn't succeeding very well.

Once the coffee was made, the group moved to

the living room. TJ and Shooter sat next to each other on the couch, while Sam and Matt took up station on a love seat across the room.

Matt leaned over and picked up the leather journal from the coffee table in front of the love seat.

"What's that?" Sam asked, running her hands over the wrinkled, ancient leather.

"Nothing less than the journal of the Vampyre Niemann," Matt said, to stunned looks from his guests.

"You're kidding!" TJ said, her face paling a bit at the mention of the monster who had tried to change her into one of his own kind.

Matt shook his head. "No. In fact, it makes for some very interesting reading."

Sam cast a worried look at TJ. "Matt, do you really think we should?"

Matt leaned forward, staring at TJ as Shooter put his arm around her shoulders. "I'll leave it up to TJ."

"What's—what's in it?" she asked, seeming to shrink as she leaned back into the crook of Shooter's arm.

"I think there are some things here that will help us understand what Niemann tried to do to you, TJ, and perhaps even help us make sure we completely undo what he did."

TJ glanced at Sam, a look of almost panic on her face. "What do you think, Sam?" she asked in a suddenly small voice.

Sam nodded. "If you're up to it, TJ, it might do some good."

"OK, then, tell us what it says," she almost whispered, a tone of dread in her voice.

Matt took a sip of his coffee and leaned back. "It's a story not unlike yours, TJ."

He began to tell the story he'd read in the journal.

"A man named Elijah Pike was born in 1801 in northern Maine. When he was about twenty years old, he was working as a woodcutter. One day, he got lost in a blizzard, and after roaming around the countryside for most of the day, he finally sought refuge in a log cabin. He was half frozen and starving. When he knocked on the door, he was let in by a strange figure who soon fed him some wine. Evidently, the wine was drugged, for he fell fast asleep and dreamed of being forced to drink of the creature's blood."

When Matt said this, TJ's hand went to her mouth and she paled further, a small gasp escaping from her bloodless lips. She remembered how Roger Niemann had opened a vein in his neck with a fingernail and put her lips to the wound. She shook her head, trying to erase the memory from her mind as she wondered again what had made her take the first drink of his tainted blood.

Shooter put her cup of coffee in her hands; Matt waited while TJ took a deep drink, then he continued.

"When Pike woke up the next morning, the man was gone and he was alone in the cabin. The storm broke and he finally made his way home. A few days later, he was seized by a strong fever and nothing the local doctors did could stop it. A week later, he was declared dead and placed in a coffin to be stored in a nearby barn until the ice melted enough for him to be buried."

"If he died, how did he come to write the journal?" Shooter asked.

Matt's lips curled in a smile without mirth as he explained. "After a few days in the coffin, Pike woke up to a ravenous hunger. He states he could 'smell' or sense people nearby. He climbed out of the coffin and discovered two young people making love in the hayloft. Out of control, urged on by something he calls 'the Hunger,' with a capital *H*, Pike attacked the couple and killed them, drinking all of their blood to assuage this so-called Hunger."

"Jesus," Sam whispered, her eyes moving to TJ, whose head was down with her eyes focused on the carpet.

"Realizing he'd become some kind of monster, but not knowing how or why, Pike ran off and left town so as not to be a danger to his wife and children," Matt continued. "Over the next fifty years, he found he didn't age and that he had some sort of mental powers that would let him know what others, people he called 'the Normals,' were thinking. He also found he could exercise some rudimentary control over their memories so that if he bit them and drank their blood but didn't kill them, they wouldn't remember."

"Christ, I don't believe it," Shooter said. "It's like some bad Bela Lugosi movie."

"I tend to agree with Shooter, Matt," Sam said. "After all, how could drinking someone's blood do all that?"

"Later in the journal, he explains how," Matt said. "Pike, after many years of living like this, either killing or assaulting hundreds of people for their blood, finally began to search for how this came to be. He discovered he was not alone, that there were others like him, creatures that lived solitary lives, preying on the Normals and trying to keep from being caught and killed by the authorities. Some of these others had banded together and formed some sort of Council to try and keep the existence of the

Vampyres a secret. From the council, Pike found out the history of his new race."

Shooter abruptly stood up. "If we're going further with this, I'm gonna need something stronger to drink than coffee."

"Me too," Sam said.

"Me three," TJ added.

"OK, that's a good idea. I'll fix us all drinks," Matt said.

"Make mine a double," Shooter said. "I'll be right back."

While Matt made the drinks, Shooter went out to his Mustang, opened the glove box, and took out a pack of Marlboros. When he took one out and put his lighter to it, he noticed his hands were shaking.

When everyone had gathered back in Matt's living room, drinks in hand, Matt noticed TJ's color was better, as if she'd somehow managed to get her feelings under control.

Shooter, on the other hand, looked like he was having trouble dealing with the revelations about the man, or creature, who had tried to take over his lover's mind and body.

"You OK, Shooter?" Matt asked.

"Yeah, but I'm startin' to wonder just how all this is gonna help us deal with what happened to TJ."

TJ gave him a smile and entwined her hand in his, giving it a light squeeze to show she was all right.

"We're coming to that part," Matt said. "In the next part of his journal, Niemann, or Pike, tells of how the Vampyre race got its start and just how the physical characteristics are generated."

Sam shook her head, a bewildered expression on her face. "Matt, I just fail to see how genetic characteristics can be passed on by the mere drinking of blood."

"It'll become obvious, dear," Matt said, picking up the journal and beginning to talk.

"According to Pike, the Vampyres are a race descended from a small group of Gypsies who lived in a mountain area in Europe called the Carpathian region."

"Carpathia?" Shooter asked. "Where the hell is that?"

"I think it's somewhere in Hungary," Matt said. "Anyway, over a period of hundreds of years, due to inbreeding, a mutant gene arose in the Gypsies that caused a rare disease known as erythropoietic uroporphyria." Matt hesitated and glanced at Sam, "The condition we nowadays call porphyria."

Sam gave a small smile, as if this explained some things to her, as did TJ.

"What is porphyria?" Shooter asked. "And what does it have to do with—"

Matt held up his hand. "Shooter, the symptoms of porphyria are pale skin that blisters and burns upon exposure to sunlight, phosphorescent teeth that glow in the dark, and congenital hemolysis, or rupture of red blood cells, causing red, bloodstained eyes and bloody tears and a progressive anemia that can be controlled only by infusions of whole blood."

"You're kidding," Shooter said. "You're describing the typical vampires of the movies."

Matt nodded. "Exactly. In addition, many of them also have elongated teeth, like fangs."

"But, Matt, what about the mental abilities Pike talked about?" Sam asked.

"Evidently, the Gypsies of the region had a high incidence of people with second sight, precognition, and even mild mind-reading capabilities, as well as extremely long lives for the times. As the inbreeding grew more severe due to their isolation, these abilities became commonplace in the community and even increased in strength over many decades."

"Still," TJ said, her eyes far away as she thought of the implications of what she was hearing, "none of this explains the transmission of these traits by drinking blood. After all, porphyria as we know it is not transmissible this way."

"Pike explains that by the occurrence of an infection in the group by some sort of mutated bacteriophage that soon included everyone in the village."

"Now you've lost me again," Shooter complained.

TJ turned to look at him as she spoke. "A bacteriophage is a microscopic viruslike particle that has the ability to transfer genetic material from one cell to another. We use it in the lab all the time to change the characteristics of bacteria."

"So these little bitty things can change a person's genetic code and turn them into these monsters?" Shooter asked.

Matt and Sam nodded at the same time. "Yeah. Sam and I discovered some of this while working to cure TJ," Matt said. "In fact, we used some antibiotics known to be effective against bacteriophages to stop her infection."

"If that's the case, then why am I still having some symptoms of the disease?" TJ asked, a look of shame and loathing on her face.

Matt frowned. "That I don't know yet, TJ, but I haven't finished studying Pike's journal. He's evidently worked on this problem for over a hundred years, and if he's found out something that might help us, I'll discover just what it is."

"Matt, why don't you make copies of the journal

for TJ and me?" Sam asked. "That way, we can all study it for clues that might be helpful."

"Good idea," Matt answered.

Shooter stood up and took TJ by the hand. "I think we've heard enough for one night, Matt. Thanks for the meal, and the info. It's certainly given us a lot to think about."

Matt and Sam walked them to the door. Sam put her hand on TJ's shoulder. "Don't worry, TJ. We'll get to the bottom of this and make you well again."

TJ smiled sadly. "I hope so."

"Good night, guys," Matt said.

As they watched the couple walk down the sidewalk toward Shooter's car, Matt turned to Sam. "We've still got some wine left."

"The hell with the wine. I need a stiff drink after hearing what was in that journal."

Matt fixed the drinks and handed one to Sam.

She took a deep draft, sighed, and leaned into him, her head on his chest. "Matt," she said in a low, husky voice.

"Yeah, babe?"

"Make love to me."

Matt raised his eyebrows. Sam had never been this forward before.

"I need to get my mind off vampires and blood diseases for a while," she added.

"Oh, so now I'm medicine, huh?" he teased, leaning back to look into her eyes.

"Of the best kind," she said, taking him by the hand and leading him into his bedroom.

As they stood next to the bed, he gently unbuttoned her blouse and slipped it off her shoulders, revealing breasts unencumbered by a bra.

He cupped one in his hand and kissed her while she undid her jeans and dropped them to the floor.

Within seconds, they were both naked and lying in each other's arms.

Matt bent his head and took her nipple in his mouth as she caressed him into full arousal.

Suddenly she spread her legs and rolled him on top of her, moaning deep in her throat as he entered her. Her fingernails dug into his back as he moved against her, nuzzling her neck with his lips.

Minutes later, Matt groaned with release and crushed her lips with his.

He rolled over onto his side of the bed, breathing heavily. Sam smiled at him, picked her drink off the nightstand, and drained it.

Then, with a wicked grin on her lips, she leaned over him. As her hair brushed his groin, she mumbled, "Now that you've had your fun, it's my turn."

Matt raised his head and watched her mouth cover him. "You're a slave driver," he said.

"You ain't seen nothin' yet," she replied, her breath warm on his loins.

Seven

Armed with fake ID, Mary Nichols sat at the bar in a saloon on St. Louis Street, just off Bourbon Street, tears running down her cheeks. She shook her head when the bartender stepped over and asked her what she wanted. She was too pissed off and hurt to order anything. Her asshole of a boy-friend had been acting like a jerk in the last bar, coming on to the strippers as if she hadn't even been sitting there. She'd run out of the place, turned a couple of corners, and ducked into this place to give him something to think about.

She looked up as a deep masculine voice next to her said, "Bring the lady a white wine."

The man sitting on the bar stool next to her was one of the most handsome men she'd ever seen. He had dark curly hair and bright blue eyes, though they did appear a bit bloodshot, as if he'd been having too much to drink. His face was creased in a slight smile, kind but not mocking.

"I find a light white wine is often the best anti-dote for sadness, don't you?" he asked gently, his hand finding its way to her shoulder.

Mary dried her tears and nodded, hypnotized by the stare of those ice-blue eyes that looked as if they could see into her very soul.

The bartender placed a glass in front of Mary,

and the stranger paid for it with a ten-dollar bill, saying, "Keep the change."

Oh, Mary thought, *kind and gentle and rich to boot, but he looks like he needs to spend a little more time in the sun.* His skin was so pale it was almost translucent.

"If you're alone, please join me at my table," the man said, and got up off the stool and strolled over to a dark corner of the saloon.

He even walks as if he owns the place, Mary thought. She picked up her wine and followed him to his table.

She sat down and took a deep drink of her wine to give her courage. She was on a senior trip with her French class from Baton Rouge; as a high schooler, she was not really accustomed to letting herself be picked up in bars by strange men.

"Hi, my name's Mary," she said, purposefully not giving her last name just in case he turned out to be a pervert.

"I am Jacques Chatdenuit," he said.

"Chatdenuit?" Mary asked, smiling. "Isn't that French for cat of the night?"

Jacques smiled and nodded. In the darkness, just for a moment, Mary thought his teeth seemed to glow.

Must be a black light in here somewhere, she thought, and raised her glass to him.

"Thanks for the drink, Mr. Chatdenuit," she said. "I really needed it."

"I know," he said. "I could tell."

Mary went on to tell him how her boyfriend had acted, and he seemed very concerned.

"Perhaps we should take a walk back to this other bar and let him see you with another man," Jacques

said. "That might make him jealous and cause him
to treat you better in the future."

"That's a great idea," Mary said, laughing at the
thought of her unsophisticated friends seeing her
in the company of such a handsome, worldly gentleman.

"Finish your wine and we'll go show them all,"
Jacques said.

Wondering if she'd voiced her thoughts out loud,
Mary upended her wineglass and drained the last
few drops. Of course, she must have. Otherwise how
would he have known what she was thinking?

Stumbling a little from the effects of the wine,
Mary got to her feet and walked out the door with
the man named Jacques.

Instead of turning to the left toward Bourbon
Street, Jacques put his arm around her shoulders
and led her to the right.

"Wait a minute," Mary protested. "The club is
the other way."

"I'm just going to take you down toward the river
to let the night air clear your head a bit before we
meet your boyfriend," Jacques said.

Mary nodded slowly. She did seem to be having
trouble focusing her thoughts. Perhaps the night air
would do her good, and the river would be very
pretty in the moonlight.

Four blocks later, they entered the Woldenberg
Riverfront Park. There were occasional couples
walking arm in arm, but for the most part, the park
was almost deserted at this time of night.

Suddenly concerned at being alone in the darkness with a man she'd just met, Mary glanced
around. "Maybe we'd better head back."

Jacques turned to her, easing her back into the
branches of a large bush, his hands moving to her

breasts. "No, I think not, Mary," he said, his voice changing, from deep and masculine to a throaty growl, like that of a lion's.

As his hands began to knead her breasts and he pushed his tumescent groin against her, Mary opened her mouth to scream; the scream died in her throat at the horror of seeing Jacques's face begin to melt and change before her eyes.

His eyes became red and piercing. He opened his mouth to reveal glowing fangs, dripping what looked like blood as he ran a long, pointed tongue over his lips.

With a sudden movement, he ripped her blouse off, along with her bra, and ducked his head to her chest. As his teeth closed over her nipple, drawing blood, Mary's mind shut down in terror and she fainted, becoming limp in his arms.

Jacques lowered her to the moist, damp earth and tore the rest of her clothes off, a frenzied rending of cloth and flesh. He stripped quickly and knelt over her nude body, caressing her firm young breasts with both his hands and his eyes. She moaned and moved slightly under his touch. When his hand moved to her groin, her eyes fluttered open and she spread her legs and pushed herself against him, though her face still wore an expression of horror.

He flicked his tongue against her lips, probing her mind with his until she wrapped her arms around him with a deep groan of desire. Grinning evilly, he pinned her arms to the ground above her head and sank his fangs into her breast as he entered her violently. While she grunted in pain with each thrust of his hips, he moved his mouth to her neck and began to feast on her blood.

When she was empty and he was satiated, Jacques

leaned his head back and howled at the moon, causing several nearby strollers to run in panic from the park.

Jacques stood over her lifeless body, got into his clothes, and wiped blood from his lips with the back of his hand. He knelt, picked up her head, and kissed her cold, dead lips, silently giving her thanks for her gift to him.

He glanced once at the moon before strolling nonchalantly toward his apartment in the French Quarter, his Hunger assuaged once again as it had been every night for the past week.

Eight

I finally finished moving into my apartment in the French Quarter. I'd found a nice one with its own enclosed garden on Dauphine between St. Peter and Orleans, one block off Bourbon. It was very expensive, but I still had plenty of money that I'd rescued from my warehouse in Houston before leaving.

I picked the French Quarter for two reasons. First, the French Quarter of New Orleans is an area that thrives on the darkness of night, as I do. My nocturnal comings and goings would hardly be noticed in such a place. Secondly, I'd taken a job at one of the outreach clinics of the Tulane School of Medicine, using my new name, Albert Nachtman. It was located only a short distance from my new abode. There I hoped to be able to continue my research into both the problems of CJD and how to reverse the disease of Vampyrism.

The one problem with my apartment was it wasn't very close to where I'd docked my ship on Lake Ponchartrain. Lake Ponchartrain isn't really a lake; it's more of a large bay off the ocean just to the north of the city. With any luck, however, I wouldn't need to go to the ship very often, or to the warehouse I'd rented just down the street from the docks.

To celebrate my new living arrangement, I walked the few blocks down Orleans, circled Jackson Square, and moved toward the French Market to enjoy café au lait and beignets at the Café du Monde.

The coffee here is dark and strong with a hint of chicory, and the beignets, small pastries covered with powdered sugar, are supposed to be the best in the world.

I took an outside table to enjoy the early-morning coolness before the ever-present summer humidity made the day miserable. After my coffee and pastries were served, I opened the morning paper.

My heart began to beat faster and my mouth became dry at the headlines: RIPPER STRIKES AGAIN.

I read the news report, my coffee forgotten and growing cold on the table. There had been a series of brutal killings on the fringes of the French Quarter over the past few weeks. All of the victims, young women, had their throats ripped out and their bodies drained of blood. The police were assuming they had a new serial killer working in the midst of the city, but I knew different.

I glanced heavenward and uttered a silent curse. It seemed lately if I had any luck at all, it would be bad. After moving to a new location to avoid the scrutiny of the police, I find there is an apparent Vampyre on a killing spree right in my new neighborhood.

I waved the waiter over and requested a fresh cup of coffee and drank it as I read the details of the killings. From the marked brutality and the very public places where the killings occurred, I wondered if the Vampyre was sick. Only the mental derangement that comes with the final stages of CJD, Creutzfeldt-Jakob disease, would make one of my kind take such chances of discovery . . . that or a supreme arrogance bordering on megalomania.

I realized I had grown lax in my daily activities of late. I'd been moving around the city with my mental abilities blocked to avoid detection should I happen to run into another of my race. Since my last confrontation with the members of the Vampyre Council, when I'd killed the leader, Jacqueline de la Fontaine, along with some others, I'd tried my best to steer clear of any involvement with the Vampyre organization. I now felt that was a mistake.

If there was, in fact, one of us acting as "the Ripper," then he was a danger to us all and steps would have to be taken to rid ourselves, and the Normals, of his activities.

I vowed to go about my business as usual, though with my mental abilities unmasked in hopes of finding either the Ripper himself or others of my kind who might help get rid of this scourge. I knew I was taking a chance, since I was almost certainly considered an enemy by the Council members.

Throughout my long life as a Vampyre, I'd shunned members of my new race, both through shame and disgust at what they and I had become, and because I'd always been something of a loner. Now my very survival, and the survival of my race, depended on my cooperating with others of my kind to find and kill the sick one known as the Ripper.

I finished my breakfast and returned to my apartment. In order to be prepared for the day when our paths would cross, I took one of my *katanas,* the Japanese long swords, and a gallon jug of gasoline and secreted them in the trunk of my car. To kill a Vampyre, one must cut off the head and burn the body, and I wanted to be ready to do just that when the time came.

From the newspaper accounts, I knew the Ripper hunted in the same haunts I did: bars and nightclubs where patrons wouldn't remember his face when he left with a potential victim. It was time for me to start frequenting such places on a regular basis. Sooner or later, I would find him, for my mental abilities allow me to sense the sickness in a Vampyre as easily as I can smell the stench of decay on a corpse.

I just hoped I would sense him before he sensed me, for surprise is the key in a fight between members of our race.

At nine o'clock in the morning, I went to my office. I'd picked an outreach clinic located in a poor part of town for several reasons. The university has a problem recruiting doctors to work in such places, so they didn't bother to check my forged credentials too closely. Also, working with the poor and downtrodden salves my conscience somewhat about my need to feed off the Normals and helps me to be able to live with my terrible needs.

As I worked my way through the pitiful patients, mostly homeless people and the very poor, my mind was already on the coming darkness and the start of my hunt for my fellow creature.

I knew I was going to have to be extremely careful. Finding the monster would necessitate unshielding my mind in order to locate his, and this would leave me vulnerable to his reading my thoughts as well. My task was going to take all the mental finesse I was capable of. A member of the Vampyre race as mentally unbalanced as the Ripper would be an extremely dangerous adversary, one I need to be careful not to underestimate.

Nine

Matt was in the doctors' lounge, discussing with Jeff Strickland how the medical students were performing on their ER rotation, when the door opened and Dr. Sheldon Silver stepped in.

Strickland grinned and raised his hand. "Hey, Dr. Silver, what're you doing here? We haven't lost anyone in the last hour or two."

He was referring to Silver's job as professor of pathology and his attendant job as the interim medical examiner of the county.

Silver smiled. "I'm not here to do an autopsy, Jeff," he said, "though from the looks of those bags under your eyes, I might be seeing you down in the morgue sooner rather than later if you don't get some rest."

Strickland got tiredly to his feet. "Comes with the job, Doc," he said. "In surgery, if you snooze, you lose."

"Actually, I'm here to see Matt," Silver said.

"Then I'll leave you to it," Strickland said. He turned to Matt. "I'll get those written evaluations of the students to you by the first of the week, Matt."

Matt nodded. "No hurry, Jeff. Whenever you get to it."

After Strickland left, Matt inclined his head at the

coffeepot in the corner of the room. "Cup of Joe, Shelly?"

Silver's expression turned wry and he wagged his head. "No thanks, Matt. I'd rather drink formaldehyde."

Silver, known as Shelly to most everyone, was as usual wearing white jeans and a Hawaiian shirt, blue with white flowers this time. His only concession to hospital protocol was a wrinkled white clinic jacket with some stains on it that no one had the nerve to question the origin of. Shelly was a rotund five feet seven inches tall. Although he appeared to be fat, he was actually heavyset, with most of his bulk being muscle rather than adipose tissue.

He had a springy, quick walk and moved with no wasted motion. His hair was dark, shot through with gray, and his blue eyes seemed to twinkle when he laughed.

Shelly had been the de facto leader of the so-called Vampire Task Force responsible for the discovery of Roger Niemann and his lair. He was Sam's boss and also her closest friend, along with his wife, Barbara.

"Well, if you don't want coffee and you're not here to do an autopsy, what can I do for you, Shelly?" Matt asked.

"Sam tells me you have some new information about the origin of the creature we knew as Roger Niemann."

"Yeah. Damon Clark found a journal Roger had been keeping for over two hundred years, if you can believe the dates in it."

Shelly took a seat across from Matt and leaned forward, his elbows on his knees. "Two hundred years, huh? That's a long time to be going around sucking the blood out of people."

"Yeah, it is," Matt answered. "But you know, Shelly? From the way Niemann wrote in his journal, he hated the fact that his disease, as he called it, forced him to attack and sometimes kill people."

Shelly leaned back, his eyebrows knitted. "Nothing forces us to kill others, Matt."

Matt gave a sad smile. "I don't know about you, Shelly, but I eat steak and chicken and fish. . . . I guess the cows and chickens and fish don't think we *have* to do that."

"Animals are a far cry from human beings," Shelly said, though his tone was not as sure as before.

"That's just it, Shelly. Evidently, Niemann now considers himself a different race, almost a different species since his conversion two hundred years ago. He wrote in his journal that the Vampyres consider us Normals an inferior species, one made to be food for them."

Shelly stared at Matt. "That may be their opinion, but that doesn't make it the correct one."

Matt sighed, looking suddenly tired. "I know, I know. I'm not saying I buy into Niemann's arguments. It's just that since I've been reading his journal, I've been trying to get into Niemann's mind. I can almost see his point of view, and, in fact, I feel rather sorry for the hand that fate dealt him."

As Shelly opened his mouth to protest, Matt held up his hand. "I agree with what you're gonna say. What he became didn't excuse what he did, but we've got to remember, he didn't ask to become one of the undead any more than TJ did."

"Speaking of that," Shelly said to change the subject, "Sam also informed me that TJ continues to show some . . . rather disturbing symptoms."

Matt's eyes dropped. "Shooter seems to think so,

though we were with them Saturday and we didn't notice anything out of the ordinary." He paused; then, with a crooked grin, he added, "Other than the fact the monkeys didn't seem to like her too much."

Shelly pursed his lips. "Still, if Shooter is worried, perhaps we ought to check it out."

"What do you mean?"

"I think it's incumbent upon us to run further tests to see if we've really cured TJ of the infection that Niemann caused, especially since you've evidently found in that journal of Niemann's some new information concerning the etiology of the infection."

"Sam and I discussed that, but so far, TJ is reluctant to be put through any more tests."

"Well, if you can change her mind, I've prevailed upon the dean of the medical school to make a laboratory available to you and Sam. One of the microbiology professors is on a sabbatical, and his lab is vacant. You and Sam can use it for as long as you need to make sure TJ is all right."

He reached in the pocket of his clinic jacket and pulled out a key. He pitched it to Matt. "Here's your key. I've already given Sam hers."

Matt glanced at the key. "Thanks, Shelly." He looked back up. "Will you be available for consultation on the blood test results and any therapy we contemplate?"

"Of course," Shelly answered. "In fact, Sam told me there was something about plasmids in Niemann's journal, so I called a friend of mine at McGill University. He's the leading researcher on plasmids in the world. He's going to send us everything he has on human infections with plasmids."

"Then I guess it's up to us to convince TJ to go through with the tests."

Shelly stood up. "I'll leave that to you and Sam. I've never had much luck trying to change a woman's mind."

"Ain't that the truth," Matt said, laughing.

Matt worried all afternoon about how he and Sam and Shooter might broach the subject of conducting more tests on TJ. Finally, he figured it might best be done over dinner and drinks. Throughout his life, he'd found that women were most susceptible to suggestions after a superb meal at a fine restaurant.

He phoned Sam, who agreed with his assessment, and then he called Shooter, who also said he was free that night. Now the only thing left for Matt to do was to pick the right restaurant. After some consideration, he settled on a seafood place, not wanting to have to deal with the sight of TJ eating a rare steak and then having to tell her she might still be infected with the Vampyre bug, be it a plasmid or whatever.

That night, the foursome met at Papadeaux's, a Cajun-style seafood restaurant off I-10, not too far from downtown. The restaurant was a huge, multistoried wooden building decorated in a seafaring mode, with all manner of stuffed and mounted sailfish, swordfish, tarpon, and sharks, as well as fishing nets and Japanese glass net-floats and starfish.

Sam glanced around at the decor. "I may grow gills just looking at all this," she said.

Matt assumed a hurt expression. "Don't tell me you don't like it," he said. "This is supposed to be one of the best seafood places in town."

"Yeah," Shooter chimed in. "Just look at all these fish on the walls. Anyone who could manage to catch these beauties must know a lot about how to cook 'em.''

TJ shook her head. "Dear Shooter," she said, "the owners didn't catch those fish, and the cook certainly didn't. They bought them from some interior-decorating shop, which, in turn, probably bought them from some garage sales in Florida."

"They just told the decorator they wanted something in macho-male fishing kitsch," Sam jibed.

Matt looked at each of the women in turn and then at Shooter. "See, pal, a man goes to extraordinary lengths to please the woman of his dreams, and what does she do? She makes fun of his choice of restaurants."

Shooter nodded in agreement. "Next time we'll just take 'em to Kip's Big Boy and let 'em eat hamburgers."

Both TJ and Sam laughed. "OK, guys," Sam said, "before you get your feelings hurt beyond all redemption, TJ and I both love the place. In fact, we've both said before we wanted to eat here, but couldn't afford it."

"Wait a minute," Matt said, looking from one to the other. "What do you mean can't afford it? Aren't you two girls paying tonight?"

"In your dreams, big guy," TJ said, giggling at the thought.

As the waiter approached with a stack of leather menus in hand, Shooter said in a whispered aside to Matt, "Uh-oh, leather menus. You know what that means, don't you?"

Matt nodded, a glum expression on his face. "Yeah. Megabucks before we leave here."

Shooter shrugged. "At least we've got women with us in case we don't have enough money and have to wash dishes."

TJ punched him in the arm. "Was that a sexist remark, Mr. Kowolski?"

"No, not at all, Shooter said. "It's just a well-known fact that washing dishes is bred in women's genes, whereas men are born to hunt and fish and gather food."

"You forgot the inbred male gene for chasing skirts," TJ said, a dangerous look on her face.

The waiter stood there, watching the byplay with a half smile on his face. "Can I get you folks something to drink, or an appetizer perhaps?" he asked.

"Gin and Seven for the other lady and me, and roach exterminator for the gentlemen," TJ said acidly.

"Will that be up or on the rocks on the roach exterminator?" the waiter asked.

"On the rocks, definitely," Matt said. "I can't stand room temperature poison."

"Scotch and water for me, and something with an umbrella in it for Matt," Shooter said.

"I'll have a gin and Seven, too, with a wedge of lime," Matt said, glaring at Shooter. He glanced at the menu. "And how about a round of those spicy crab cakes for an appetizer?"

"You got it, sir," the waiter said, and walked off, shaking his head.

Shooter watched him. "Probably gay," he said.

"Why do you say that?" TJ asked.

" 'Cause he looked like he couldn't believe the way you women were acting. If he were straight, he'd have a girlfriend or a wife and would know it's par for the course."

TJ punched Shooter again, and as he rubbed his arm and moaned, she muttered, "Butt lick."

When the waiter brought the drinks, Matt held

his up for a toast. "To good friends and good times," he said.

They all clinked glasses and took a drink.

When the waiter brought the crab cakes, they ordered. Matt asked for the blackened redfish; Sam ordered swordfish, brushing aside Matt's concern about the level of mercury in it; Shooter decided on shrimp Creole; TJ scanned the menu for a moment, then pitched it on the table. "I'll just have a steak, rare, with French fries and a salad," she said.

The rest of the group stared at her, and then glanced at each other, worried expressions on their faces. Shooter leaned over and put his hand on her shoulder. "TJ, baby, this is a seafood place. Why don't you order something they specialize in?"

TJ shrugged, not meeting his eyes. "I just feel the need for some meat, Shooter. Don't make a federal case out of it."

When Shooter started to speak, Matt shook his head.

The group's earlier jovial mood was broken when the food was served and TJ tore into the bloody meat, a look of intense concentration on her face.

After the meal was finished, the foursome ordered Key lime pie and coffee. While they were eating it, Sam decided it was time to broach the subject of further testing on TJ.

"TJ," Sam began, "Matt and I have some news about what we can do to make sure you're completely cured."

TJ looked up from her pie, an anxious expression on her face. "Oh?"

"Yeah. Dr. Silver has procured a lab for us to use from the microbiology department, and he's enlisted the help of a professor from McGill University."

"The man's supposed to be the world's greatest authority on human infections with plasmids," Matt added.

"You think he can help me?" TJ asked, glancing at Shooter, who put his hand on hers in silent support.

Both Matt and Sam nodded. "We haven't heard from him yet, but Matt's already downloaded everything he's written on the subject off the Internet."

"Anything useful?" TJ asked.

Matt smiled. "I think so. Several of his articles deal with different type of plasmids that carry genes that keep other plasmids from conjugating."

"Conjugating?" Shooter asked. "Is that what it sounds like?"

TJ smiled for the first time in a while. She looked at him. "Conjugating is the term used for plasmid reproduction," she explained.

"Yeah, and if we can stop that," Sam said, "then sooner or later all the plasmids in TJ's body will die a natural death and she'll be totally cured."

"So you two do think there are still some of these plasmid whatchamacallits floating around in TJ's bloodstream?" Shooter asked.

Matt shrugged. "It could account for some of the symptoms that have you and TJ worried."

TJ's eyes dropped. "I was hoping all that was behind me," she said in a low voice. "It just makes me feel so . . . dirty to think I might still be infected."

"Nonsense," Sam said quickly. "We're not saying you are definitely still infected, TJ. But, if there are still some plasmids we didn't get rid of the first time, this may be a perfect way to ensure they don't cause you any further trouble."

TJ glanced at Shooter. "Do you think I should go through with more tests and treatment, Shooter?"

Shooter shrugged, his face blushing red. "Jeez, I don't know, sweetheart," he said. "I'm just a flatfoot cop; you guys are the medical experts—"

"What can it hurt, TJ?" Matt interrupted gently. "The worst that can happen is you'll go through some unnecessary blood tests."

Her eyes stared into his, troubled. "But what about injecting me with more plasmids? I'm not so sure I like that idea."

Sam shook her head. "That's gonna be our last resort, TJ, and only if this professor in Canada and Dr. Silver and Matt and I all agree it's necessary."

TJ bit her lip. "All right, I'll do it," she said, her eyes turning to Shooter. "I don't want you to have any doubts about me, Shooter."

He leaned over and kissed her lightly on the lips. "I've never had any doubts about you, TJ."

Ten

The Louisiana chapter of the Vampyre Council decided to meet in New Orleans, since the most important business they had to discuss was what to do about the new threat to their existence, the rogue Vampyre the media had dubbed the Ripper.

The leader of the chapter, who also happened to live in New Orleans, was Carmilla de la Fontaine. She was the niece of the leader of the Texas Council, Jacqueline de la Fontaine, who'd been killed along with several other members of her council a few months previously by the rogue Vampyre Roger Niemann.

Carmilla owned an antique shop in the French Quarter, where she housed a collection of the precious antiques she'd acquired over her many years of life.

Carmilla was worried that the members of the Council might guess that the fate of the Ripper wasn't the only thing on her mind. She had a deep and abiding hatred for the Vampyre known as Roger Niemann ever since he'd killed her aunt. In fact, she was so obsessed with him that she couldn't believe he was dead.

When she found out how he'd killed her aunt, the one who was responsible for her own transformation, she made herself a promise she would personally destroy him, and she didn't intend to rest until she'd done just that. She had a sneaking feeling that Niemann had somehow survived the attack by the Houston police and was now acting as the Ripper in New Orleans. In fact, that was just what Niemann had been doing in Houston that caused the Council there to confront him. Carmilla saw no reason he wouldn't continue his rapacious killings if he was still alive.

Another reason behind Carmilla's calling of a meeting at this time was her desire to consolidate her control over the group. There had been recent rumblings of a revolt among her followers, instigated, she felt, by Michael Morpheus and his followers.

As members of the Council began to arrive, she showed them to a back room used for such meetings. The room was outfitted with a large Georgian dining table and had a small kitchen and several settees and easy chairs scattered around on exquisite Persian rugs.

The Vampyres were introduced to each other as they arrived, since names were changed as years went by to preclude drawing attention to their long lives. The Vampyres tended to take names of characters in old vampire novels or Greek mythology, or sometimes just names that had double meanings in different languages. It was a sign of their contempt for humans that they would take such names and risk exposure—though it was a small risk, for most humans doubted their very existence.

The first two to arrive were Jean Horla and Peter Vardalack. Jean was a tall black-haired man, thin to the point of emaciation, who looked like a mortician. Peter, on the other hand, was short and pudgy, with rosy cheeks, bright blue eyes, and a merry expression. He always seemed to be thinking of a joke that no one else knew. They were both from the Baton Rouge area.

As Carmilla was pouring chicory coffee into china cups, she slyly probed the surface of their minds to see if they were among those who were tending to listen to Morpheus's talk of defection. She had a light touch with her mental probing and only went deep enough to gauge their emotions, not deep enough to alert them to her invasion of their thoughts. They seemed to have no animosity toward her and she found no trace they were anything other than what they seemed.

The bell on the front door tinkled as Adeline Ducayne and Sarah Kenyon entered. Adeline and Sarah were almost never seen apart, and rumor among the Vampyres was that they were more than just good friends. Adeline was petite and pretty, with dyed blond hair, pale skin, and a doll-like face; Sarah was broad and stocky, with large arms and hands, and hair cut very short.

Carmilla greeted them warmly, declining to try and read their minds. Women tended to be more sensitive to such intrusions and she didn't want to alienate them unnecessarily if they were on her side.

While she was helping them to coffee, Michael Morpheus arrived alone, as usual. Michael was olive-skinned with jet-black hair worn long and pulled back into a ponytail. He had a single gold stud earring in his left ear. He rarely took part in Council meetings and was known as something of a rogue who rebelled at the Council's pacifist notions of nonlethal feedings. Carmilla was sure it was he who was fomenting rebellion at her leadership, since they'd disliked each other from the first time they met.

Soon after their first encounter, Michael had suggested they become mates. Carmilla, who found his oily good looks and his bloodthirsty nature repulsive, declined. They'd been enemies ever since.

Shortly after Michael's entrance, a group of several men and women arrived together: Christina Alario, Theo Thantos, and Gerald Enyo, laughing and talking among themselves as if coming to a party.

When Carmilla greeted them, Theo said, "Louis Frene will be a little late. His plane was held up in Alexandria."

Carmilla waved them into the back room with a sweep of her hand. "Come on back and we'll go on and get started without him. The others are having coffee."

"Some of your special chicory blend, I hope?" Christina asked.

"Of course, along with some beignets I had delivered from the Café du Monde."

Once the group had all gotten coffee and pastry, they took seats around the room, with Carmilla sitting at the head of the table.

She tapped a Mont Blanc pen on the table lightly, calling the meeting to order.

"We will get started without waiting for Louis, since we have an extensive agenda to cover."

Michael snorted, his obsidian eyes boring into hers. "I hope you haven't called us here for more bullshit about how we should feed and how we need to keep a low profile," he said. His dislike of taking orders was well known and he rarely tried to hide his disdain for Carmilla's campaign to keep the Vampyres from killing Normals.

Carmilla ignored him. "The first item on the

agenda is what we should do, if anything, about this killer known as the Ripper."

"Are we sure he's one of us, and not just another crazy Other?" Adeline asked, using another Vampyre term for humans.

Peter laughed dryly. "If he's not one of us, then he ought to be, for he certainly appears to like the taste of blood."

"I think we have to assume the worst, Adeline," Carmilla answered, scowling at Peter's levity.

"I don't see what the problem is," Sarah said. "How does this person's actions impact us?" She looked around at the group. "As far as I can tell, all of us are abiding by the Council's decision to pursue only nonlethal feeding."

"That's the point," Carmilla said. "I know that there are members of this body who do not agree with our decision on how to feed inconspicuously." She stared pointedly at Morpheus as she said this, and then continued. "But so far, everyone has gone along with the decision of the majority. If there is now a rogue out there who doesn't accept our sovereignty in these matters, then sooner or later, he or she will have to be dealt with."

"Does anyone have any idea who this 'rogue' might be?" asked Gerald, glancing around at the others. As he spoke, Carmilla got a mental whiff of anger in his mind and made a mental note to check him out later. Perhaps he was one of the members who were leaning toward Morpheus's viewpoint that the Normals, an inferior breed, were their rightful prey and that they should feed on them at will.

Everyone shook their heads at Gerald's question, except Carmilla, who frowned as she surveyed the group around the table, wondering who else might be against her.

"I have an idea who it might be," she finally said.

As all eyes turned to her, she elaborated. "As you all know, a few months back, in Houston, a rogue there named Roger Niemann killed my aunt and several other members of her Council over just such a disagreement—"

"But," Peter interrupted, "wasn't Roger killed by the Houston police?"

Carmilla shrugged. "That's the story, but we all know how hard it is for an Other to kill one of us. What if he somehow managed to escape and made his way here to New Orleans?"

An excited murmur spread around the room, until Carmilla held up her hand. "I yield the floor to Theo. He's told me something I think you all should be aware of."

Theo cleared his throat. "A few nights ago, as I was entering the Café du Monde, a man brushed by me on his way out. I was almost sure it was Roger Niemann, but by the time I'd turned around, he was gone."

"Did you scan his mind?" Peter asked.

Theo nodded. "I tried, but all I got was a blank."

"That's hardly proof it was Roger Niemann," Michael said scornfully.

Theo gave him a flat look. "The only minds I've ever encountered that I've been unable to read have been among the Vampyres. If this wasn't Roger, then he was one of us."

"And if he's one of us, with nothing to hide, why was he blocking his thoughts?" Carmilla asked.

"Even if this Roger Niemann is now living here, that doesn't mean he's the Ripper," Sarah said.

"He ran amok in Houston, and now I'm telling you he's doing the same thing here!" Carmilla said with some heat.

Jean reached across the table to put his hand on her arm. "Carmilla, you must admit you've been obsessed with this Niemann ever since he killed your aunt. Aren't you perhaps overreacting?"

Carmilla took a deep breath. "Perhaps, but the fact remains that my aunt and her followers braced him over such behavior, and were killed for their interference in Niemann's lifestyle."

Michael glanced at the Rolex on his wrist, a bored expression on his face. "Let's get on with the rest of the meeting. We'll all keep our eyes and our minds open to see if we can locate Niemann . . . though," he added, glancing scornfully at Carmilla, "we all know how obsessed you are with this particular Vampyre. I, for one, believe you're letting your desire for vengeance against him rob you of your common sense."

Carmilla's lips pressed tight at the insult, but she knew he was right. However, she still felt she was justified in her beliefs about Niemann being alive. "Think what you will, Michael, but our next speaker may change your mind. I'd like to introduce a friend from Houston, Ramson Holroyd."

From out of the shadows of a corner stepped a large black man, well over six feet tall, with broad shoulders and heavily muscled arms. He inclined his head at the group.

"Why have you asked an outsider to our meeting, Carmilla?" Michael asked. "This has always been a closed association."

He just can't help trying to undermine my leadership, Carmilla thought, but kept her feelings deep within her mind so he couldn't read them. "He has information that is vital to us all," she replied.

Ramson, ignoring Michael's protest at his presence, spoke in a deep, sonorous voice. "While our

Houston Council was investigating the Roger Niemann mess, we came upon some facts that shook us to our very core. Roger had begun the rite of Transformation on a woman he wanted for his mate. It was almost complete when he was attacked and possibly killed."

"So what?" Michael asked. "We've all done much the same over the years."

Ramson smiled slightly. "Yes, but to our knowledge, no one has ever been able to reverse a Transformation once it's taken place. Our information is that the medical group in Houston that was responsible for Niemann's killing was able to do just that."

There was a gasp around the room and the members looked at each other, expressions of wonder on their faces. "But . . . but that's impossible!" Peter said.

"If that is true," Adeline said with a hint of awe in her voice, "then maybe the same process could be used to cause us to no longer be Vampyres."

"Those were our thoughts," Ramson said. "In fact, before he attacked us and killed several of our members, we had information that Niemann himself was working on just such a process."

"Bah!" spat Michael. "So what? Why would any one of us desire to become an Other again? With their mayfly lives and their lack of mental abilities—I'd rather be dead!"

Adeline turned to him, fire in her eyes. "Yes, but you don't speak for us all, Michael, as has been shown many times in the past. I, for one, would give anything to be cured of this curse of a lust for blood that consumes my every waking moment."

There were several nods around the table, showing general agreement. Carmilla watched her group carefully, trying to figure out who might be on her side and who might be inclined to move with Michael. Of the group, she noticed frowns on the faces of Jean Horla, Sarah Kenyon, and Christina Alario. Christina's eyes sought Michael's and Carmilla thought she saw a slight nod pass between them.

"Ramson has a plan that I think we should all hear," Carmilla said into the hush that followed his words, still troubled by the seeming split within her group.

As all eyes turned to him, Ramson began: "I would like the Council's permission to contact the members of this medical team and to ask them to visit us here in New Orleans and to share with us their secret for reversing the Transformation."

"If this is such a good idea, why didn't your own Council in Houston do it?" Michael asked.

"My Council doesn't exist any longer," Ramson said with a sad, defeated look in his eyes. "Niemann, before he died, managed to kill all the leaders of the Council, and the rest disbanded in disagreement over how to proceed in the future." He stared at Michael. "Like you all, there were some in our group who felt open war should be declared on the Normals. The disagreement finally led to the disbanding of our Council."

"There is a second advantage to having the Houston medical team come here," Carmilla said quickly. She didn't want to get into a discussion just yet on the merits of either argument; she needed time to find out who her allies were. "If Roger Niemann is still alive and is here acting as the Ripper, these people who knew him best will be able to help us locate and, if need be, destroy him."

A murmur of agreement passed through the room. Michael jumped to his feet, his face flushed with anger. "You cowards sicken me!" he said loudly, scorn dripping from his words. "Sitting around and whining about your need for blood, when fate has made you into beings far superior to those we feed upon. Count me out of your little scheme to become Normals again."

He whirled on his feet and walked rapidly from the room without looking back.

Carmilla watched him leave. She glanced at Jean and Sarah and Christina, half expecting them to follow. When they didn't, she sighed and turned back to the others. "Can I have a vote on Ramson's plan? All in favor signify by raising your right hands."

"Before we vote," Adeline interrupted, "we must consider the wisdom of approaching humans and letting them become aware of our existence."

Carmilla waved her objection away with the flick of a wrist. "I do not think that is a problem, Adeline. After all, this team we're discussing is already aware of us through their intervention with Niemann's mate. Evidently, they've either managed to discount the fact of our existence, or they've had no luck convincing the authorities of it."

"That's right," Sarah agreed. "We all know how dumb the Normals are when it comes to the possibility of believing in us. In spite of hundreds of years of evidence to the contrary, they still prefer to ignore our presence."

Carmilla nodded, pleased that the mood of the group seemed to be in her favor. "Could we vote now, please?" she asked agreeably.

Every hand in the room went up, some rapidly, some slowly, as the members of the Council thought about what such a decision might mean to them.

Eleven

Matt inserted the key Shelly had given him into the door marked MICROBIOLOGY LAB and pushed it open. He and Sam entered and turned the lights on.

"Wow!" Matt said, glancing around the large equipment-filled room.

Sam smiled and began reading the labels. "Hey, Matt, here's an old electron microscope," she said, grinning. "I haven't seen one of these since my med school days."

Matt was astounded at the wealth of equipment Shelly had put at their disposal, but after watching TJ at dinner the other night, he was convinced Shooter was right to be worried. Her behavior, though not outrageous, was certainly not normal for her. She was entirely too hungry for bloody, half-cooked meat to suit Matt's mind; moreover, she seemed listless and distracted lately, not at all the bubbly TJ he used to know.

As his thoughts ranged back to that night, Sam walked up to him and snapped her fingers. "Hey, are you with me?" she asked, smiling at his dreamy, disconnected expression.

"Huh? Oh, yeah, sure," he said, snapping out of it. "I was just thinking. Do you think TJ will really let us run the tests on her when it gets right down to it?"

"That's what I was about to tell you," Sam answered. "I don't believe we're gonna have any problems with her. She woke me up last night, dripping with sweat and with a terrified expression on her face."

"Oh?"

"Yeah. Seems she's been having these dreams, almost every night, and they've really got her spooked."

"What sort of dreams?"

Sam bit her lip. "I'm not supposed to tell anyone, but they concern her acting in an . . . unusual manner."

Matt stared at her, trying to read between the lines of what Sam wasn't telling him. After a moment, he thought he had it. "You mean, she's been dreaming of sucking the blood out of people?"

Sam gave a slight nod, uncomfortable even talking with Matt about what TJ had told her in confidence. "That's pretty close. In any event, the dreams have made TJ want to be checked out. She's as afraid of becoming like Niemann as we are for her."

"When did you tell her we'd start?" Matt asked.

"After she gets off duty today. Her shift ends at five."

Matt glanced at his watch. "I've got a one o'clock class to teach; then I'll go down to the lab and get what we need to draw blood and bring it up here."

Sam glanced around at the counters and tables covered with equipment. "Good. I'll spend my time trying to figure out how to use this stuff. Hopefully, there'll be some manuals scattered around somewhere."

Matt grinned. "If you get stuck, call Shelly. Some of these machines look as old as he is."

Sam frowned, taking Matt's joke seriously. "You know, that's not a bad idea. After all, Shelly's probably forgotten more about lab tests and microbiology than either of us know."

"Do you think TJ would mind?"

Sam shook her head. "No. TJ loves Shelly. I'm sure it'd be all right with her, especially since Shelly was in on all this from the beginning."

Matt leaned over and gave Sam a quick kiss. "OK, babe, I've gotta go."

She grabbed him by the front of his white clinic jacket. "No, you don't mister!" she growled, her voice husky. "I want a better good-bye kiss than that."

"You modern women are *so* demanding," Matt said, shaking his head. He stepped closer, put his arms around her, and kissed her as she wished to be kissed.

When they broke, Matt's face was flushed. "Maybe I could get someone else to give that lecture, and we could . . ."

Sam shook her head. "No, we've got too much to do, big boy. But," she added with a mischievous smile, "that'll give you something to look forward to tonight."

"Promise?"

"Yes. Now go teach the med students something useful and then we'll meet back here to get ready for TJ this afternoon."

TJ was terrified at the changes she felt taking place in her body lately. Her dreams were filled with visions of blood-drenched necks and bodies torn asunder; her days were spent with a deep hunger gnawing at her insides, a void that could only be satisfied by meat cooked so rare the blood dripped and pooled on the plate around it. The image of Roger Niemann and his black, piercing eyes consumed her mind from the time she awoke until she drifted into fitful, restless sleep. At times, her loins ached with remembrance of the passion they'd shared in his lair when she was his prisoner. She still couldn't understand how she'd responded to his lovemaking when she despised him and everything he stood for, but she couldn't erase her memories of their wild coupling.

The only thing that scared her more than these recent changes was the thought of undergoing more laboratory tests with Matt and Sam. It wasn't the tests that frightened her, but rather the chance that the tests would determine there was no hope; she feared she would end up like Roger, skulking about in the darkness, looking for hapless victims to assuage her hunger for blood.

She took a deep breath, smoothed her hair, and opened the door to the microbiology lab. Sam and Matt glanced up from a computer on a gray metal desk in the corner of the room.

"Hey, TJ," Sam called cheerfully, as if they were two girlfriends meeting for a casual lunch, instead of a doctor and her patient about to undergo tests that would determine her fate.

"Hi, TJ," Matt said, barely taking his eyes off the computer screen.

"Hi, guys," TJ replied, trying to sound more hopeful than she felt.

"Come on in," Sam said, beckoning to her. "We've just gotten an e-mail from the doctor in Canada that Shelly referred us to. He's the world's leading authority on plasmids."

"Canada?" TJ asked, walking over to read behind Matt's shoulder.

"Yeah," Matt answered, wondering if she'd forgotten their conversation at the restaurant the other night. "His name is Professor Bartholomew Wingate, M.D., Ph.D., and no telling what else. He teaches micro at McGill University Medical School in Montreal."

"What's he say?" TJ asked, trying to keep the fear out of her voice.

Matt shrugged. "He's asking me to fax him all your previous lab results as well as whatever other information we might have on the origin of your infection."

Sam put her hand on TJ's shoulder; her sympathetic smile showed she understood what TJ was going through. "We're gonna send him some copies of the journal pages in Niemann's book in which he tells how the whole thing started, as well as some of the symptoms he describes."

"What else does he say?" TJ asked.

"He attached some of his research papers to the e-mail," Matt said, clicking on the icon of the paper clip in the upper right part of the screen. "I already had most of them from the Internet, but he included some that haven't been published yet. Mainly, they deal with different kinds of plasmids that are used to stop conjugation among other plasmids."

TJ nodded slowly, smiling as she remembered how Shooter had misunderstood the term conjugation, thinking it had some sort of sexual meaning. "Yeah, that's a good idea. Plasmids reproduce by conjugation; so if we can stop that, all the plasmids left will die of old age eventually, just like blood cells do, and I'll be cured."

"The only problem is, the anticonjugation plasmids are very specific. Wingate says he'll need to know quite a bit about your particular plasmids before he can grow some anticonjugation ones to combat them."

TJ's forehead wrinkled. "But didn't the tests you took earlier, when I was really sick, give us that information?"

Sam shook her head. "I'm afraid not, TJ. About all we could find out was the infection had something to do with plasmids. Our equipment wasn't delicate enough to determine the specific type of plasmids involved."

"What about Niemann's journal?" she asked, looking from one to the other. "Didn't he say he'd been doing just this kind of research for many years? Maybe he's got the answers we need."

Matt glanced at Sam, a troubled look on his face. "No doubt he did, TJ, but he didn't put his research results in his journal."

TJ snapped her fingers. "I know. They're probably in the warehouse he used as a safe house. We could look there."

Matt grimaced. "Yeah, we could. Except, Damon told me that someone took all the stuff outta Niemann's warehouse a couple of days after he was killed. It was picked clean."

Sam stared at Matt. "You didn't tell me that," she said. "Who would do such a thing?"

Before Matt could reply, TJ's face paled and she stumbled to a seat in front of the desk. "Roger," she said, her voice croaking on the word.

"TJ, Roger is dead," Matt said gently.

Her tortured eyes turned to him. "Did the police ever find his body?" she asked.

"Well, no . . . ," Matt began.

TJ buried her face in her hands. "I knew it!" she moaned.

"TJ, don't go jumping to conclusions," Sam said.

She looked up, a haunted look in her eyes. "He'll come for me. He told me we'd be together forever." She closed her eyes tight, trying to shut out the memory of his naked body pushing against hers, and of her frantic response to the feelings it stirred in her.

Sam turned to Matt, tears in her eyes at the pain her friend was going through.

Matt came around the desk and laid his hand on TJ's shoulder. "If he does, TJ, Shooter and the police will get him again, just like they did before."

Sam knelt in front of TJ to get her attention. "TJ, Roger is dead. There have been no further killings in Houston since the police shot him. If Roger were still alive, we'd know it by the bodies he'd leave behind."

For the first time, a hopeful gleam appeared in TJ's eyes. "That's right. If he were still alive, he'd be feeding and we'd read about it in the newspapers."

Sam stood up. "Sure, so quit worrying about it. What we've got to do now is draw some of your blood and send it to Dr. Wingate so he can start classifying your plasmids."

"Did he say how long that would take?" TJ asked.

"Unfortunately, several months at least," Matt said. "It would be much quicker if we could somehow find the results of Niemann's research."

TJ grabbed Matt's arm. "We could go look in the

warehouse. Maybe the police missed something or the robbers left something behind."

Matt glanced at Sam, and then he shrugged. "I guess so. I don't see what harm it could cause."

"First," Sam said firmly, "we're going to draw some of your blood and get it sent on the way to Wingate. Then we can go to the warehouse."

"All right," TJ said, her mood upbeat at the thought of going to look for Niemann's research papers. She felt sure if they could just find them, they would show a way out of her present predicament.

She brushed aside a momentary dread at entering the place where Niemann had so debased her. She took a deep breath and squared her shoulders. She knew in order to survive the ordeal facing her, she was going to have to be stronger than she had ever been before. But it would be worth it if she could somehow be cured of the curse Niemann had put on her.

TJ sat in a chair and stuck out her arm, grimacing as Matt approached her with a needle and syringe in his hand.

Twelve

Jacques Chatdenuit took his time dressing for his night out. His Hunger, though becoming more insistent, was still manageable, so he was in no hurry. In fact, he thought, anticipation of his hunt and later feed made the actual event even more piquant.

As usual, he put on dark jeans, a dark shirt, and a black leather jacket. Practice had taught him that blood spilled on dark clothes does not show up at night, and he fully intended to spill some blood tonight.

Combing his dark, curly hair before a mirror, he stared into his ice-blue eyes, wondering not for the first time how they'd come to be. His background was French Canadian, and both of his parents had dark eyes and hair, as most of the people did in his native Quebec.

He'd been born in 1932, in the midst of the Great Depression. His early childhood years were uneventful, though his family was as poor as most everyone he knew. Things were getting better when he was twenty-five and secured a job on a tramp steamer out of the port city of Montreal. As the ship sailed up the Street Lawrence toward the open ocean, the young man stood on the deck, the salty sea air blowing in his face as he dreamed of the adventures he was going to have.

It was in his first port of call on the western coast of Africa that he decided to go to a waterfront bar in the seedier part of the small city.

While in the bar, a lovely black woman approached him and offered to buy him a drink. One thing led to another, and before long she took him to her house on the outskirts of town.

She seemed intrigued by both his boyish good looks and his brilliant blue eyes, stating she'd never seen such a combination before.

As they made passionate love on her large, down-filled mattress, Jacques started and drew back as her teeth bit into his neck. Soothing him and murmuring sweet words in his ears, she told him to lie back and enjoy the night, for she had something special in mind for him.

For some reason, he didn't think it strange when she opened a small vein on her wrist with teeth suddenly long and sharp, then placed his lips to the wound. He drank greedily, as if consumed by a thirst he couldn't understand.

Jacques awoke two weeks later, after she'd nursed him through the high fevers and night sweats and chills of his Transformation.

Then, with loving tenderness, she began to teach him what a great gift she'd given him: immortality and the dominion over lesser beings of the world, who were forever more going to be his prey.

Jacques stayed with her for four years, until the number of people dying of horrible neck wounds began to alarm the local authorities. Though his mate was indeed beautiful, she was uneducated and simple, and Jacques was soon tired of her lack of sophistication. The search by the local authorities for the killers who drank their victims' blood gave him the excuse he needed.

Sneaking out in the middle of the day, covered from head to foot with long, flowing clothes against the tropical sun, he made his way to the port and secured a job on a freighter headed for the United States.

By the time the freighter pulled into a Virginia port, almost a third of its sailors were missing and the rest were so frightened they'd taken to sleeping with knives by their bunks.

Jacques jumped ship and began to make his way across the United States, leaving a trail of bodies in his wake. His mate had taught him that Normals were his natural prey, so he had no trouble with his conscience over his need to kill. In fact, he'd never even given thought to the possibility of feeding without killing.

Occasionally, in his travels, he came across others of his kind, but he avoided any protracted contact with them. His experience in Africa had taught him that two Vampyres drew too much attention. He preferred to live and hunt alone.

When he finally arrived in New Orleans, he found there were already many Vampyres living there. At first, he figured he'd move on, thinking that many of his kind hunting in one place would be too obvious to the authorities. However, he discovered by discreetly reading the minds of his fellow hunters, they'd come to some arrangement among themselves to pursue only nonlethal feeding. Not fully understanding the reasoning behind their reluctance to kill, he decided to hang around for a while and see what he could discover.

Using his own mental abilities very carefully while keeping his innermost thoughts blocked, he realized these Vampyres had formed a Council that decided when and how they could hunt. Disgusted with their timidity and fear of the Normals, whom he considered his rightful prey, he kept apart from the others of his kind. He moved alone through the dark streets of New Orleans and fed as he always had, totally and without pity.

Living among members of his own kind without being discovered meant he had to use his mental capabilities very carefully, lest one of them "smell" him out with their own psychic abilities. Therefore, he went about his business with his mind locked down most of the time, only unleashing his powers when he was on a hunt. This self-enforced isolation caused him to be lonely, but he had yet to come across anyone who impressed him enough to consider the long process it would take to make them his mate.

After moving to New Orleans, he decided to take a job as a private investigator, specializing in industrial espionage. With his mental ability to see into others' minds, it was easy for him to acquire the information that heads of companies would pay dearly for, and it had a side benefit of allowing him to use his new skills to find and keep tabs on the other Vampyres in his area without risk of discovery. He knew at some point in the future, such information might be crucial to his survival.

Tonight he planned to go to Pat O'Brien's, a popular nightclub frequented mostly by tourists and college kids. It was very crowded, always noisy, and almost everyone there was usually drunk. It was an excellent place to find young women suitable for a feed, and the number and closeness of the crowd would shield his use of his psychic abilities should another Vampyre happen to be nearby.

As he walked down Bourbon Street on his way to the nightclub, he hummed a song from his childhood, "Papa Joe's," about a famous bar in New Orleans.

Since it was a weeknight, there was no line waiting to enter Pat O'Brien's, but the room was packed with almost every table full. Jacques shoved his way through the crowd and moved to the left, stationing himself at the bar, which commanded a view of the entire room. In this way, he could observe the patrons without being noticed.

"What'll it be?" the barman asked.

"Double Jack and Coke," Jacques said, placing a twenty-dollar bill on the bar. One of the more pleasant aspects of being a Vampyre was the almost total lack of effect alcohol had on him. He could get a slight buzz, but there were no nasty aftereffects no matter how much he drank.

The room was dark, except for the stage upon which two pianos faced each other with middle-aged women singing college fight songs the audience called out for. The darkness didn't bother Jacques, for he could see as well in total darkness as the Normals could in full light.

He sipped his drink, letting his gaze roam the room looking for his next victim. He would refrain from using his mind until he'd singled out one of the many young women present to be his "date," as he liked to think of them, for the night.

I entered the nightclub, the sixth one of the night, and hoped that I would somehow come across the man, or woman, the police were calling the Ripper. I wasn't searching for him out of any desire to do a good deed for the Normals or to save any lives, other than my own. I knew that if the Ripper wasn't stopped, before long the authorities would put two and two together and come up with the same answer the Houston police had: there was a monster loose in their city. I wanted to prevent that from happening so I wouldn't have to move again. I was anxious to get back to work on my research and I wasn't about to let some crazy Vampyre delay it any longer.

My mouth had an awful taste in it from all the cheap liquor I'd consumed on my quest for the Vampyre killer. Most of the establishments I'd been in didn't serve Martell brandy, so I'd been drinking house whiskey, usually watered down and raw to the throat.

My nose wrinkled at the smell of stale cigarette smoke and the overly sweet drink served at Pat O'Brien's known locally as a Hurricane. The crush of the crowd unnerved me somewhat, since I'd long since given up letting myself frequent such places. I guess it was the thought of being in the midst of so many Normals, surrounded and squeezed in, and knowing that they would kill me without a second thought if they knew what I was.

But, unlike me in the days when I used to hunt and kill these innocents, the Ripper seemed to pick his victims from tourists and the well to do rather than the dregs of society as I had. So I was here in the most popular tourist nightclub in the city, nervous and uncomfortable as I searched for a being who would kill me without hesitating if I were to let my guard down.

An older black waiter moved toward me, dancing and jiving to the music. He held a metal serving tray over his head. It was covered with hundreds of coins and he tapped on the bottom of it with his fingers, which had thimbles on them, in time to the music that was being played.

With a wide grin, he leaned over to ask me what I wanted to drink. Suddenly his eyes widened and his face sobered for a moment, as if he could sense I wasn't the usual type of person he waited on. Even in the short time I'd been in New Orleans, I'd found the blacks in the area seemed to be especially sensitive to mental intrusion, and to have an almost second sight when it came to "smelling" out my kind. Perhaps it was the all-pervasive belief in voodoo that permeated their society and their lack of disbelief in things supernatural that enabled them to sense our presence when more sophisticated white Normals couldn't. In any case, after a moment, he shook his head and his eyes cleared.

"What can I get you, sir?" he asked, having to talk loudly to be heard over the music and conversation in the room.

I decided to switch drinks. "A vodka martini, with two olives, please."

"Yes, sir!" he said cheerfully, evidently suppressing his instinct about my wrongness.

While I waited for my drink, I surveyed the room, not knowing exactly what I might be looking for. The Ripper could look like anyone: Vampyres came from all walks of life and were Transformed at all ages, so the creature could be almost anyone in the room. The only way I was going to discover if the Ripper was present was to use my mind, but I wanted to wait for a while so as not to give myself away.

After the waiter brought my drink, I sat back in my chair and continued to observe the crowd, reflecting on the irony of a being such as I, who'd killed hundreds over the years, sitting here trying to stop another from doing what I'd done so many times.

I opened my mind slightly, just enough to receive any psychic vibrations, but not enough to emit any of my own. I don't know quite how to explain what it feels like to have someone in your mind: almost like a tickle, or a feather stroking the brain, that's about as close as I can come to describing it. I felt that tickle now and immediately shut my mind down and forced myself to remain calm and centered, at least outwardly.

Inside, I was on red alert. The battle was about to begin. . . .

Thirteen

By seven o'clock in the evening, Matt and Sam had just about finished with the first round of tests on TJ. Matt was bandaging the puncture wound on TJ's iliac crest, from where he'd drawn a sample of her bone marrow, when Shelly and Shooter entered the lab.

"Look what I found wandering around the halls," Shelly said, his hand on Shooter's shoulder.

"You guys didn't tell me where the lab was, so I had to ask Shelly," Shooter said, his eyes on TJ as he checked to see how she was doing.

TJ jumped up from the examining table and ran to throw her arms around his neck. "Hey, Shooter," she murmured in his ear. "I'm really glad you came."

Matt and Sam both said hello. While Matt packed away the specimen he'd taken, Sam said to Shooter, "TJ's been a real trouper, Shooter. She let us poke and prod and stick her all day without a single complaint."

As Sam talked, Shelly noticed the Band-Aid on Shooter's neck and the spot of dried blood on it. He frowned as he thought of the implications of such a wound, but decided not to mention it, for the moment.

Shooter kissed TJ on the cheek and rubbed the

back of her neck with his hand. "You about ready for dinner, babe?" he asked.

She nodded vigorously. "Yeah. I think I'm about a quart low on blood, so we'd better do something to replace it," she answered.

"You guys want to come along?" Shooter asked.

Matt shook his head. "Not now, Shooter. Sam and I've still got some work to do to label and collate some of the samples we've taken. I want to get them packed up and sent to Dr. Wingate in Canada as soon as possible. How about a rain check?"

"You got it," Shooter answered. He took TJ's hand and they left the lab together.

As the door closed behind them, Sam noticed the worried look on Shelly's face.

"What's up, boss?" she asked. "Trouble in the morgue?"

He shook his head, his eyes still on the door Shooter and TJ had gone through.

"Did either of you happen to notice the bandage on Shooter's neck?" he asked, turning his attention to them.

Matt shrugged. "No. Why?"

Sam was more astute to Shelly's implied meaning. "Do you think—"

"I don't know," Shelly interrupted, "and I don't want to jump to conclusions, but the wound was in the same location as the bites we found on all those vampire victims last year."

Matt's eyes widened. "You think TJ's been feeding on him?" Matt asked.

Shelly shrugged. "Certainly not in the fullest meaning of the word, since Shooter shows no signs of acute anemia. But I wonder if TJ's not starting to show more serious signs than just an appetite for rare meat."

"Maybe he just cut himself shaving," Matt said, though it was plain even he didn't believe that explanation.

Shelly stared at the door again. "Perhaps." He glanced back at Sam and Matt. "If I were you two, I'd do those tests just as fast as you can. We may be running out of time with TJ."

Matt and Sam looked at each other, their minds filled with horror at what they were thinking.

"Shelly," Sam said, "would you mind giving Dr. Wingate a call and impressing on him the urgency of the samples we're sending him? We need him to run them through as fast as possible."

Shelly nodded, his expression serious. "Certainly, though I wonder if he'll believe what we have to tell him."

"It'll probably depend on just what's in these samples we're sending him," Matt said. "If, as I suspect, TJ's bone marrow is infected with the plasmids, it will mean our original treatment failed and we don't have much time."

"I'll call him first thing in the morning and tell him the samples are on their way," Shelly said.

Shooter and TJ stopped at a small steak house on Westheimer for dinner. TJ, as usual, ordered a sirloin steak, rare, while Shooter had a New York strip, medium.

While they waited for their food to arrive, Shooter studied TJ in the low light of the eatery. She seemed pale and drawn, with bloodshot eyes, as if she wasn't getting enough sleep.

He reached across the table and covered her hand with his. "Are you still having those dreams?" he asked gently.

TJ's eyes dropped and she nodded slowly. "Yes."

"Are they still too bad to talk about?"

She glanced up at him, her eyes watery with tears. "Oh, Shooter. I don't know what's happening to me," she moaned. "I used to be so happy . . . so carefree. Now it's as if I have the weight of the whole world on my shoulders."

He squeezed her hand, trying to smile. "Don't worry, babe. We'll get through this together. Before you know it, that doctor in Canada will send Sam and Matt some medicine that'll make all this go away."

TJ smiled back at him sadly. "I hope so, Shooter. I want us to have a good life together."

"We will, sweetheart, I promise."

After the meal, Shooter and TJ walked to his car. "You want me to take you home, or would you rather stay the night with me? I'm working the late shift tomorrow, so we can sleep in."

For the first time that night, TJ smiled happily. "Let's go to your place. I need you to hold me."

Shooter grinned lasciviously. "In that case, you've come to the right man."

When they got to Shooter's apartment, TJ walked straight toward the bedroom, unbuttoning her blouse as she went. "I don't know about you, but I feel grimy after spending all day in the lab. I'm gonna take a shower."

Shooter was right behind her. "Last one in is a rotten egg," he shouted, stripping off his shirt before he finished the sentence.

He stepped into the shower, turning the water on as hot as he could stand it, knowing that's how TJ liked it. As the steam billowed up in thick clouds, fogging the shower door, TJ entered with him.

He turned, letting the water cascade off his back,

turning it the color of a fresh-cooked lobster, and stared at her. She was naked, standing in the open door, hip cocked in a provocative pose, staring at him.

Shooter felt himself harden at the sight of her nudity and couldn't keep his eyes off her breasts as the water splashed over them, tiny droplets hanging from her nipples, which were hard with desire.

As he opened his arms, she moved against him, nuzzling his neck with her lips as her hands took hold of him, gently massaging and kneading and stroking.

She let go long enough to pull the bandage off his neck and place her lips against the small twin scabs where she'd bitten him the night before. She licked and sucked until his blood began to run again. The taste made her wild; she grabbed his shoulders and hoisted herself up onto him, spearing herself upon his manhood as he gasped in sudden pleasure.

The steam prevented him from seeing how her teeth slowly elongated and her nails grew into claws as her features began to change and coarsen under the influence of the blood on her tongue.

She ground her pelvis against his, grunting and growling deep in her throat, visions of the Vampyre Niemann in her mind as she recalled a similar coupling in the shower of his lair months before.

Shooter, unaware of the changes taking place in his lover, grasped her buttocks in his hands and pulled her tight against him as his penis swelled and exploded inside her.

TJ had to use all her willpower not to rend and tear his back with her claws as she sucked his neck and continued her wild pumping against his pelvis.

Finally, she leaned her head back and howled as

she came with him, clutching him tightly with her legs around his waist.

Shooter, exhausted with the effort, fell back against the wall of the shower, eyes closed in ecstasy and fulfillment.

TJ laid her head on his neck as the water from the shower washed the remnants of blood off her mouth, and her features gradually changed back to normal.

"Jesus!" Shooter whispered into her ear. He turned the water off and carried her, still pressed against him, into the bedroom. He laid her, still dripping wet, on the bed, and flopped down on his back next to her. "That was incredible."

TJ opened her eyes, still dazed from her visions of Niemann and the violence of her orgasm. She saw twin drops of blood ooze from the wound on Shooter's neck and slowly trickle downward. Her nipples hardened and she felt her sex throb and become wet again. Rolling on her side, she placed her hand on his groin and slowly moved it back and forth.

Shooter turned his head to stare at her. "You want more?" he asked incredulously.

"Not just yet," TJ said in a husky voice. "I'll give you a few minutes to recover."

"A few minutes, hell. I may need a week," Shooter protested weakly.

TJ felt a stirring beneath her hand, and she grinned up at him. "Oh, I don't think it'll take quite that long," she murmured, burying her face against his neck and rolling on top of him, pressing her breasts against his chest.

As he entered her, Shooter grabbed her hips and gasped in pleasure, hardly noticing the stinging in his neck.

Fourteen

I slowly let my eyes wander over the crowd in the bar; sipping my drink, I searched as if I were just another horny tourist on the lookout for a willing date.

Finally, I found him. He was sitting at the bar and the stench of his blood lust was so strong I wondered why the Normals couldn't smell it. He was young-looking, with dark curly hair, and his blue eyes sparkled as he panned them over the young women in the club. I had no doubt he was trying to decide on just which one to pick for his meal of the night.

My fists clenched under the table in disgust at what he was doing, though I'd done the same thing thousands of times before. It's odd how perversion in others seems so much worse to us than our own sins do. Perhaps it's because we can almost always find a suitable excuse for our own transgressions against others, no matter how disgusting.

I forced myself to look away, lest he notice my attention. I'd already risked far too much by using my mental powers to smell him out, and I had to be careful not to tip him to my presence now. If my plan to kill him was to succeed, I had to catch him by surprise.

Out of the corner of my eye, I saw him get to his

feet and carry his drink over to a table where three young women were sitting. He smiled and gestured at the empty chair and took it when one of the girls nodded at him.

I could tell by the way his eyes glittered when he looked at the young lady it wouldn't be too long before he found some excuse for them to leave, so I threw a couple of dollars down on my table and walked outside.

Hurrying to my car just down the street, I opened the trunk and took out my *katana* and slipped it under the edge of my overcoat. I grabbed a one-gallon can of gasoline and carried it with me as I walked back to an alley just past the door to Pat O'Brien's. I eased back into the darkness, where I could see the door, unnoticed, and waited. I knew it wouldn't be long now.

As I waited, I tried to figure out whether I was really doing this to protect myself from his drawing unwelcome attention to our existence, or whether I was in some obscene way trying to kill the very thing in him that I detested in myself. After a while, I came to the conclusion it really didn't matter one way or the other, so long as he was stopped before he could kill again.

I was right. In less than fifteen minutes, my quarry emerged from the club with the young woman from the table on his arm. She was laughing and talking animatedly, clearly excited to be with such a handsome man. I wondered briefly what her thoughts would be if she knew what he had planned for her this night.

My fingers found the hilt of my *katana* under my coat and I was surprised to find they were damp with sweat. I guess it's never easy to kill one of your own kind, no matter the provocation. Always before when I'd done this, it'd been to put one of my fellow Vampyres suffering from CJD out of their misery. Never before had I killed for such a selfish reason.

I stepped from the shadows and unshielded my mind, issuing a mental command to halt.

The Vampyre stopped, his eyes momentarily confused as he searched the darkness for the origin of the mental shout.

When his eyes found mine, his lips curled in a sneer and he half-turned to his companion. She stopped talking and her eyes became blank at his psychic order. He left her standing in the middle of the sidewalk and slowly approached me.

"What do you want, interloper, and why do you interrupt my quest for prey?" he asked in a harsh voice, as if to intimidate me by his manner.

"You endanger us all by your indiscriminate killing," I answered in a low, calm voice as I pulled the sword from beneath my coat.

He stopped, the sneer leaving his face to be replaced by an expression of doubt.

"Are you one of those Council lapdogs?" he asked, his eyes boring into mine as he tested my strength with a mental command to give way.

I brushed his order aside, noting it was weaker than I'd feared. "No. I am here on my own."

"Then I suggest you go on your way and mind your own business if you value your life," he said gruffly.

"Not until I put an end to your existence."

Now he smiled, glancing around at the people walking along the nearby sidewalks. "In front of all these Normals?" he asked, spreading his arms wide.

I slowly shook my head, issuing at the same time my own mental command for him to go into the alley.

His smile melted and he showed his teeth in a grimace as he fought to resist, but my mental strength was greater than his. With halting steps, he moved slowly but steadily out of the light of the street and into the semidarkness of the alley.

I followed and set the can of gasoline on the concrete as I drew back the *katana* for a killing stroke.

The Vampyre's face contorted with supreme effort and he forced me out of his mind for a moment. He bent and quickly picked up a length of pipe lying on the ground next to him and swung it at my head.

Surprised by his ability to overcome my mental control, I ducked and parried his blow with my blade, sending sparks glittering into the darkness.

I whirled and swung backhanded at his head, missing him by inches when he threw himself backward against a wall behind him.

I had readied myself for another strike when I heard a shout from behind me, "Put your weapon down and step back!"

I glanced over my shoulder and saw a New Orleans policeman crouching and holding his pistol in a two-handed grip—it was pointed at me.

I lowered the blade and saw my opponent take off at a dead run down the alley.

"I said, put the weapon down, now!" the cop repeated in a loud voice.

With another mental command, I froze him for the briefest moment—when awaking, he wouldn't even be aware of this inconvenience. Then I took off after my prey, holding my blade in front of me against a surprise attack.

After running for a block, I turned a corner and came out onto Royal Street into a crowd of drunken revelers. The Vampyre was nowhere in sight, but I caused quite a stir in the crowd when they saw my sword.

I hurriedly stuffed it out of sight under my coat and continued running until I was out of the crowd and on a dark side street.

Damn, I thought to myself. I'd alerted the creature to my plans and he wouldn't be nearly so easy to find again. I decided to leave my car for a while and go back for it after the police had left the area.

I headed for my apartment to shower and change clothes before returning to pick up the car, shielding my mind and keeping a close lookout in case my quarry was still nearby. There was no way I was going to let him find out where I lived.

William P. Boudreaux, the chief of detectives, stepped from his car and let his eyes take in the scene before him. There was the usual crowd of gawkers and interested bystanders, five or six radio patrolmen milling around trying to look busy as they chatted with any pretty girls who happened to be in the crowd, and, the bane of his existence, TV news reporters.

Bill, as he was called by almost everyone, took a deep breath and motioned one of the patrolmen over to him.

"Yes, sir?" the man asked.

Bill checked his name tag; he made it a point always to call his men by name, a fact that made him very popular with the uniforms. "Sonny, would you get me a cup of coffee from that diner over there while I go face the vultures?"

Sonny glanced over his shoulder at the newspeople and grinned. "I see Melissa Faraday is there, Chief," he said, referring to a very pretty blond woman holding a microphone in her hand and talking into a camera. "If you want, I'll *handle* her for you."

Bill grinned, enjoying the double entendre. He replied in his deep Southern drawl, distinctive to people who'd been born and raised in New Orleans, "That's OK, Sonny. You just get me my coffee an' I'll take care of Ms. Faraday."

"Yes, sir," Sonny replied, and walked off toward the diner down the street.

Bill, who stood six feet four inches tall and had a barrel chest and shoulders as wide as an ax handle, hitched up his pants and pulled the edges of his suit coat together. He noticed the coat was getting tight around his middle and vowed for the hundredth time to start a diet . . . tomorrow.

He sauntered toward the crowd, letting his eyes roam over the people, knowing that often a perpetrator of a crime would hang around to see the excitement he'd caused.

He noticed a rat-faced, thin man moving through the people, and he called out, "Jimmy, come here a minute."

Jimmy Fingers looked up, a furtive expression on his face. Jimmy was a well-known pickpocket who worked the tourists in downtown New Orleans.

"Uh, hi, Chief," Jimmy said, his beady eyes looking everywhere except at Bill.

"I hope you're not here working tonight," Bill said evenly, staring at the man whose head barely came up to his chest.

"No, sir, I wouldn't do that."

"Good, 'cause it's much too nice a night to spend in our jail."

"Uh, I was just leaving, Chief," Jimmy said, and moved quickly off into the darkness.

Bill felt a hand on his arm and turned to look into the bright green eyes of Melissa Faraday, who immediately poked a microphone under his chin.

"Chief Boudreaux," she began in the stilted voice of one who is on camera, "could you tell us what happened here tonight?"

Bill smiled for the camera. Though he detested reporters in general, and Melissa Faraday in particular, he made it a practice to try to stay on good terms with the media as much as was possible.

"Good evening, Ms. Faraday," he said agreeably. "Now, as you can plainly see, I've just arrived here at the scene. Why don't you give me a little while to get up to speed on what happened and I'll be more than happy to give you an interview when I'm done."

Faraday made a cutting motion with her finger across her throat to the camera and smiled sweetly up at Bill. "You promise?" she asked.

"Of course. When have I ever lied to you?"

She laughed, low in her throat in a sexy manner that Bill was sure she'd practiced in front of a mirror for hours. "Only when you think you can get away with it, Bill."

Bill chuckled and moved off, not letting her know how much it pissed him off when she called him by his first name.

Sonny appeared and handed him a cup of steaming coffee.

"Chicory?" Bill asked as he took a sip.

"Of course," Sonny said. Everyone knew the chief drank only chicory-flavored coffee.

"Good. Now see if you can get that crowd cleared away," Bill said.

He walked over and stood next to a heavyset man

in a plaid sport coat who was talking to an elderly couple; the seniors were obviously tourists.

Jim Malone, detective second class, was the officer in charge and was the one who'd called Bill away from his home at this ungodly hour.

"Hey, Chief," Malone said.

"What've we got, Jim?" Bill asked. "Where is the body?"

"Excuse me a minute," Malone said to the couple, and pulled Bill off to the side where they could talk.

"There ain't any bodies, Chief," Malone said.

"Then why in hell—" Bill began, until Malone held up his hand.

"Hold on a minute, Chief. Like I said, there ain't any bodies, but you said to call you on anything that might be related to these Ripper killings."

Bill's eyes narrowed and his heart beat a little faster. "Go on," he said, taking another long drink of his coffee.

Malone inclined his head toward a young woman off to the side who was being checked out by a couple of paramedics. "Seems that couple over there came upon that girl standing on the sidewalk in a sorta daze. When they approached her to see if they could help, they heard a commotion in the alley and saw a couple of men fighting there."

"So?" Bill asked.

"Uh, one of the men appeared to be attacking the other with a sword," Malone answered.

"A sword?"

"Yep."

Bill took a deep breath and let it out, his excitement fading. "You sure it wasn't just a machete? You know how some of the sugarcane workers fight with those."

"Not unless the machete is four feet long," Malone answered.

"Well, what makes you think this is Ripper related?"

Malone pulled a small notepad out of his coat pocket and read his notes. "Looks like that girl was picked up in Pat O'Brien's by this fellow. When they left the club to go listen to some jazz, this other fellow stepped outta the alley and braced the first guy."

"Uh-huh," Bill said, finishing his coffee and crumpling the cup.

Malone shrugged. "That's all the girl remembers. She says all of a sudden her mind went blank and she don't remember nothin' after that."

"Is she drunk or on drugs?" Bill asked, his eyes flicking to observe the girl by the ambulance.

"Not according to the people she was with. They said she'd only had one Hurricane and wasn't known to use any drugs of any kind."

Bill pursed his lips, thinking. "Have the paramedics do a blood test for alcohol and drugs. Maybe he slipped her a Mickey or that new date-rape drug."

Malone made a note in his pad. "Reason I called you is this is the first time we've been able to get a description of the man who walked out with the girl. If it is the Ripper, it'll be a major break in the case."

"Yeah, an' it could just be a horny tourist who happened to get mugged before he could score with his pickup," Bill said, disgust in his voice.

"There's something else, Chief."

"Yeah?"

Malone led him over to the alley. "The men were fighting here until the couple called the cops on them." He pointed down at the ground, where a can of gasoline sat next to a length of pipe that had a deep groove cut in it.

Bill took a handkerchief out of his pocket and used it to cover his hand as he picked up the pipe. "Jesus," he said in a low voice.

Malone nodded. "The couple said he used the pipe to fend off the sword. Said it threw sparks all over the place when they hit together."

"This pipe is galvanized steel," Bill said. "It'd take a hell of a sword to make this cut in steel."

Bill put the pipe down. "Check the pipe and the can for prints."

As Malone made another note in his pad, Bill thought out loud. "So what we've got is some guy picks up a girl, walks out, and another guy braces him. Then something happens to make the girl go blank and the two go at each other with a sword and a pipe, an' one of the perps brought a can of gasoline to the fight."

"Uh-huh." Malone nodded.

"And you think this may have something to do with the Ripper killings?"

"Well, if the guy who took the girl did something to her mind, hypnosis maybe or used some drug we don't know about, it might explain why none of the victims of the Ripper called for help or tried to get away."

Bill looked at him. "None of the autopsies showed any evidence of drugs or alcohol."

Malone shrugged. "It's just a thought, Chief."

Bill smiled and patted Malone on the shoulder. "No, you did good, Jim. You're thinking, and I like that." He glanced around. "Next, have your men search the alley and especially that Dumpster over there to see if the men left anything else behind besides the gasoline." He paused. "And, Jim, have one of your men take down the license plates of all the cars parked within two blocks. I don't believe that man walked too far carrying a four-foot-long sword and a can of gasoline. Not with all these tourists around."

"Good idea, Chief."

"And in the morning, send the details out over the wire. Maybe some other police force will have some information on a man who uses a sword and a can of gasoline for his muggings."

"Right."

Bill sighed. "I guess it's time to face the media."

Malone chuckled. "Good luck."

Bill went over to Melissa Faraday, and held up his hand when she told the cameraman to turn on his camera.

"Just a minute, Ms. Faraday," Bill said.

"But you promised to give me an interview," she said, a note of whining in her voice.

"And I will," he said, "but there's nothing much here. Some guy picked a girl up in Pat O'Brien's and when they came out, another man attacked him and they got in a fight." He shrugged. "Sounds like a routine mugging to me."

Faraday's eyebrows went up in disbelief. "And they called out the chief of detectives for a mugging?"

"Can I tell you something off the record?" Bill asked.

Faraday hesitated.

"If you agree to keep this under your hat for the time being, I promise to give you an exclusive if anything important comes of it."

She nodded. "OK, but I'll hold you to that," she said.

"Fair enough. They called me out because the

lead detective on the case thought it might be related to the Ripper killings."

"What?"

"Yeah. I don't buy it myself," Bill said, trying to keep his voice casual, "but Malone thought since it involved a pickup in a bar, the same MO as the Ripper, he ought to notify me."

"Then you don't think it was the Ripper?" she asked suspiciously.

"Ms. Faraday, do you have any idea how many young women are picked up in bars in the French Quarter every night?" Bill asked.

"Then why did Malone think this one was special?" she asked.

She's sharp, Bill thought, *I'm gonna have to be careful with this one.* "Because after the mugging or fight, the first man ran away when the police arrived. Malone figured he had something to hide or he would've stayed to talk to us."

Faraday nodded. "OK, I can see that."

Bill put his hand on her arm. "Like I say, if anything comes of our investigation into this, I'll give you a shout. But, if this does happen to have something to do with the Ripper, I can't afford to have it broadcast on the evening news and tip him off."

She glanced down at his hand on her arm and smiled. "OK, but remember how I cooperated, Chief, 'cause if you stiff me on this one, paybacks are hell."

Fifteen

Shooter swung by the medical center to pick up Matt and Sam and TJ for the trip out to the Houston Ship Channel to explore the warehouse where Roger Niemann had held TJ prisoner.

As Matt and Sam got in the backseat of Shooter's Mustang convertible and TJ climbed in front, Matt noticed the bandage on Shooter's neck. He nudged Sam with his elbow and inclined his eyes at the wound.

Her eyes narrowed and she took his hand in hers and squeezed it to show she'd seen it, too. When he opened his mouth to speak, Sam warned him off with a frown. She silently mouthed the word "later" to indicate he should not say anything to Shooter until they were alone.

Matt nodded and leaned back in his seat, trying to relax. Every muscle in his body seemed tense at the thought of returning to the scene of their final confrontation with the Vampyre Roger Niemann. He glanced at TJ, wondering to himself how she'd handle seeing once again the place where the monster held her prisoner and did unspeakable things to her for several weeks.

Shooter must've felt the same anxiety, for he tried to keep up a jovial conversation on the trip out to the dock area, but TJ just sat staring off into space, her mind on only God knew what. Finally, Shooter stopped trying to talk and drove in stony silence the rest of the way.

When they finally arrived and Shooter pulled to a stop in front of the warehouse, Matt was amazed to see yellow crime-scene tape still adorning the outside of the building and crisscrossing the doorway.

The lock that had been broken when someone burglarized the place had been replaced and several chains were fastened across the doorway.

"You're sure this is all right?" Matt asked Shooter.

Shooter nodded and held up a key in his hand. "Yep. Talked to Chief Clark myself an' he said it'd be OK. He just asked if we remove anything to let him know in case they need it for evidence."

The four friends got out of the car and walked up to the door. When Shooter put the key in the lock, Sam placed her hand on TJ's shoulder. "You sure you're going to be all right?" she asked.

TJ nodded, but didn't speak. Sam noted her lips were pressed so tightly together they were white and her eyes were wide with anticipation.

The lock popped open and Shooter removed the chains and pulled the yellow tape away from the doorway. When he opened the door, it creaked and groaned like a scene from an old horror movie.

He stepped back, covering his nose as a strong, dusky smell of musk and old blood poured from the open door. "Jesus," he said, "it smells like an animal's den in there."

Matt wrinkled his nose at the strong odor and Sam put her hand to her face. She glanced at TJ and saw her nostrils flare and her eyes become hooded as she took a deep breath and entered the warehouse.

Sam followed her inside, watching her to see how

she reacted. TJ slowly turned, looking into the darkness as if she could see in spite of the lack of light in the room.

"Here's a light switch," Shooter said from behind them. When he flicked it on, Sam noticed TJ had a strange half smile on her face. She glanced down and saw TJ's erect nipples under her blouse. She thought with horror, *My God, the smell of this place is arousing her.*

The four began to move through the empty warehouse, pausing momentarily at the chalk outline of a body on the floor and the dark brown stains of spilled blood surrounding it.

"This is where they found the policewoman's body," Matt told Sam.

Shooter stared down at the floor, his eyes wet with remembrance of his friend who'd died here months before.

TJ averted her eyes and moved slowly toward the back of the room, toward the small cubicle where Niemann had held her prisoner while he performed the Rite of Transformation on her.

Shooter looked worriedly at Matt and Sam; then he followed TJ. When she got to the small table and chairs, and the shower stall where Niemann had raped and defiled her, she stood in front of it, a strange expression on her face.

If I didn't know better, I'd think she was enjoying the memories this room evokes, Sam thought.

Matt stood with hands on hips, turning slowly as he surveyed the empty warehouse. "Doesn't look like whoever robbed this place left very much behind."

There were a few old pieces of furniture, some cardboard boxes that'd been opened and left empty, and various pieces of paper strewn around the room.

"I doubt if we're gonna find anything useful here," Shooter said with disgust. "It looks like it's been pretty well cleaned out."

"Let's split up and see what we can find," Matt said. "Sam and I'll take this side, and you and TJ can look over there."

"OK," Shooter replied, moving to stand behind TJ with his hands on her shoulders as she continued to stare at the small room with a mattress on the floor next to the shower stall.

Matt and Sam began to walk around, stopping occasionally to bend and pick up pieces of paper or small objects. There were some old newspapers and magazines dating back over fifty years, but nothing they thought might be of any use, no notes or other evidence of any of Niemann's research findings.

TJ, followed by Shooter, stepped into the small room and stood over the mattress on which she'd coupled with such wild abandon with Niemann. Tears slowly formed in her eyes and trickled down her cheeks.

Shooter didn't know what to say, so he busied himself searching the room. Just as he was about to leave, he saw a small corner of some paper sticking out from under the mattress. When he picked it up, he saw it was a map of the United States.

He stepped over beneath one of the lights in the ceiling and unfolded the map. On it, he saw several cities circled in black India ink with small precise notations next to each one.

"Hey, Matt," he shouted. "Look at this."

He spread the map out on the table and they all gathered around to look at it.

"What do you make of those markings?" Shooter asked.

Matt leaned closer and peered at the map for a moment. When he stood up, his eyes were wide. "It looks like Niemann marked all the coastal cities from Houston to Florida. Next to each one, he wrote in the longitude and latitude and something that looks like a compass direction to them from Houston."

Shooter smiled grimly. "That makes sense," he said. "He was figuring out an escape route in case he ever had to leave Houston. Those notations are what he'd need to pilot his ship to any one of those ports."

Matt snapped his fingers. "Speaking of his ship, where is it? I didn't see it when we drove up."

"I guess the Port Authority had it towed off when Niemann didn't pay his dock fees."

"Are you sure that's what happened to it?" Sam asked.

"Why?" Shooter asked. "You don't think somebody stole it, too, do you?"

Sam shrugged. "No, not really." She paused. "But don't you think it a bit strange that a few days after you kill Niemann, everything in his warehouse disappears along with his ship?"

Matt's face paled. "You think he's still alive, don't you?"

Sam stared back into his eyes. "It would make more sense than thinking someone just happened to rob this particular warehouse, with chains and crime-scene tapes all over the doors, and then to find his ship is missing, too."

"Sam," Shooter said, "you didn't see his body. The man was literally torn apart by a machine gun, and then he fell into the water and never came up. He was definitely dead as a doornail."

"What if he wasn't, Shooter?" Sam asked. "Wouldn't the first thing he would do upon recovering be to get his stuff and put it on his ship and take off for parts unknown?"

Shooter shook his head. He didn't want to hear that the monster who almost killed all of them might still be alive. "I'm sure you're wrong, Sam."

Matt glanced from his best friend to the woman he loved. "Hey, it's easy enough to find out what happened to the ship. Why don't you put in a call to the Port Authority and see if they moved it?"

Shooter glanced at his wristwatch. "OK, but it's after five now. I'll do it first thing in the morning."

While Shooter and Matt were talking, Sam turned to TJ. Was that an expression of hope in her eyes? Was she hoping that Niemann was still alive?

Sixteen

Shooter got to his office an hour early so he could get in touch with the Port Authority. He looked up the number and dialed.

"Hello, this is John Sloan," a voice answered.

"Mr. Sloan, I'm Detective Steve Kowolski with the Houston Police Department and I wonder if you could give me some information?"

"Sure, Mr. Kowolski," Sloan answered. "What do you need to know?"

"We had an incident a few months back at a dock on the Houston Ship Channel involving a ship named the *Night Runner.*"

"Yeah, I remember it. Quite a shoot-out from what I heard."

"The problem is, the ship is no longer berthed at the dock. I was wondering if you guys moved it or had it moved."

"Give me a minute to check the records, Mr. Kowolski."

Shooter heard the sound of computer keys being hit over the phone. After a moment, Sloan was back on the line.

"No, I can't find any record of us doing anything with the ship."

"Mr. Sloan, a few days after the incident, a nearby

warehouse was broken into and cleaned out. Do you think the same people could have stolen the ship?"

Sloan laughed over the phone. "Now, that's a new one," he said. "I've never heard of a ship being stolen. Matter of fact, I don't think it'd be possible."

"Why is that?" Shooter asked.

"Well, first off, you'd have to have an experienced crew and captain to run the ship, and second, every ship leaving the port has to check in with us so we can track it and keep the shipping lanes safe from collision."

"And you have no records of a ship by that name leaving the port?"

"Nope."

Shooter gave him the date of the assault on Niemann's ship and the current date. "What other ships left the port between that time."

"You want *all* of them?" Sloan asked in amazement.

"Why, are there a lot?" Shooter asked.

"Mr. Kowolski, the port of Houston is the second or third most busy port in the States. There have been hundreds of ships in and out of here since then."

Shooter thought for a moment, and then it came to him. "Mr. Sloan, if someone took that ship out under a false name, then there would have to be a record of it leaving but no record of it arriving, wouldn't there?"

"Hey, that's right," Sloan answered. "You are a detective, Mr. Kowolski."

"If it's not too much bother, could you run a cross-check against any ships leaving in that time frame against any arrivals for the past twelve months?"

"No bother at all since we're computerized now.

But it'll probably take a couple of hours to run the program. Can I call you back?"

"Sure, I'll be at this number until noon at least," Shooter said, and gave him the police station phone number and his extension.

After he hung up, Shooter grabbed a cup of coffee and began to go through the paperwork on his desk.

Matt and Sam were in the lab going over the test results on TJ when the phone rang. Matt answered it.

"Hello, is this Dr. Matt Carter?" a voice said.

"Yes, I'm Dr. Carter," Matt answered.

"I'm Dr. Bartholomew Wingate," the voice said.

"Oh, hi, Dr. Wingate."

"Please, call me Bartholomew," Wingate said. "If we're going to be working together, I think we can do without the formality."

Matt motioned for Sam to pick up the extension. "Great, Bartholomew, I'm Matt and on the other line is Dr. Samantha Scott, known locally as Sam."

"Glad to talk to you both," Bartholomew said.

"Have you got any news for us?" Sam asked.

"Not anything good, I'm afraid. I've received the samples you sent and I've begun processing them, but without more information it is going to take some time to determine exactly what strain of plasmid is infecting your friend."

"How long are we talking about, Bartholomew?" Matt asked.

"A couple of months, at least."

"Oh, no," Sam sighed into the phone.

"Is that a problem?" Bartholomew asked.

"Yes, sir," Sam said. "TJ, the one who's infected,

has begun to show some troubling signs of the infection."

"I'm sorry to hear that," Bartholomew said. "But, unless you can get me some more specific information about just what strain she was infected with, I'll have to do it the slow way."

"OK, Doctor, just please find out as soon as you can."

"I assure you, Matt, I'll work on nothing else until we've solved the mystery. This is the most exciting thing in plasmid research I've ever come across, so I'll pull out all the stops and get back to you as soon as possible."

"Thank you, Bartholomew," Sam said, dejection evident in her tone.

"Is there no way to find out from the person responsible for the initial infection?" Bartholomew asked.

Matt looked at Sam across the room. "No, sir. I'm afraid he's dead."

"Oh, I'm sorry to hear that. It would speed up the process of growing some conjugation-blocking plasmids if we knew the DNA structure of the infecting organisms."

"Well, if we come up with anything we'll let you know immediately," Matt said.

"Thanks, Matt. Keep in touch, and if any new symptoms arise, be sure and let me know."

Sam slowly replaced the phone in its cradle and hung her head, clearly saddened by the news of how long it would take to get results that would help TJ.

Matt stood up and walked over to put his arms around Sam. "It can't be helped, Sam," he said gently. "I'm sure he's working as fast as he can."

She looked up at him. "I know, Matt, but TJ is

changing. She's turning into someone I don't know."

"What do you mean?" he asked, sitting his hips on the desk next to her.

Sam looked around the room as she tried to find the right words to describe the changes taking place in her best friend. After a moment, she focused on Matt. "I don't know quite how to describe it, Matt. It's almost as if she's a completely different person."

"How so?"

"She seems locked off in her own world. She no longer seems interested in her patients or her residency, and she's more . . . closed off. We used to confide in each other, but now it's as if she's so afraid of what's been happening to her that she's decided to go it alone. She won't even talk about the changes and she no longer tells me about the dreams that plague her and keep her from sleeping."

"You think the infection is growing, making her change into the type of creature that Niemann was, don't you?"

Slowly, Sam nodded. "Yes, and I'm afraid if we don't find some sort of cure soon, there won't be any more of the original TJ left to save."

Matt took her hand. "Then we'll just have to work harder and faster and make sure that doesn't happen."

Sam was about to reply, when the door opened and Shooter walked in, accompanied by Chief Damon Clark. Clark looked much better than the last time Matt had seen him. He'd gained some weight and looked stronger since his surgery.

"Hey, Shooter, Chief," Matt said.

Sam turned her head and discreetly wiped the

tears from her eyes, then smiled at Shooter and Damon. "Hi, guys," she said.

Matt, noticing the serious expressions on their faces, asked, "What's up? You two look like you're carrying the weight of the world on your shoulders."

"We need to talk," Shooter said.

Matt got up off the desk and moved to the small conference table in the corner of the room where he and Sam went over lab reports and research notes. He swept the papers on the table into a pile in one corner and motioned for everyone to take a seat.

Once they were seated around the table, Matt said, "Go ahead."

Shooter opened a manila folder he was carrying and laid a sheet of paper out on the desk. "After our visit to Niemann's warehouse the other day, I checked with Chief Clark and he said he wasn't aware the ship was gone, so I called the Port Authority to see what had happened to it."

"Had they moved it?" Sam asked, looking down at the paper and trying to read it upside down.

Shooter shook his head. "Nope. So I got to thinking and had the man there run a check on all the ships that'd sailed out of the port since our fight with Niemann."

"What'd you find out?" Matt asked.

"There was no record of any ship by the name of *Night Runner* having left the port."

"Maybe someone just took it and didn't check in with the Port Authority," Sam offered, playing devil's advocate.

Shooter shook his head. "Not possible, at least not for a ship as big as Niemann's."

"Get to the point," Damon said irritably.

"Anyway, I figured whoever took the ship might have changed its name, so I had them run a cross-check of any ships that left that didn't have a record of having arrived."

"Smart move," Matt said.

"Tell them what you learned," Damon said.

"Only one ship left that hadn't arrived. It was named the *Moon Chaser* and it left two days after our shoot-out."

"Where was it headed?" Sam asked.

"Officially, Naples, Florida," Shooter said. "But I called the port there and they had no record of it ever getting there."

"Maybe whoever it was just changed the name again before getting to Florida," Matt said.

"I thought of that, but first I called all the ports that were marked on that map we found in Niemann's warehouse to see if a ship named *Moon Chaser* had berthed."

"And?" Matt asked.

Shooter smiled grimly. "I hit the jackpot. The *Moon Chaser* arrived in the port of New Orleans three days after it left Houston."

"And who was listed as the owner?" Sam asked.

Shooter shook his head. "Some corporation registered in Nigeria. That turned out to be a dead end, so I called Chief Clark to see if we could get the New Orleans police to check it out for us."

Both Matt and Sam turned their attention to Damon, who opened a leather briefcase he'd set on the floor next to him and pulled out a sheet of paper.

"Just before Shooter called me, I received a bulletin from ViCAP."

"ViCAP?" Sam asked.

"The Violent Criminal Apprehension Program,"

Damon explained. "It's a computer network run by the FBI and shared with local law-enforcement agencies in which criminals are tracked across the country by means of their MOs, the type of crimes they commit."

He handed the bulletin across the table for Matt and Sam to read.

After he scanned the report, Matt glanced up with fear in his eyes. "This can't be."

Damon nodded, his lips tight. "I know. The police chief in New Orleans is investigating multiple killings where the necks are slashed and all of the blood drained from the victims, just the type of killings Niemann was doing here before we stopped him."

Sam pointed to the bottom of the bulletin. "He also had a query here about any history of assaults with swords and gasoline, just like the one we had where the man was beheaded and his body burned with gasoline. The one where the DNA tests showed the victim was over a hundred years old."

"Exactly," Damon said.

"What do you think this means, Damon?" Matt asked, though he was afraid he knew the answer.

"One of two things," Damon replied. "First, and I have to admit most likely, is we have a copycat murderer. Either someone who was in Houston at the time of our killings and who read about them and is killing in the same manner as Niemann was, or it's another creature like him who has the same MO."

"What's the second possibility?" Sam asked, her face pale.

"That Niemann somehow survived our assault, cleared out his belongings from his warehouse, sailed his ship to New Orleans, and picked up right where he left off in Houston."

"But," Matt protested, "that's impossible, Damon. You saw how his body was riddled with machine-gun bullets. Hell, his head was almost severed from his body."

Damon shook his head. "I know, Matt. And for the record, I don't believe it, either. But the coincidence of all of Niemann's belongings being removed, and his ship being taken to New Orleans, and the simultaneous beginning of killings similar in nature and method to those he performed, is just too great to ignore."

"Besides, Matt," Shooter said, "six months ago you would have said the presence of a Vampyre in Houston who sucked the blood out of his victims and seemed to be one hundred fifty or more years old would have been impossible." He shook his head. "I hesitate to use the word 'impossible' in conjunction with anything concerning Niemann."

Matt spread his hands, frustration written all over his face. "So what are we gonna do? Call the New Orleans police and tell them we think their killer . . . what do they call him, the Ripper, is a vampire that we let get away and now he's busily biting necks in their city?" He laughed harshly. "Hell, they'd think we were nuts."

Damon glanced at Shooter and said, "You tell them."

Shooter stared at Matt and Sam. "I think we should go to New Orleans and track down the owner of the *Moon Chaser*."

"What?" Sam asked, her mouth open in amazement.

"It's the logical thing to do," Shooter explained. "After all, we know what Niemann looks like, and more importantly, we believe in what he *is*. Something we'll never be able to convince the New Orleans police about."

"OK, I can see the rationale in you going, Shooter," Matt said. "But why Sam and I?"

Damon interjected, "Because if our perp is Niemann, he's likely to be using the same dodge he did here, working as a doctor somewhere. You and Sam, as docs, can get entry into those places better than a cop."

"I don't know," Matt said, his heart beating rapidly at the very thought of again confronting the monster Roger Niemann.

Sam put her hand on his arm. "Matt, I think we should go. If it is Roger, we may be able to gain access to his research. It might save TJ's life."

Matt stood up and began to pace the room. "Jesus, guys, I just don't know if I can face that again," he said, remembering the terror he felt the night he'd climbed on Niemann's ship and faced the monster head-on.

Shooter got up and walked over to stand in front of Matt. "You can do it, pal. We've got to do it. For TJ, if nothing else."

Matt chuckled, shook his head, and turned to Damon. "If we go, Chief, I'm gonna want a *really* big gun!"

Seventeen

I waited until four in the morning to return to the French Quarter to pick up my car. When I got there, I found a business card under the windshield wiper. It belonged to William P. Boudreaux, Chief of Detectives of the New Orleans Police Department. I turned the card over and on the back was written: "Please call me at your earliest convenience."

I checked to make sure I wasn't illegally parked; I wasn't. I stuck the card in my shirt pocket and got behind the wheel, wondering what Detective Boudreaux wanted with me. Had I been seen earlier when I got the gasoline out of the trunk, or had someone somehow connected me to the fight outside of Pat O'Brien's?

No, if that were the case, the police would have been knocking on my door instead of leaving a note on my car.

As I drove the several blocks to my apartment, I considered my options. I could pack up and leave again, abandoning all the efforts I'd made to create a new life here, or I could brazen it out and go see what the policeman wanted.

I laughed to myself. Neither option particularly appealed to me, but at least seeing this Boudreaux would let me know where I stood.

I decided to go and see the man, but I was going to do it on my terms. I certainly wasn't going to walk into his office where I'd be trapped if they were on to me. This was going to take some careful planning.

The next morning, I went to the police station and told the officer at the information desk I had an appointment with Detective Boudreaux. He told me his office was on the third floor, in the homicide division. I followed his directions and entered a large room; there were desks arranged in orderly rows throughout the area, and a glass-enclosed office at the far end of the space. I could see a large, broad-chested man in shirtsleeves and a tie behind the desk, working on some papers. He had sandy brown hair and a close-cropped beard. The nameplate on the door read BOUDREAUX.

Before anyone could ask me what I wanted, I turned and made my way back down the stairs to the first floor and then out the door.

Taking up station at a small restaurant across the street, I ordered a cup of coffee and sat by a window where I could see the door to the police station.

It was 12:30 and I was on my third cup of coffee when I saw Detective Boudreaux come outside. He was with two other men and they stood on the stairs talking for a few moments before going their separate ways.

I threw a couple of dollars on the table and walked over just as Boudreaux was opening the door to his car.

"Detective Boudreaux," I said, forcing my face into a smile.

He turned and gave me a quizzical stare. "Yes?"

I stuck out my hand. "Hi, I'm Dr. Albert Nachtman. You left one of your cards on my windshield last night."

He took my hand, nodding. "Yeah. You were parked near a crime scene and I have a few questions to ask you about what you saw last night." He hesitated. "Uh, how did you find me?"

"I arrived at the information desk just as you were leaving. When I told the man there I was supposed to see you, he pointed you out to me."

"Oh. Well, Doctor, I was just heading for lunch. . . ."

"Me too, Detective. I work at a clinic and rarely take lunch, but this was the only time I could get away. How about we eat together and you can ask me your questions?"

"Well, I—"

"Today is red-beans-and-rice day at the Court of Two Sisters," I said, mentioning one of the more exclusive restaurants in the Quarter. "I'll treat you since I'm imposing on your lunch break."

He grinned. "That's a deal. I don't get to eat at the Court very often."

"I'll meet you there," I said, and walked off toward where I'd left my car.

On the way, I breathed a sigh of relief. If the detective had any suspicions about me, he would never have agreed to meet with me away from his office. Still, I would have to be very careful. One didn't get to be chief of homicide without being very smart.

We met at the entrance and I suggested since it was such a nice day that we eat outdoors in the courtyard. After we ordered, Boudreaux got right to the point.

"Dr. Nachtman, there was a disturbance last night down the street from Pat O'Brien's. Two men got into a fight. Afterward, my men canvassed the area and found your car parked nearby."

I nodded. "Yes. I drove there directly after work, Detective. My clinic was exceptionally busy yesterday and I felt the need to unwind before heading home. I spent the evening listening to some jazz at a blues club on Dauphine Street."

"What time did you get there, Doctor?" he asked, taking a small notebook from his coat pocket and making some notes in it as we talked.

"Oh, about six or six-thirty, I think," I answered.

"And when did you pick up your car?"

"Not until this morning."

That got his attention. "Oh?"

I gave him a rueful grin. "Yes. I'm afraid I had several drinks in the club and I didn't think I should drive in that condition, so I walked home."

"You live in the Quarter?" he asked.

I nodded and gave him the address of my apartment.

"And, when you parked, did you see anything suspicious? Any unusual characters hanging around?"

I laughed, trying to keep it light. "In the Quarter?" I asked, smiling. "There are always strange people on the street, but I saw nothing that aroused my suspicions." I waited a beat, and then asked, "What do you mean?"

He sat back as the waiter brought our food. Once he'd left, Boudreaux chuckled. "Oh, like a man carrying a sword and a can of gasoline."

I shook my head. "Now, *that* I would have noticed," I said humorously.

He put his notebook away and bent to his food. "Well, it was just a shot in the dark. No one else seems to have noticed him, either."

As I ate, I asked casually, "I understand you're head of homicide. Was there a killing last night?"

He shook his head. "No, but one of my men thought the fight might have something to do with the Ripper killings."

I shuddered. "I hope you found some clues to the identity of that fiend."

"Unfortunately, no," he said, mopping up the last of his red beans and rice with a roll. "But we did get a good description of one of the men."

"That's good," I said. "Perhaps you can catch him before he kills again."

"We're doing our best, Doctor," Boudreaux said, standing up and reaching into his back pocket for his billfold.

I held up my hand. "No, sir. This is on me. It's the least I can do for our men in blue."

He grinned and stuck out his hand. "Well, thanks again, Doctor Nachtman. I'll let you know if we have any more questions."

I stood up and took his hand. "Anytime, Detective, anytime."

After he left, I sat back down and ordered a cup of coffee and let my muscles relax. It was obvious he had no suspicions about my story. Evidently, the witnesses hadn't gotten a good look at me or he would have asked more questions about my alibi. Hopefully, this was the last I'd see of Detective Boudreaux.

As I sat there in the courtyard, drinking my coffee, I began to plan how I might go about locating the Ripper. Now that he knew I was after him, it was going to be much harder to catch him unaware.

I went back over our conversation in my mind. I remembered he'd mentioned something about a Council. Perhaps it was time for me to approach the local group and seek their assistance in ridding New Orleans of this scourge. After all, from the way he talked, they had to be as concerned about the unwelcome attention he was getting as I was.

My only decision was whether I wanted to get involved with another Vampyre Council. The last time I'd done that, it hadn't gone so well.

Eighteen

After seeing my last patient and telling my staff good evening, I closed and locked the front door to my clinic. I turned off the lights and went into the back room where we kept our blood samples taken during the day until they could be sent to a lab for analysis.

Opening the refrigerator, I took out a rack of test tubes containing a variety of blood samples and set them on a table. From my coat pocket, I took out a list of patients' names that I'd previously tested and found to be free of both the CJD prion that causes spongiform encephalopathy, or Mad Cow Disease, and of the virus causing AIDS.

I took the vials from the patients on the list and arrayed them before me and sat at the table. Looking at the blood-filled vials made my stomach growl and the Hunger within me begin to grow.

My hands trembled and I could feel my face and hands begin to change into my Vampyre form as I uncapped the first vial and raised it to my lips. It'd been almost a week since I'd fed and my mouth was watering already at the coppery scent of the blood.

As the blood poured onto my tongue, it had a bitter taste due to the chemicals in the vial, which prevented it from coagulating, unlike the sweet, spicy taste of blood fresh from a victim's neck.

I shuddered at the taste and forced myself to swallow the life-giving fluid. Soon I'd emptied all of the vials known to be safe from disease and the Hunger subsided enough to let me think clearly.

I fought the urge to sweep the vials off the table and head out onto the streets and rend and tear the first person I met and take a blood feast sweetened by the heady aroma of adrenaline and fear.

My mind, when the Hunger was not in control, knew rationally that if I was to live in New Orleans and continue my research into finding a cure for Vampyrism, I would have to feed like this for the foreseeable future. It was not something I looked forward to.

I leaned back in my chair and let my mind remember kills of the past, when I'd fed on fresh blood whenever I felt the Hunger. My loins grew heavy with remembered lust and I could feel the Hunger stir within me once again.

I shook my head and sat up, forcing the images of my victims from my mind. I got up and went into my office and booted up my computer, loading my research program.

The Hunger subsided as I pored over my notes and some of the papers on plasmid research I'd downloaded off the Internet. I knew there must be an answer here, if I could only find it.

Michael Morpheus pulled his Lincoln Navigator to the corner and waited while Jean Horla, Sarah Kenyon, and Christina Alario climbed in. Jean got in the front seat and the women in the rear.

As he pulled back out into traffic, Jean looked at him. "Just why did you ask us to meet you, Michael? Does it concern Council business?"

"In a way," Michael answered, an enigmatic smile creasing the corners of his lips.

"Are we going to meet the other members of the Council?" Sarah asked.

"No, this meeting is just between us and must remain a secret," Michael said. "Now sit back and relax. All of your questions will be answered shortly."

He turned the next corner and got up on the freeway headed out of New Orleans toward Baton Rouge. After driving for about twenty minutes, he took an exit toward a town named Liberty.

Just before he entered the city limits of the small community, he turned down a dirt road and drove for another five miles. Finally, he pulled to a stop in front of an old wooden house set back in a grove of oak trees.

As they got out of the car, Jean looked at the place skeptically. With hands on hips, he demanded, "Why in hell did you bring us all the way out here?"

Michael smiled and gestured toward the front door. "Come inside and I'll show you."

He unlocked the door and stood aside as they entered. Inside, the house was furnished comfortably but not extravagantly.

Michael led them through the living room and kitchen and out the back door onto a porch overlooking a dock that stretched out into a small bayou.

Christina laughed low in her throat. "Have you taken up fishing, Michael?" she asked, leaning on the porch rail and staring down into the water ten feet below.

"Not exactly," Michael replied. "I want to show you something."

He stepped into the house and returned a few

moments later with several dead chickens in his hands.

"What the hell?" Jean said. "You're not going to perform some weird voodoo ritual, are you?"

Michael shook his head and then pursed his lips, letting out a loud whistle. Suddenly, from the banks of the bayou, several dark forms materialized and moved slowly into the water, causing ripples and small waves to form.

Michael held the chickens up for a moment before pitching them out into the bayou.

The dark water seemed to come alive as three large alligators rose to the surface and began to tear the chickens apart, writhing and churning the water with their tails.

His guests gasped and stepped back from the porch rail at the sight of the ferocity with which the gators tore into the meat.

Sarah looked at Michael. "Does all this have a purpose?" she asked.

"Come inside and let's talk," Michael said.

He showed them into the living room and poured them all glasses of wine as they sat on his couch while he remained standing.

"First, a toast," he said, holding his glass up. "To the Vampyres, long may we reign."

The others glanced uneasily at one another before finally drinking the wine.

After the toast, Michael took a seat in an easy chair across the room from the others. "During the last several meetings of the Council, I've probed each of your minds enough to know that you all are unhappy about the restrictions on our feedings imposed by Carmilla de la Fontaine."

Jean glanced at the women sitting next to him and frowned. "That may be, Michael, but we are also realistic enough to know that nonlethal feeding is the only way to keep the authorities from finding out about our existence."

Michael held up his hand. "What if there was some way to feed as we used to and still remain safe?"

Christina shook her head. "That's impossible, Michael. With the advances in forensics and the way the police departments are all linked together by computers, it would be impossible to hide our killings from the authorities for long."

"Let me suggest a way," Michael said, noting the effect his words had on his guests. "I rented this place from a Realtor in Baton Rouge, making all the arrangements over the phone under an assumed name and paying the rent for a year in advance. For the past month, I've trained the alligators in the bayou to come to my call, ready to eat."

"So what?" Jean asked. "What do they have to do with our method of feeding?"

"Let me finish. There are two main problems with feeding as we were intended to. First, there is the problem of the bodies. As Christina says, there is no way to hide the fact that we leave behind bodies drained of their blood. Even if we fake an accident to account for their deaths, the lack of blood in the bodies would leave a trail the police would soon follow. Secondly, the procuring of victims is problematic. Most people will be missed by someone, sooner or later, leaving yet another trail for the police to follow."

Sarah nodded impatiently. "Yeah, that's the reason Carmilla has decreed we engage in only non-lethal feedings."

"What if I tell you I've solved both problems?" Michael asked.

Jean leaned forward in his seat, becoming more interested. "Go on."

"There is an entire class of people who live off the radar screen of the authorities," Michael said. "Poor people who live in rural areas, criminals and deviants who rarely if ever go to the police for help, and transients who have no family or friends to be concerned if they turn up missing."

Jean smiled. "I think I see where you're going with this."

Michael inclined his head at a hallway leading off the living room. "I have four bedrooms in the rear of the house. In each of them, I've placed such a person. People whose absence will never be reported to the police, or if reported, are of such insignificance the police will expend little energy searching for them."

"What kind of people?" Sarah asked, turning her face toward the hallway and sniffing as if she could smell their blood through the walls.

"Two of the women are prostitutes, the man is a Vietnam veteran who lived on the streets, and the third is a young girl just off a bus from a small town in Alabama, a runaway."

He raised his glass in another toast. "I shall let you take your pick of the delicacies I've procured."

Sarah, whose sexual predilections were well known, stood up, her eyes glittering. "I'll take the runaway female," she said, scarlet drool already dripping from her lips.

Christina stood up and fluffed her hair. "I'd like to try the man." She smiled grimly. "I've always loved soldiers."

Michael grinned at Jean. "That leaves the other two women for us, Jean."

Jean smiled without speaking, a bulge evident in

his pants from the Hunger/lust that was building. "I can hardly wait," he said, his voice husky. "It's been so long since I've fed properly."

Michael stood up and took some keys from his pocket. Each had a tag with a number attached. "The rooms are numbered," he said, handing each of them a key. "And don't worry if your . . . guests become noisy. There are no other houses nearby for anyone to hear their screams."

Nineteen

Sarah took the key with a numeral 1 on it and walked down the hall to the first door. A piece of paper was taped to the door with a 1 printed on it. She put the key in the lock and opened the door and stepped inside.

A girl about sixteen years old was lying on the bed. She looked up and it was evident she'd been crying. Her hair was mussed and her eyes were bloodshot.

When she saw it was a woman who entered, the look of fear and dejection on her face was replaced with an expression of hope. She jumped off the bed and ran toward Sarah. "Oh, please, miss. You've got to help me," she cried, grabbing Sarah's shoulders. "A man kidnapped me and has been holding me prisoner here for days."

Sarah smiled sweetly and pulled the girl to her, holding her in her arms and murmuring soothingly. "Don't worry, dear," Sarah said in a low voice. "Everything is going to be all right soon."

The girl leaned back and wiped tears from her eyes. "My name's Jill," she said. "Can you keep that awful man from hurting me?"

Sarah smiled. "Of course, Jill. Take my word for it, you have absolutely nothing to fear from the man who brought you here."

"Oh, thank God," Jill said as she turned to pick up her purse from the bed.

Sarah stepped in close behind her and reached around her, cupping Jill's breasts with her hands as she nuzzled her neck with her lips.

"What—what are you doing?" Jill asked, stiffening and trying to pull away.

"I'm going to love you, Jill, dear," Sarah murmured against the young girl's skin.

"But I've never done that before. . . ."

Sarah put her hands on Jill's shoulders and turned her around. "Trust me, Jill. You're going to love what I'm going to do to you."

Jill's eyes widened and she shrank back as Sarah moved in close and pulled the girl to her once more, fastening her lips on Jill's in a deep kiss.

After a moment, Jill relaxed and moaned when Sarah's hands gently undid her blouse and slipped under her bra to squeeze her nipples while they kissed.

Slowly, never taking her lips from Jill's, Sarah moved her back toward the bed as she continued to caress Jill's breasts.

When she felt the edge of the mattress press against the back of her knees, Jill lay back on the bed, pulling Sarah with her.

Sarah pushed her tongue between Jill's lips and moved her right hand down between Jill's thighs. Jill moaned again and spread her legs, pushing her sex against Sarah's hand as it slipped inside her shorts.

"Oh, that feels so good," Jill cried out, putting her arms around Sarah and pulling her down tighter against her.

Sarah reached up and ripped Jill's blouse and bra

off, then pulled her shorts and underwear off and threw them on the floor.

Jill, writhing in pleasure at the feeling Sarah's fingers were causing, shut her eyes and arched her back when Sarah circled her nipple with her lips and began sucking on it.

She cried out in surprise and pain when Sarah's teeth bit down on the nipple, causing blood to spurt onto Sarah's tongue.

Sarah, excited beyond all control by the taste of Jill's blood in her mouth, rolled on top of her and buried her face in her neck.

Jill hunched up against Sarah's pelvis, grinding and moaning as Sarah put her lips to her neck.

A sharp pain in her neck made Jill cry out again and she turned to look at Sarah. Her eyes widened and she began to scream in earnest when she saw Sarah's face melt and change, with her teeth elongating, dripping with red drool.

Sarah growled once, then fastened her teeth into Jill's flesh while she pumped her groin against the girl's. Jill stopped screaming and began to whimper as her mind retreated into insanity at the sight of the monster feeding on her. She lay there limp and unresponsive, her eyes blank and sightless.

Within minutes, Sarah climaxed with a scream and tore out her victim's neck with one mighty bite, exulting in the taste of Jill's blood as it pumped all over her face.

Christina entered room 2 and locked the door behind her. She saw a man with several days' growth of beard sitting on the floor, leaning back against the wall. He had bushy, unkempt hair and a sallow complexion indicating years of alcohol and drug abuse.

He turned reddened, bloodshot eyes on Christina

and grinned, revealing yellow teeth. "Hey, lady," he said in a hoarse, gravelly voice. "You wanna tell me what's goin' on here?"

Christina's nose wrinkled at the sour, fetid smell of the man. "I'm here to set you free," she said, walking toward him.

His eyes brightened and he struggled to his feet. " 'Bout time," he said sullenly.

Christina moved toward him, licking her lips at the sight of his carotid artery pulsing in his neck. She stepped up to him and put her hands on either side of his head. Slowly, never taking her eyes off his, she opened her lips and planted a kiss on his.

For a moment, surprise showed in his eyes, but then he responded as all men do. He put his arms around her and pulled her breasts against his chest and thrust his hardening penis against her.

"Is that a knife in your pocket, or are you just glad to see me?" Christina teased.

The man leaned back and looked at her. "Lady, next to a drink, you're 'bout the best thing that's happened to me in—I can't remember when," he said.

Christina stepped back, undid her dress, and let it fall to the floor. She was naked underneath.

"Jesus," the man said, his voice husky with desire.

Christina turned her back to him, sauntered over to the bed, and lay down on her back, her legs spread for him.

It took him less than a minute to shed his clothes and join her on the bed. He fastened his lips on her right nipple and got between her legs, pushing his penis against her.

Christina grinned. "Wow, that's some foreplay, mister," she said.

"Huh?"

"Never mind," she said, shifting slightly so his penis entered her as she pulled his head down and placed her lips against his neck.

"God almighty," he cried as he began to pump as fast as he could against her.

Suddenly he felt her bite his neck; he jerked his head back. "Hey, no biting," he complained.

Christina shook her head. "No, you don't understand."

"Understand what?" he asked, starting to grind against her again.

"Biting is what this is all about," Christina said, and she jerked his head down and fastened her lips to his neck, piercing the skin and entering his carotid artery in one convulsive bite.

He had time to scream once before Christina jerked her head from side to side, ripping out his artery as her claws dug into his hips and buried him deeper inside her.

His erection outlasted his life long enough for Christina to groan in sexual release as she gulped and swallowed his blood.

Jean Horla put his key in the lock of room 3, opened it, and entered, closing it behind him.

A black woman, dressed in the traditional garb of the street prostitute—a miniskirt that barely covered her hips and a halter top, which exposed more breast than it covered—was sitting on the bed, leaning back against the headboard, filing her nails.

She glanced up at Jean. "Mister, I don't know who the hell you think you is, but my man gonna cut you up into little pieces for what you done to me," she said in a nasty voice, her eyes narrow with hate.

Jean held up his hands, "Whoa, little lady. No need to get upset," he said in a reasonable voice. "I'm just in from out of town and I asked my friend to line me up with some entertainment for the night. Don't worry, I'll pay you double your usual rate for the time you've been here."

She frowned in suspicion. "Double?" she asked. "In advance?"

"Sure," Jean said, reaching into his pocket. "How much will that be?"

She hesitated, trying to decide how much she could get. "I usually get two hundred a night, an' I been here for three days."

Jean chuckled to himself. He knew she was lucky if she got fifty a night, but what the hell. She'd never live to spend it.

He unfolded a wad of hundred-dollar bills and slowly counted out ten of them. "I'll give you a thousand if you show me a really good time."

Her eyes widened at the sight of the stack of hundreds he laid on the dresser against the wall. It was more money than she'd make in a month giving blow jobs to johns in their cars. She was already figuring how much she could hold out on her pimp as she got to her feet and peeled out of her top and miniskirt.

"For that kinda money, you can do whatever you want, sweetie," she purred, batting her eyes at Jean in what she thought was a sexy manner.

"Good," Jean said, stripping off his clothes.

Her eyes dropped to his penis, which was almost twice as large as any she'd ever seen. "Hoo, boy," she exclaimed, moving across the room and taking it in her hands. "Maybe I oughtta be payin' you, big boy."

Jean bent down and flicked out his tongue, licking her lips as he turned her toward the bed and gently pushed her down onto her stomach.

"Uh, wait a minute there," she said, a worried

look on her face as she looked back over her shoulder. "I don't know if'n you're gonna fit back there."

Jean grasped her waist and pulled her up onto her hands and knees as he fitted himself behind her. He cupped her pendulous breasts in his hands and rammed into her, causing her to screech in pain as the tender flesh between her buttocks ripped open.

Her eyes were closed and she grunted and groaned when he began to pump against her. His hands became claws, which pierced her breasts as he pulled her back against him.

"Sweet Mary!" she yelled, trying to pull away, "You're killin' me!"

"Not yet," Jean replied through teeth that'd grown down past his lips, "but soon."

After a moment of wild coupling, he came with a groan and let her flop on her face. She scrabbled on hands and knees away from him, turning in time to see his features melt and coalesce into a monster, with a long pointed tongue flicking in and out as he moved toward her.

"Oh, God . . . No-o-o!" she screamed, her hands going to her face, the pain in her backside forgotten.

He dived on top of her, ignoring her as she clawed at his face with her fingernails and jerked and fought for her life.

He put a claw in her hair and yanked her head back, exposing her neck to his fangs. He lowered his head and began to feed.

Slowly, her screams diminished into grunts and groans, and her legs and arms became limp at her side.

When she was lying empty on the bed, he stood up and licked the remains of her blood off his lips.

Sighing in complete satisfaction, he picked up his clothes and got dressed. He walked to the dresser and stood in front of the mirror and combed his hair. When he was satisfied with his appearance, he picked up his thousand dollars and put it in his pocket. He left the room without looking back.

Michael Morpheus, unlike most Vampyres, didn't associate feeding with sex. In fact, he never had sex with his victims, thinking them an inferior species not deserving of such an honor. He saved that for members of his own species.

He entered room 4 and didn't bother to lock the door behind him. He found the other prostitute he'd kidnapped sitting on the edge of the bed, her eyes fearful as she watched him move across the room toward her.

"What you want with me, mister?" she asked, tears forming in her eyes.

He shook his head. "Nothing much. Just your miserable life."

"What?" she asked, starting to get to her feet.

Michael let himself change, enjoying the look of terror in the woman's eyes when his hands became claws, his face elongated, and his fangs appeared.

"Oh, Jesus!" she said, her mouth dropping open.

Michael slashed sideways with his claws extended, severing her carotid artery and almost tearing her head off at the neck.

As she flopped backward, he caught her in his arms and pulled her to him, fastening his teeth on her neck and swallowing her blood as it pumped out of her ruined neck.

Within minutes, he was done and he carried her lifeless body out of the room and onto the back porch.

He whistled shrilly, waited for the movement in

the reeds at the bayou's edge, and then casually tossed her body into the water.

The others, finished by now, walked out onto the porch to see what he was doing.

Suddenly the woman's body was ripped apart by gigantic jaws that emerged from the dark water.

Michael dusted his hands off, grinning at his friends. "There, you see? Nothing for the forensic pathologist to examine."

Christina grinned. "I love your garbage disposal," she said, and she left to get her victim's body from the bedroom to feed to the alligators.

Once all the bodies were gone, Michael and the others met back in his living room.

"I suggest we plan to meet here once a week," he said. "That should be enough to satisfy the Hunger."

The others nodded and prepared to leave. Just before Christina got to the door, Michael put a hand on her shoulder. "Christina, why don't you stay for a while?" he asked.

She glanced down at his lap and saw the large bulge there. "Certainly, Michael," she replied with a sardonic smile. "What kind of a girl would I be if I didn't thank a gentleman for taking me out to dinner?"

Twenty

Matt, along with Sam, Shooter, and TJ, arrived in New Orleans and checked into the Royal Orleans Hotel in the middle of the French Quarter.

As they stood in the opulent lobby waiting for their keys, Shooter glanced around at the lavish furnishings. "Jeez, guys," he said, "I'm not used to this kinda luxury."

Matt smiled. "Well, I hear there's a Motel Six down the road if you'd rather stay there."

TJ grabbed Shooter's arm and hugged it as she nestled next to him. "Nothing doing," she said. "This is the first time we've traveled together and I want it to be special."

Shooter and TJ were rooming together, as were Matt and Sam. Shooter held the receipt up and grimaced. "Look at this. Three hundred fifty dollars a night! That's pretty damned special."

TJ leaned her head back and batted her eyes at him. "Aren't I worth it?" she asked.

"There's only one answer for that, Shooter," Sam said gaily, "that is, if you don't want to end up sleeping in the lobby."

Shooter grinned down at TJ. This was the most normal she'd acted in weeks, and he didn't want to spoil the mood by being grumpy. "Of course you are, sweetheart," he answered. "Nothing is too good for the woman I love." He grabbed her hand. "Come on, let's go check out the gift shop while they get our rooms ready."

After they walked off, Sam punched Matt on the shoulder. "Why can't you be romantic like Shooter?"

"It's a mite difficult to be romantic when we're up here on a trip trying to track down a homicidal maniac who's supposed to be dead," he said.

Sam smiled knowingly. "Just wait until we get to our room. I've brought something that'll make you forget all about Vampyres."

He raised his eyebrows. "Oh? What's that?"

"Just a little something I picked up at Victoria's Secret the other day."

Matt took a deep breath and turned to the desk clerk. "You got those keys ready yet?" he asked anxiously.

When they got to the room, after promising to meet Shooter and TJ in the restaurant after unpacking, Matt tipped the bellman, then shut and locked the door.

He turned to find Sam standing by their window, which overlooked Bourbon Street. He walked up behind her and circled her with his arms, letting his hands cup her breasts.

"Now, what was that you said about Victoria's Secret?" he murmured in her ear.

She turned and kissed him lightly on the lips. "Uh-uh, that's for later. Now I've got to unpack and get settled in."

"Promises, promises," he grumbled. "That's all I ever get."

Sam opened her suitcase and pulled out a sheer black nightie that would barely cover her hips. She held it up. "Think about this while you wait," she said. "Anticipation is the best part of making love."

"Well," Matt said, smiling at the nightie, "maybe not the *best* part, but it ranks right up there."

After Sam got their clothes arranged in the closet and dresser drawers, she glanced at her wristwatch. "Time to meet Shooter and TJ downstairs."

"Yeah, I'm so hungry I could eat a horse," Matt said. "The peanuts on the plane didn't do much to satisfy my appetite."

After he locked the door behind them, they walked down the corridor arm in arm, as so many lovers before them had done.

They found Shooter and TJ in a corner booth, next to a window that also overlooked Bourbon Street. They were laughing and pointing at some of the strange-looking people walking down the sidewalk.

Sam whispered in Matt's ear, "Doesn't TJ look good? It's as if this trip has brought her back to her senses."

Matt nodded. "Yep. She's like the TJ we used to know."

TJ noticed them standing in the entrance and waved them over.

After they were seated, Shooter grinned at Matt. "You're not gonna believe some of the people walking around the streets here. It's like a costume party."

Matt laughed and picked a menu off the table. He gulped and shook his head. "Boy, Shooter, if you think the room rates were pricey, just wait until you see what they get for a burger and fries in this joint."

Sam cleared her throat. "OK, boys, here are the ground rules. We're here on business, as well as pleasure, and I don't want any more grousing about what it's costing us. TJ and I will split the expenses, so I don't want to hear any more about it."

"That's right," TJ agreed, staring at Shooter with narrowed eyes.

The men held up their hands. "All right, all right," Shooter said as a waiter appeared ready to take their orders.

"And no burgers and fries," Sam said. "When in Rome, and all that stuff."

To make her point, Sam ordered shrimp Creole. TJ said she'd have trout Ponchartrain. Matt grinned and ordered oysters Rockefeller. When Sam looked at him, he spread his arms. "I've gotta get ready for that new nightie you showed me up in the room."

Shooter looked at TJ. "Did you hear that? Sam bought a new nightie."

TJ patted his arm. "Don't you worry, Shooter. We went shopping together."

"Oh," Shooter said, mollified. He looked up at the waiter. "I'll have the oysters, too."

When they'd finished the food, which all agreed was beyond compare, Matt ordered after-dinner cocktails for everyone.

After the drinks were served, he said, "Now let's decide how we're going to go about finding Roger Niemann, if he is, in fact, still alive and here in New Orleans."

"The first thing we've got to do is check in with the local police," Shooter said. "Chief Clark told me the man to see is the chief of detectives, William Boudreaux. According to Damon, he's the man heading up the Ripper investigation."

"You think he'll agree to see us?" Sam asked.

Shooter nodded. "Yeah. Damon called him and told him we were coming up here to check on someone wanted in connection with a series of murders in Houston. He said there'd be no problem."

"I think Shooter and I should tackle that. You girls go to the local medical society and see if you can get a line on any new doctors in town. If Niemann is here, it's my guess he'll be here as a doctor."

"But, Matt," TJ said, "in a town this size, there's bound to be lots of new doctors coming here every year. How'll we know which ones to check out? Roger is sure to have changed his name."

"First we'll look at hematologists and internists," Matt answered. "I doubt he'd change his specialty. If that doesn't work, we'll just have to get names and addresses of all the new docs and see if we can get a look at them. It's my guess he won't have bothered to change his appearance too much."

"And while you guys are doing that, I'll see if I can find out where that ship, the *Moon Chaser*, is berthed. I'll set up surveillance on it. With any luck, if it is Niemann's ship, he'll make a visit to it and I can follow him to his home."

"That's all well and good," Sam said, "but, since this is our first night here, I propose we act like regular tourists and enjoy it."

"What did you have in mind?" Matt asked.

Sam glanced at TJ and smiled. "TJ and I would like to see a couple of strip clubs and maybe take in some jazz or ragtime bands."

Matt frowned. "Jeez, Sam. I'm awfully tired. Don't you think we should turn in early?"

She patted his hand. "Don't worry, dear. We won't keep you out too late, and I promise you the nightie will be waiting for you when we get in."

The night of fun started out fine, with everyone enjoying the strip clubs along Bourbon Street.

Shooter let the others know he was mightily impressed with a certain brunette at one club, until he found out the strippers were all female impersonators. He immediately suggested they try Al Hirt's club down the street and see if they could find some good jazz to listen to.

TJ started out the night in a very good mood, considering the serious purpose of their visit to New Orleans. She was laughing and teasing Shooter, until she found herself becoming increasingly disoriented.

It began after they were seated at a table for four at Al Hirt's. They'd ordered drinks and were enjoying the band's first set of the evening, when suddenly TJ began to get mental impressions. It was as if someone else was in her mind with her, and she began to get double images of the club, like she was seeing it through someone else's eyes.

She squeezed her eyes shut, but the images remained and even began to be accompanied by emotional responses foreign to her.

Rubbing her forehead, as if that would make the images disappear, she glanced around the dimly lit room. After a moment, she found a dark-haired woman staring at her; she became convinced she could see herself and Shooter through that pretty woman's eyes.

Flustered, she shook her head and got up to go to the ladies' room to splash cold water on her face. Once she was in the rest room, the images and feelings vanished and she began to believe she'd only imagined them.

She was resting her hands on the sink and staring at herself in the mirror when she noticed a reflection of the dark-haired woman entering the room.

TJ turned and the woman walked up to her and

stared at her without saying a word. Then, she smiled, reached into her handbag, and pulled out a business card. She handed it to TJ without speaking and left the room as suddenly as she'd appeared.

TJ read the card: DE LA FONTAINE ANTIQUES. The name was spelled out in fancy gothic lettering, with an address and phone number embossed underneath.

Taking a deep breath, TJ placed the card in her purse and went back to join the others.

Twenty-one

When they got back to the Royal Orleans, the two couples separated at their doors, promising to meet at nine for breakfast.

TJ walked into their room and threw her purse on the dresser. "I'm going to take a quick shower," she said. "I'll be out in a minute."

Shooter nodded and made his way to the bed, then flopped down on it. He was more than a little drunk and the room was spinning like a top.

He was just starting to doze off when TJ stepped from the bathroom fifteen minutes later. He opened bleary eyes and saw her standing in the doorway, dressed in a sheer white nightgown that flowed around her figure like clouds on a windy day.

The hair on the back of his neck stirred. She looked exactly like the females in the old vampire movies who ran around broken-down castles in white nightgowns, chasing hapless villagers.

Ashamed of his thoughts, he shook his head to clear it and took a longer look at her. He focused his eyes on the dark spots at her chest and groin where her nipples and pubic hair could plainly be seen through the gauzy fabric. This had the desired effect and all thoughts of vampire films were banished from his mind by the immediate and powerful feelings of lust.

"How do you like it?" she asked in a husky voice.

"It's terrific," he croaked, rolling off the bed and moving toward her.

He took her face in his hands and gave her a deep, lingering kiss, feeling her hands moving to his groin and cupping his manhood.

She leaned her face back and whispered, her breath warm on his lips, "I think you're overdressed for the occasion."

While he got out of his clothes as fast as he could, TJ moved to the bed and lay back with her hands behind her neck, watching him with hooded eyes.

Suddenly she blinked and shook her head. She found she was able to see herself through Shooter's eyes and even feel his lust for her in her mind. This was incredibly erotic and she felt herself become immediately wet with reflected desire for him.

She reached down and caressed her breasts, feeling her nipples spring to life as he stepped out of his shorts and stood naked before her.

"Hurry, Shooter," she moaned, rubbing her breasts with her palms.

He quickly lay next to her on the bed and pulled her against him as he kissed her. She could feel him pressing hard against her and she pressed back, making him moan in pleasure as she ground her pelvis against his.

As they kissed, tongues intertwining, he lowered the strap of her gown and exposed her breast to his view. He moved his head and took the nipple in his mouth, cupping and kneading the breast with his hand while he suckled.

TJ groaned and felt herself begin to change, staring at his neck in front of her face. She quickly reached up and turned the light off, lest he see what she was becoming.

She pushed him over and rolled on top of him, burying her face in his neck as her hand sought and found his penis. Shooter laid his head back and gave himself up to his feelings as she caressed him with her hand and bit gently into his neck with teeth that had grown into fangs.

As her hand moved faster and faster, and she sucked harder and harder, Shooter's hips began to move in rhythm with her hand.

TJ, almost delirious with lust, opened her mouth and was about to rend and tear when she suddenly realized what she was doing. With a mighty effort, she pulled her lips back from his neck and moved her head down across his stomach.

Breathing heavily with the effort to control herself, TJ took him in her mouth, covering her fangs with her lips to keep from hurting him.

Shooter groaned and grabbed TJ's thighs, spreading them and burying his head between her legs to give her the same pleasure she was giving him.

Minutes later, TJ screamed as they came together, climaxing at almost the same instant. TJ turned her head to the side and rested it on Shooter's groin as he grew soft, giving her time to change back into a human again.

Once the change was complete, she reversed positions and straddled him, leaning her face down to kiss his lips. "Now I want you inside me," she whispered.

He shook his head weakly. "I don't think . . . ," he began.

TJ decided to try to impose her mental emotions on him, as she had read his before. She concentrated, thinking of her lust for him and projected it at Shooter mentally.

Within seconds, he was growing rigid beneath her, his lips curled in a silly grin.

She smiled back and lifted her hips slightly and then brought them down on him, impaling herself on his penis.

He reached up and jerked the top of her gown down and she leaned forward, letting his lips cover her breast as they coupled again and again.

Afterward, with Shooter asleep next to her, TJ lay in the darkness thinking about what was happening to her. The blood lust coupled with her changing appearance and her new mental abilities told her that if they didn't find some way to cure her soon, her soul would be lost forever.

Once Matt and Sam were in their room, she turned to him and kissed him lightly. "You know what, Matt?" she asked.

"Uh-uh," he said, moving his lips to her neck.

"I'm starved," she said.

"What?"

"Why don't you order us a hamburger and fries from room service while I change?" she asked.

"You want to eat? Now?" he asked, his disappointment evident.

"You order the food," Sam said, "and I'll change into the nightgown I showed you earlier."

"OK," he said, though it was clear food was the last thing on his mind.

By the time the waiter had brought the food, Sam had taken a quick shower and reappeared wearing the black see-through nightgown as she promised.

They set up trays on the bed and proceeded to scarf down hamburgers, fries, and some chili Matt had added to her request.

When they were done, he put the tray outside the door in the corridor and turned to find Sam lying in bed propped up against the headboard, the top of her nightie barely covering her breasts as she smiled invitingly at him.

"Aren't we supposed to wait an hour or something?" he asked as he walked toward her.

"Nope, silly. That's before swimming," she replied.

"But I do intend to dive right in," he said, grinning as he slipped out of his clothes.

"In that case," she said, lowering the top of her gown to her waist—"come on in, the water's fine."

Twenty minutes later, they both stopped in the middle of making love and looked up as they heard a muffled scream from next door.

Matt grinned at Sam. "I see TJ's having fun."

She shrugged and pulled him to her with a laugh deep in her throat. "How do you know that wasn't Shooter screaming?" she asked.

Twenty-two

Matt and Sam were already at breakfast when Shooter and TJ joined them. Both Matt and Sam noticed Shooter looked a little haggard, and there was a fresh bandage on Shooter's neck.

Sam nudged Matt and raised her eyebrows, but he shook his head. He'd discuss it with Shooter later when they were alone.

"Good morning," TJ said brightly, looking fresh and radiant in the early-morning sunshine streaming through the window.

"Morning," Matt said while Sam just smiled.

"Jesus, I need some coffee," Shooter moaned, holding his head.

"A little hungover this morning?" Matt asked.

"A lot hungover," Shooter replied.

When the waiter appeared, Shooter told him to leave a carafe of coffee because he was going to need a lot to get his motor going.

"Did you sleep well?" Sam asked, grinning at TJ. TJ blushed. "Yes, we did."

"We didn't," Matt said. "Too much noise from the room next door."

Shooter smiled for the first time that morning. "Yeah. We must've left the TV on too loud."

"Watching a porno channel, were you?" Matt asked with a chuckle.

TJ glanced at Shooter and covered his hand with hers. "No, actually, Shooter is being gallant. We both got a little . . . carried away last night, it being our first night in a hotel together."

Sam laughed. "Well, at least these two have something in common. Hotels seem to make them horny."

Matt winked at Sam. "It's not the location, sweetheart, it's the company."

Once the waiter served their food, they all dug in with hearty appetites, except Shooter, who stared at his food with a sour expression on his face. "I don't know if my stomach will tolerate food for a while."

"The best cure for a hangover is to eat," TJ said.

Matt nodded. "Listen to your doctor, Shooter. She knows best."

After they were through eating and were on their after-meal coffees, Matt asked, "OK, team, what's the plan of action for today?"

Shooter reached in his pocket for a cigarette, until a stern look from TJ made him change his mind. "I thought Matt and I'd go check in with the police, and you girls head to the medical society offices."

While waiting for the doorman to get them a cab, TJ turned to Sam. "Sam, would you mind going to the medical society by yourself? There's someone I've got to go see."

"Uh, sure, TJ," Sam said. "But I didn't know you knew anyone in New Orleans."

"I don't," TJ replied. "But last night, some strange things were happening to me, and this woman appeared in the ladies' room and gave me a card," she said, pulling Carmilla's card out of her purse and showing it to Sam.

"Did she say anything?" Sam asked.

TJ shook her head. "No, but there was something about the way she acted that told me she might be of help to us."

Sam cocked her head. "What kind of strange things are you talking about?"

The cab pulled up and TJ placed her hand on Sam's arm. "Please bear with me for a while, Sam. I don't have time to explain right now, but I'll tell you all about it tonight."

Sam patted her hand. "OK, TJ, but you be careful. Remember, we're dealing with forces and people here that are very dangerous."

"I promise I'll be very careful," TJ said, and jumped into the taxi.

While they were waiting for their bill to arrive, Matt peered at Shooter over the rim of his coffee cup. "What's with the bandages on your neck, Shooter? Cut yourself shaving?"

Shooter fingered the bandage, his eyes avoiding Matt's. "Uh, not exactly."

Matt leaned across the table and spoke in a low voice so nearby diners couldn't overhear. "Come on, pal. You've been sporting wounds on your neck for a couple of weeks now. What gives?"

Shooter finally looked at Matt, his eyes tortured. "It's TJ, Matt. When we make love, she just goes wild and gives me a little love nip on the neck. It doesn't mean anything."

"That's bullshit and you know it," Matt said. "You know what TJ's been through and what that son of a bitch did to her. This could mean she's changing again into something like Niemann."

Shooter shook his head vigorously, but it was clear the thought had occurred to him. "I don't want to even think about that," he said.

"Look, Shooter, I know you love TJ, but you've

got to be realistic about what's going on here. If she's sucking your blood, then we need to reinstitute therapy as soon as possible before she gets so far along it won't work."

Shooter's hand went to his neck. "It's not like that. It's just a little tear in the skin. She doesn't actually suck the blood out."

"Does she show any other signs of progression of her illness?" Matt asked.

Shooter thought about the deep scratches on his back and how TJ always turned the lights out so he couldn't see her when they made love, but he shook his head. "No, not really."

"OK," Matt said, "but we've got to know if she continues to want to taste your blood. It'll mean our time is shorter than we first thought."

"I'll let you know," Shooter said, hating to lie to his friend, but afraid of what the truth might be.

When Matt and Shooter checked in at the front desk of the New Orleans police station, the desk sergeant said, "Go right on upstairs, the chief is expecting you."

They entered the chief of detectives' office and William Boudreaux rose to greet them. He was a huge bear of a man, standing well over six feet tall and almost as wide. He was wearing a short-sleeved dress shirt that appeared a couple of sizes too small, and his belly protruded over his belt, threatening to send buttons popping everywhere.

He had a file open on his desk, and Matt, reading upside down, saw it had Roger Niemann's name on it.

"Howdy, men," Boudreaux said in a thick New Orleans accent.

"Hello, Chief Boudreaux," Shooter said. "I'm Detective Steve Kowolski and this is my friend, Dr. Matt Carter."

Boudreaux stuck out his hand. "Call me Bill, boys, everybody does," he said, grinning, "an' I'll call you Shooter."

Shooter smiled back. "I see you've been talking to my chief."

Boudreaux laughed. "That's quite a story, 'bout how you got your name."

"Yes, sir, it's funny now, but it didn't seem so at the time," Shooter said.

"I was working robbery back in my early days on the force and my partner and I answered a call to a liquor store. About the time I got out of the car, this perp comes running out waving a shotgun at me. Well, needless to say, I grabbed for my .38 and somehow the son of a bitch went off. I ended up shooting the little toe on my right foot clean off."

"No shit?" Boudreaux asked, laughing out loud.

"Yeah," Shooter answered, "and the funny thing is the perp was so startled when my gun went off he dropped the shotgun and surrendered right there."

Matt added, "And Officer Kowolski has been called Shooter ever since."

"Take a seat, boys," Boudreaux said as he sat in his desk chair and leaned back, his hands folded across his ample stomach. "You want some coffee? It's made with chicory and guaranteed to put hair on your chests."

Both Matt and Shooter shook their heads.

"I've been reading this file Chief Clark over-nighted to me. It makes a hell of a story."

Shooter nodded. "Yes, sir. We think he was responsible for dozens of killings in the Houston area."

Boudreaux picked up a sheet of paper from the file and peered over it at them. "According to this medical examiner's report, the wounds this Niemann inflicted were remarkably similar to the ones we've been seeing in our Ripper killings."

"That's one of the reasons we've come to your city," Shooter said. "The similarity of the murders, plus the fact that we have some evidence Niemann may have traveled to New Orleans after our confrontation with him in Houston."

Boudreaux's forehead wrinkled. "But, according to your chief, this Niemann was shot several times with a machine gun and fell into the Houston Ship Channel. You think he may have survived that?"

Shooter shrugged. "I didn't think it was possible at first, Bill, but we never found a trace of his body, and with the problems you've been having here, we thought it worth a shot to come up here and look around."

Boudreaux nodded. "Tell me about this body y'all found with his head cut off and the body burned with gasoline."

Shooter turned to Matt. "That was handled by Matt," he said.

Matt went on to describe how they'd found the body partially consumed by a gasoline fire after his head had been severed.

"You run any tests on the remains?" Boudreaux asked, leaning forward and putting his elbows on his desk.

Matt took a deep breath. He knew what he was about to say would be hard for the policeman to believe.

"Yes, sir. We did DNA testing and found evidence the body was over a hundred years old."

Boudreaux pursed his lips. "Could someone have

dug the body up out of a grave and cut it and then burned it?"

Matt shook his head. "The medical examiner didn't think so. The tissues in the body showed evidence of a recent infection with an organism that wasn't around a hundred years ago. It was, and is, our belief the man was alive when he was killed and that he was, in fact, well over a hundred years old at the time."

Boudreaux tapped his index finger on the file. "I'm readin' between the lines here, boys, but I get the impression you and your chief think there was more to this Niemann character than a run-of-the-mill serial killer. There's some stuff in here 'bout records of this guy goin' back a long, long time, too."

Matt and Shooter glanced at each other. Shooter shrugged. "You might as well level with him, Matt."

"Chief, without getting too technical, we believe there exists in America a group of people infected with a disease that leaves them with symptoms very similar to the myth about vampires. These people live an extraordinary length of time, and because of their infection, they need fresh blood to live. It is our belief Roger Niemann was one of these people and that he killed like he did in order to survive."

Boudreaux smiled. "So, to cut to the chase, you think this Niemann fellow was a vampire, and that either he or one like him is responsible for our Ripper murders?"

Matt held up his hand. "Not a vampire in the supernatural sense, Bill. It's just a disease that causes some of the same characteristics of the old fables."

"Chief," Shooter added, "I hope you won't dismiss our concerns or think we're nuts because of this."

Boudreaux shook his head. "Not to worry, Shooter. I've lived here in New Orleans for all of my life, an' I gotta tell you I've seen some things that'd make the hair on the back of your neck stand up plumb straight. Remember, this is the land of voodoo, and New Orleans is the capital." He grinned. "No, I don't dismiss nothin' out of hand, but I do like to see some proof 'fore I go off half-cocked."

"All we're asking is for you to allow us to do our own investigation," Shooter said. "We'll keep you informed of anything we find out, of course."

"Are you carryin', son?" Boudreaux asked.

"Uh, no, sir," Shooter said. "But I did bring my service revolver with me. It's in my suitcase at the hotel."

"Well, I suppose if you're gonna go nosing around our city, you oughta have some protection. Stand up, Shooter."

Shooter got to his feet, a puzzled expression on his face.

"Raise your right hand and repeat after me: 'I solemnly swear to uphold the laws of the commonwealth of Louisiana.' "

Shooter held up his hand and repeated the words.

"Now," Boudreaux said, "you're an honorary deputy and that allows you to go armed in our state."

"Thanks, Chief," Shooter said.

"You can thank me by findin' the bastard who's killin' my citizens," Boudreaux said. He fished in his shirt pocket and brought out a card, which he handed to Shooter. "Here's a card with my home number and cell phone number. You'll be able to reach me twenty-four hours a day."

Matt got to his feet. "Chief, before we go, let me just emphasize how powerful Niemann is. When we tracked him to his ship and the SWAT team attacked him, he fought back with only a sword."

"He went up against a SWAT team with a sword?" Boudreaux asked unbelievingly.

Shooter nodded. "Yeah, and he managed to take out eight men before we got him."

Boudreaux looked from Matt to Shooter. "In that case, maybe I'd better swear your friend in, too. You may need all the firepower you can carry if you manage to find this guy."

Twenty-three

TJ got out of her cab and checked the address against the card the woman had given her. It was correct and the sign over the small storefront office read DE LA FONTAINE ANTIQUES

When she put a hand on the doorknob, TJ got such a feeling of foreboding she almost turned around and left, but she forced herself to open the door and enter. After all, she told herself, her life might depend on what she learned inside.

A couple was inside, walking the aisles and occasionally picking up objects and checking the price tags. They were obviously tourists, with the man wearing Bermuda shorts and the woman in a dress of outlandish colors.

The attractive dark-haired woman from the other night appeared from behind the counter and smiled at TJ. When TJ started to speak, the woman shook her head, cast her eyes at the tourists, and motioned TJ through a door into a back room.

"Make yourself comfortable, dear," she said in a voice devoid of accent. "I'll be with you in a moment."

TJ took a seat at a large, ornately carved table in the rear of the room and glanced around her at the antiques, which filled every corner. She was no expert, but she thought the pieces were exquisite and knew they were probably worth a small fortune.

After a few moments, TJ heard the front door shut. Seconds later, the woman appeared. "I've put the Closed sign on the door so we won't be disturbed," she said.

When TJ said nothing, the woman approached and held out her hand. "I am Carmilla de la Fontaine," she said.

TJ shook her hand. "I'm TJ O'Reilly."

"Yes," Carmilla said. "I know."

"Have we met?" TJ asked.

"No, dear. I got that from your mind the other night."

"You read my mind?"

Carmilla made a dismissive motion with her hand. "Not exactly, but I was able to get certain impressions."

TJ put her face in her hands. "I'm so confused," she moaned.

Carmilla moved to a counter. "Would you like some hot tea? I've always found tea to be very soothing in times of crisis."

TJ nodded and watched as Carmilla prepared two cups of tea and served them on an elaborate silver service.

"Milk or sugar?"

"Sugar and lemon, please," TJ answered, amazed that they were sitting here having tea after the woman had just told her she could read her mind.

As she poured, Carmilla said, "I sense you are very confused and somewhat disoriented about what happened to you last night."

"Yes."

"First let me say that I am like you," Carmilla

said in a low, calm voice. "That is, we share certain characteristics through no choice of our own."

"Are you . . . are you a vampire?" TJ asked.

"We prefer the term Vampyre, with a *Y,*" Carmilla said with a smile. "And, yes, I am, and I suspect you are, too, my dear."

TJ, surprised at Carmilla's openness, took a deep drink of her tea. It was delicious and the warm liquid did seem to calm her a bit.

Carmilla stared at her for a moment. "How is it you are one of us and don't know it?" she asked.

TJ shook her head. "I'm not one of you. . . . At least, I don't think I am yet."

"But one of us must have taken you through the Rite of Transformation?"

TJ grimaced at the word. "Yes. Several months ago, in Houston, a man who is . . . a Vampyre named Roger Niemann kidnapped me. He did perform certain rituals on me, against my will, of course."

She hesitated at the look of hatred that came over Carmilla's face at her mention of the name Roger Niemann.

"Is something wrong?" TJ asked, wondering if she'd said something to anger the woman.

"No, not with you, my dear," Carmilla said, reaching across the table to pat TJ's hand. "It's just that I've had some dealings with this Roger Niemann, and 'dislike' is much too mild a word for how I feel about him.

"However," Carmilla continued, "you say Niemann did perform the Transformation ritual on you, and yet you don't think you have been changed by it?"

TJ's face sobered. "Oh, I was changed all right. But, soon after he finished with me, some friends found me and treated me with medications that made most of the symptoms go away—at least for a while."

Carmilla's face lit up with excitement. "You say these friends have a treatment that can reverse the Transformation?"

TJ nodded. "At least, partially. Now, however, some of the symptoms are returning. That's why we're here looking for Roger. We know he's been experimenting with procedures to reverse the Transformation and we want to get some information from him."

Carmilla's face paled and TJ noticed her hand begin to shake, spilling her tea. "You say, Roger Niemann is here in New Orleans?" she asked in a hoarse voice.

"We're almost sure he is," TJ replied, "but we don't know just where yet."

Carmilla took a deep breath, forcing herself to calm down, and poured them both more tea.

"Now, TJ, you must start from the very beginning and tell me everything you can about what happened to you and how your treatment affected your Transformation."

It took TJ over an hour and a half to explain to Carmilla how Roger, racked with guilt over his need to kill to satisfy his lust for blood, had chosen her to be his mate. How out of both a physical attraction for her and a desire to have another doctor to help him in his research, he hoped to find a cure for Vampyrism. Though she didn't remember her treatment, she told Carmilla what Sam and Matt had told her about how they'd used antibiotics to kill the plasmids that carried the DNA genes that caused the symptoms of Vampyrism.

When she was finished, Carmilla was clearly excited about what she'd heard. "And did the treatment work?" she asked.

"Only partially, and the cure was only temporary," TJ answered. "I find myself again exhibiting some of the symptoms, and that is why we hope to find Roger. We believe if he will share some of his research with us, we'll be able to effect a permanent cure."

"Oh, my dear," Carmilla said, taking both of TJ's hands in hers. "If only that is true."

"Now that I've told you my story, perhaps you can explain to me why you hate Roger so much," TJ said.

"That, too, is a long story, TJ. Basically, there are two types of Vampyres. Those that revel in their differences and think that normal people, those we call Normals, or Others, are our legitimate prey. The second type, and by far the most prevalent, are those like Roger and myself. Those who despise what we are and hate taking other lives so that we can survive.

"My aunt Jacqueline De La Fontaine headed a council in Houston of those who wanted peace with the Normals. Roger, when they approached him and asked him to cease his killing of innocent people, savagely murdered my aunt and some of her followers." Carmilla's face reddened and she gritted her teeth. "For that, I have sworn to kill Roger myself."

TJ leaned forward and spoke earnestly. "But, Carmilla, if Roger holds the key to undoing the Transformation, you must not kill him. He seems to be the best hope for you and me and all of us who want to become human again."

Carmilla nodded gravely. "You are correct, of course. And, my dear, if Roger does hold this key you speak of, then I may be inclined to spare his life if he shares it with the rest of us."

When TJ started to speak, Carmilla held up her hand. "But, TJ, I must warn you. Recently, we've begun to have some killings in New Orleans that almost certainly are being done by one of us. If Roger is here in the city, then I will bet that it is he who is murdering these people. If that is so, then I fear he no longer wishes to revert to normal, for only someone who relishes killing can be committing these atrocities."

"I cannot believe that, Carmilla. When I was undergoing the Transformation, Roger and I . . . Well, we became very close. I just know that he is innocent of these murders. He hated killing and was doing everything in his power to stop."

Carmilla sighed. "I hope you are right, my dear. But now, you have given me much to think about, and to share with the members of my own Council. Where are you staying?"

"My friends and I are at the Royal Orleans."

Carmilla rose. "Then go back to them, and not a word about what we've spoken about. I will get in touch with you after I've spoken to my Council. If they agree, we'll help you find Roger and see what he has to say for himself."

As TJ left the antique shop, Carmilla reminded her. "Remember, not a word to your friends. The other members of our race are very strict about secrecy, and I wouldn't want you to put your friends' lives in danger."

With that chilling warning ringing in her mind, TJ made her way back to the hotel.

Twenty-four

It was well past midnight when Albert Nachtman switched off the DNA sequencer in his home lab. He'd inserted samples of his own blood into the machine and had been using it to try and determine the DNA code of the plasmids infecting his bloodstream that caused his Vampyre symptoms. After many tries and hundreds of hours of work, the machine had finally succeeded in the identification.

Albert booted up the Dell Inspiron notebook computer he used to record his data and began to write:

> I have finally made a significant breakthrough in my research into the causes of Vampyrism. The DNA sequencer has identified the plasmids coursing through my blood as belonging to the so-called F-like plasmids, which are relatives of the prototypic fertility factor, F. Plasmids replicate by conjugation, or splitting apart. The good news is that in their wild form, the F-type plasmids' ability to conjugate is repressed; that is, only about one out of a thousand of the F-type plasmids are able to conjugate and reproduce. In theory, this should make them easier to control once I've

been able to synthesize some sort of repressor
for conjugative DNA transfer.

Researching the Internet, especially the work
of Dr. Bartholomew Wingate at McGill University, I found that in the F-type plasmids, gene
19 is the one that regulates fertility and conjugation. His papers speak of work on an anti-
sense RNA, called FinP (fin: fertility
inhibition), which, in conjunction with the protein FinO, might constitute a repressor for conjugative DNA transfer and thus stop the
propagation of plasmids in my bloodstream.

Whether or not Bartholomew has achieved
this synthesis of FinP and FinO yet is not indicated in his published work, nor is the question
of whether it will work on F-type plasmids addressed.

I have been debating whether to call him directly for the answers, but that would pose
problems of how to explain my situation without exposing myself to detection by the
authorities.

Albert saved his work and then turned off the
computer. He used the Dell laptop for security reasons. It was easily portable and could be carried with
him in the event he had to vacate his home in a
hurry.

He stretched and yawned. He was getting close
to solving the problem of reversing Vampyrism, but
he knew he still had a long way to go to actually
begin the process.

He checked his watch. It was too late to go hunting for the Ripper. If he was on the prowl tonight,
he'd probably already chosen his victim and was
somewhere he couldn't be found. Albert knew full

well the Ripper's need for privacy when he fed, for he'd faced the same situations many times himself.

He got up from his desk and went into his bedroom. He decided to get some sleep and recharge his mental batteries. Though his Vampyre body needed little rest, he found his mind was sluggish and his thoughts muddled if he didn't sleep occasionally.

TJ had wrestled with her conscience all afternoon about whether to inform her friends of what she'd learned from the Vampyre known as Carmilla de la Fontaine.

When they met back at the hotel, the four friends gathered in Matt and Sam's room and ordered sandwiches from room service.

Once the food had been delivered and they were sitting around the coffee table in front of the couch, Sam asked the boys how their day had gone.

Shooter shrugged and then spoke around a mouthful of ham and cheese on rye. "All in all, not too bad. At least Chief Boudreaux didn't throw us out on our ears when we told him of our suspicions about Roger Niemann being a Vampyre and perhaps being his elusive Ripper."

"Yeah," Matt added. "He even promised to share whatever clues he came up with concerning the Ripper killings if we did the same with whatever we turned up."

Shooter grinned. "Hell, he even deputized me so I could legally carry a gun while we hunt the bastard."

"What about you, Matt?" Sam asked, a glint in her eye. Matt knew she abhorred guns and violence, so he shook his head. "He offered to deputize me, too, but I declined. I told him I'd just probably shoot myself or some innocent bystander if I tried to fire a weapon."

TJ looked over at Shooter. "And did you bring a gun with you?"

He nodded. "Yep, but I told the chief a little white lie. I said I had my service revolver with me."

"You don't?" TJ asked.

"Nope. I borrowed one of the SWAT team's new fifty-caliber Smith and Wesson automatics and a supply of dumdums and Glaser Safety Slugs."

"What are dumdums and Glasers?" Sam asked.

"Dumdums are soft-nosed bullets with hollow points that expand when they hit. They'll leave a hole in flesh and blood you can put your fist through. Glasers are like little shotgun shells. The slugs are hollow and contain dozens of small pellets floating in liquid Teflon. They're not very good against bulletproof vests, but they're hell on flesh and blood. When they hit, the nose opens up and sends all the little lead shot spreading out in a cone-shaped path of destruction. Afterward, it looks like the target was put through a meat grinder."

Sam shuddered. "I don't like the thought of going around hunting a man like he was a wild animal."

Shooter's face became sober. "You didn't see what that son of a bitch did to my friend Sherry or those SWAT team men who got in his way," he said grimly. "And, Sam, I need to remind you we're not exactly hunting a man here. From all accounts, Niemann is more like a wild animal than a human—"

To change the subject, Matt interrupted. "And how did you ladies do on your mission to get a list of the new docs in town?"

Sam glanced at TJ, but didn't say anything about her going off on her own. "Not too well. With Tulane School of Medicine here and the large number of private clinics, there have been over two hundred doctors in and out of town in the past three months, and that's not counting the ones who didn't join the medical society."

"I guess, then, we'll just have to find him the old-fashioned way," Shooter observed.

"Which is?" Matt asked.

"We'll stake out his boat and hope he visits it soon."

"That could take weeks," Sam protested.

Shooter shrugged. "I'm open to other suggestions."

TJ bit her lip. It was now or never, she thought to herself. "I need to tell y'all something."

"What is it, baby?" Shooter asked.

"I didn't go with Sam today."

Shooter cocked his head to the side. "Oh?"

TJ took a deep breath and then explained how her mental abilities had been growing, and of the meeting she had with Carmilla. She held nothing back and told them everything that'd been said, including Carmilla's threat if she told them about the Vampyres.

"Jeez," Shooter said when she'd finished. "There must be a whole lot of these creatures if they have a Council and everything."

"Did she say how many there were?" Sam asked.

TJ shook her head. "No, but I got the impression there were quite a few."

"All this mental stuff must've been awfully hard on you, sweetheart," Shooter said. "Why didn't you tell me . . . us about it?"

TJ dropped her eyes, unable to meet his gaze. "I didn't understand it myself at first, and when I did finally realize what was happening, I didn't tell you because I didn't want you all to think I was a freak."

They all immediately commiserated with her and told her they would've thought no such thing.

She looked up, her face a mask of determination. "The reason I'm telling you now is that I see a way to find Roger without waiting for him to visit his ship."

"What's that, TJ?" Sam asked.

"I could start projecting my mind out, calling to him as I go around town, telling him to come see me."

Shooter jumped to his feet. "No way!" he almost shouted. "I'm not about to let you set yourself up as bait for this monster."

She set her tortured eyes upon him. "But don't you see, Shooter? Roger has the same mental abilities I do, only much more powerful. I don't think there is any way you could find him and follow him without his knowing about it. Your mind and thoughts would give you away."

"But he didn't hear the SWAT team coming when we fought him last time," Shooter protested.

"That's because you went immediately to his ship and boarded it," TJ said. "You didn't try to follow him around the city first. By the time he knew you were on to him, you had him trapped on his ship."

Matt sighed. "She's got a point, Shooter."

Shooter glared at Matt. "Don't tell me you're on her side in this crazy idea, pal."

"Hold on, Shooter," Sam said thoughtfully. "I think TJ has a point. If this Carmilla lady could pick up her thoughts and find her, Roger is going to sooner or later. I think it's better if we fix it so when he does hear her, we'll be there to protect her."

"How can we do that if he's such a great mind reader?" Shooter asked.

"I think I know a way . . . ," Sam said, and then she explained her idea.

Twenty-five

Jacques Chatdenuit paced back and forth in his apartment. The recent confrontation with the other Vampyre had caused him to refrain from feeding for several days. He was unsure of just how much the creature knew about him and his habits, and didn't want to go out until he knew how much danger he was in.

Ordinarily, Jacques wasn't afraid of anything; his megalomania wouldn't allow him to think anyone was as strong and intelligent as he was. However, the force of the other Vampyre's mind had surprised and dismayed him. He knew that in a force of wills and strength, the match was too close to call, and he wasn't ready to put it to the final test and risk his life finding out who was the stronger.

He tried to eat some normal food, but his stomach rejected it. As he knelt over the toilet throwing up, his Hunger made itself known. It started as an empty feeling in his gut, followed by a slight tremor in his hands and a flushed feeling. Soon his mind could think of nothing else but blood. He found himself growing hard with the thought of once again going on the hunt.

"Fuck him!" he growled. "If he wants a fight, then it's a fight he'll get."

He put on his hunting outfit of black jeans and

shirt, and started to leave his home. He stopped just before shutting the door behind him, thought for a moment, then reentered his room. He went to a closet and took out a .357 revolver loaded with wad-cutter slugs, put it in his belt in the small of his back, and threw a sport coat on to cover the weapon.

He knew the pistol wouldn't kill another of his kind, but the force of being hit with five or six of the big slugs would slow the other down long enough for him to make his getaway.

A grim smile curled his lips as he left and went out into the darkness to satisfy his growing Hunger. He only hoped it would give him time to make a safe acquisition without risking his identity.

As he walked down the street, Jacques decided to change his method of picking his prey, just in case his new enemy was watching the places he usually frequented on his hunts. He walked past Bourbon Street, keeping his mind tightly blocked to prevent any others of his kind from learning of his inten-tions, and moved toward the Hilton Hotel on Street Charles Street.

He entered the hotel and went straight to the bar area. He knew there were always tourists staying at the popular hotel and thought maybe he'd have some luck with some who hadn't gone out for the night yet.

He took a seat at the end of the bar where the light was dim and the bartender wouldn't be able to get a good look at him. Ordering a double Jack Daniel's and Coke, he turned on his bar stool and surveyed the room.

Sure enough, there were three couples sitting at a large table in the rear of the room. Any of the three females would do; each of them was young, pretty, and full of life.

Jacques felt his heart begin to pound. He hoped his Hunger could be held off long enough for him to make his move safely.

Just as he was finishing his drink, the girl on the end, with long, blond hair, got up from the table and walked toward the rest rooms at the other end of the bar.

Jacques threw a ten-dollar bill on the counter and followed her, hoping his luck would hold and there'd be no one else back there. He knew there was a back door near the rest rooms that opened onto an alleyway. Only seconds would be needed if the area was clear.

He waited outside the ladies' room, pretending to use the pay phone. Five minutes later, the blonde came out of the room, looking down as she replaced a compact and comb in her purse.

Jacques glanced over his shoulder and saw that they were alone.

"Pardon me, miss," he said in his most agreeable tone as he moved toward her.

She looked up, an expression of mild surprise on her face. "Yes?"

Jacques pointed over his shoulder. "Your friends asked me to tell you they'd meet you outside . . . right through that door."

"What?" she asked, puzzled.

"They said they'd explain when you got there." He stepped past her and opened the door, standing to the side so she could step through.

"That's funny," she said slowly as she moved by him. "They didn't say anything about leaving."

He followed her out and shut the door behind him.

She turned. "I don't see . . . ," she started to say.

He made a fist and hit her square in the jaw, knocking her unconscious and catching her in his arms as she fell. As quick as a wink, he threw her over his shoulder and ran at a lope, deeper into the alleyway. He made two turns, moving ever farther from the busy streets near the door.

He came to a Dumpster and set her down on the ground next to it. As she moaned and shook her head, he stripped off his clothes and stood over her, letting his body change as she came awake.

"What—what happened?" she moaned, holding her jaw and trying to get to her feet. When she looked up and saw him standing naked before her, his face a horrible monster mask and his fangs drooling red liquid, she put her hands up and started to scream.

Jacques stepped forward and clamped his left claw over her mouth while he ripped her clothes off with his right.

She struggled and fought, laying the flesh of his cheek open with her fingernails as she tried to escape his grasp.

He grinned, exposing his mouthful of fangs, and flicked his long, pointed tongue out at her. "Oh, you're a feisty one," he growled, his breath smelling like a charnel house to her.

"I like that," he said, moving up against her and pinning her to the brick wall behind her. He put his mouth on hers and fondled her breasts as he ground his penis against her groin.

Slowly, his mind forced her to relax and stop fighting him. Her eyes became glazed and she moaned with pleasure as he grabbed her thighs and spread them. He lifted her in the air and pulled her down onto him, kissing her deeply as he slid inside her.

She groaned and put her hands on his back and pulled him deeper into her as his lust was transmitted to her mind.

"Oh, God," she almost screamed as he began to pump against her, his claws digging into her breasts as he pinched and pulled her nipples.

"Don't stop," she gasped, beginning to climax.

In the background, Jacques could hear a male voice calling, "Sally . . . Sally, are you there?"

He leaned his head back and stared into her sightless eyes. "I'm afraid I must, my dear," he said in a voice husky with lust and desire. "All good things must end," he added, opening his mouth wide and bending to her neck.

She bucked against him, still in the throes of her orgasm, as he ripped her throat out and drank her life.

Minutes later, as he rounded a corner fifty yards from Sally's body, he heard her boyfriend scream, "Oh, God . . . No-o-o!" when he found her ravished and torn remains.

Twenty-six

Once all of the members of Carmilla de la Fontaine's Council were present and had been served the drinks of their choice, Michael Morpheus called out, "I really must protest your calling another meeting so soon after the last, Carmilla." He glanced around the table as if to judge how much support he had among the other members. "After all, some of us do have lives separate and apart from belonging to this group."

Carmilla gave a mild smile. "You're welcome to leave at any time, Michael, or for that matter, not to attend at all," she said pointedly. "I'm quite sure we can come to any decisions we need to without your input, if that is what you desire."

Michael waved a languid hand as he yawned to show he gave very little importance to whatever she might have to say. "Oh, do go on, Carmilla. You're wasting time."

Carmilla cleared her throat and began to tell them of her discovery of and meeting with TJ the previous day.

"And is this woman absolutely sure that Roger Niemann is in town?" asked Peter Vardalack.

"No," Carmilla answered, "but she and her friends were sure enough to leave their jobs and travel here in hopes of contacting him."

"The more important question," began Adeline Ducayne, "is are you convinced she was somehow able to cause her Transformation to regress."

Carmilla inclined her head. "Yes, though the effects were only temporary. She is definitely in the very early stages of Transformation, though the actual ceremony took place almost a year ago."

"That's unheard of," Louis Frene said. "I myself have never seen the complete Transformation take more than several weeks, and it is usually much shorter than that."

Michael spoke up again. "Are you sure this is not just wishful thinking on your part, Carmilla? After all, we all know how you long to return to being one of the Normals again, though I cannot imagine why."

"Of course I'm sure, Michael. Otherwise, I would not have called this meeting of the Council. And, for your information, I'm not the only one here who would be interested in a process that would make us normal humans again."

Theo Thantos spoke for the first time. "But, Carmilla, as you yourself said, the reversal of the Transformation was only temporary. Of what possible use is that?"

"TJ and her friends are certain that Roger Niemann has information that will enable them to make the reversal permanent."

"Carmilla, if this Roger Niemann is here as this woman says, and if he is in fact the Ripper, aren't we obligated to eliminate him?"

Carmilla inclined her head, her face set and grim. "If Roger is here, whether he is the Ripper or not, I will terminate him. I owe that to my friends and relatives he murdered in Houston." She held up her hand. "But if he has information that is useful to us, there is nothing to prevent us from gaining that information and then taking him out."

"I'm still not sure why you called us here today," Gerald Enyo said. "What would you have us do about all this?"

Carmilla looked around the table at the members of the Council. "We need to find Roger Niemann, and we need to be involved with this woman in her search for the ability to reverse the Transformation."

When Michael opened his mouth to speak, she interrupted him. "Yes, Michael, even those of you who are perfectly happy to remain as you are need to be involved in this. Whatever research Niemann has done has vital importance for all of us, even if we elect not to use it. So what I'm asking is for each of us to open our minds more than ever before as we go about the city. We must find Roger if he is here, and we must determine if he is the Ripper or not. If he is not, then we can also use our search to find whoever is the Ripper."

As the members began to talk among themselves, Carmilla saw Michael passing strange looks with Christina Alario, Jean Horla, and Sarah Kenyon. She wondered just what was going on between them, but put it out of her mind for the present.

"Does anyone have any objections to my proposal?"

No one spoke up, so she called the meeting to an end. "If any of you come up with anything, please call me immediately," she said as she showed them out the door.

After she closed the door, she peeked out the blinds and saw Michael and the three other members standing in a small group talking. Something was definitely strange about the furtive way they glanced over their shoulders as they talked. She decided she'd better do some sleuthing so she wouldn't be caught unaware by whatever they were planning.

Shooter got back to the hotel just after five in the afternoon after spending most of the day searching for Roger Niemann's ship.

He went to his room and woke TJ up from her nap and they went to Matt and Sam's room.

"Did you find it?" Matt asked as he showed them into the room.

Shooter raised his eyebrows and grunted. "Do you have any idea just how many places there are to dock ships in the New Orleans area?"

"No, but I have a feeling you're gonna tell us," Sam replied with a laugh.

Matt fixed them all drinks from a makeshift bar he'd made on the dresser. Shooter and TJ sat on the couch while he and Sam pulled up easy chairs across the coffee table from them.

"Over twenty," Shooter said, "but there were only four or five places a ship as large as Niemann's could be berthed." He took a long swig of his drink. "And, of course, I finally found it at the last place on my list."

"Are you sure it's the same ship?" TJ asked.

"Yep. The name's been changed to *Moon Chaser*, but it's definitely the same ship we boarded the night of the attack."

"Where is it?" Sam asked.

"It's berthed at the docks on Lake Ponchartrain, and let me tell you, it's not a place I'd want to be alone after dark. There's nothing around the area but a row of bars frequented by sailors and longshoremen. Definitely not listed on tourist attractions."

"Do you think he might be living on it?" Matt asked.

Shooter shook his head. "I don't think so. The gangplank had a fence across it and it looked like it might be wired to an alarm, so I didn't try to get aboard."

"So our next step will be to try and put Sam's plan into action," TJ said, her eyes worried as she sipped her drink.

Shooter put his hand on her arm. "Are you sure you want to try this, babe?"

She looked up at him. "I don't see any other way."

"Let's go over it one more time," Sam said. "We're going to leave a note attached to the gangplank asking Roger to meet you at some very public place, with lots of people around."

TJ nodded. "I've been doing some experimenting with this mind-reading stuff. It appears to work about the same way conversation does. If I'm more than a few feet away, I don't get anything."

"That means if we're in the immediate area but not too close, and there is a crowd of people around, he won't be able to pick up on our thoughts, right?" Matt said.

Before TJ could answer, Shooter looked closely at her. "Does this mean when we're close, you're able to read my mind?" he asked.

TJ grinned and patted his leg. "Believe me, Shooter, honey, you don't have to be a mind reader to know what you're thinking about. Ninety percent of the time, it's one thing."

Shooter blushed crimson red as Matt and Sam and TJ all joined in laughter.

"I know what you mean," Sam agreed, glancing at Matt. "It seems all men are the same."

"I resemble that remark," Matt said, grinning. "I occasionally think of things other than sex."

"Only when you're hungry," Sam said, "and even then, it's not far in the back of your mind."

Shooter laughed, glad to see TJ so relaxed before they tried such a dangerous maneuver. His face sobered and he asked, "OK, so you guys will take up positions in some crowded club and I'll hang out near the ship. When I see Roger get the message, I'll hightail it back to join you and let you know he's on the way."

"Remember, stay far enough away so he can't pick up on your emotions or thoughts," TJ reminded him. "His abilities may be stronger than mine, so I don't know just how far out he can 'hear' things."

"Well, all that's left now is for us to pick a spot to meet him at. We want one that's crowded, but not too noisy. You two have got to be able to talk."

"It should be relatively dark, too," Shooter added. "Otherwise, Roger may see us and recognize us in the crowd."

"That won't matter once he's taken his seat," Sam said. "Because as soon as he's seated, we're all going to join the party."

"What if he gets rough?" Matt asked.

"I don't see that happening," Shooter said. "For one, I'll let him know I'm armed, but I think he truly cared for TJ and I doubt he'd try anything too violent with her present."

"Especially if we let him know right away we're not there to threaten him, but to ask for his help," Sam said.

"And remember, Roger's been working on reversing his sickness for many years. Once he finds out we may have a way, I think he'll be more than happy to cooperate," TJ said.

Shooter got to his feet and picked up a tourist magazine from the dresser. "Now, I guess it's time to pick our spot and then I'll go take up station near the ship."

After thumbing through several pages of the magazine, Sam said, "There!"

On the page was an ad for Top of the Sheraton. "That's perfect," she said. "See, it's a piano bar and it's on the top floor of a hotel. It's bound to be crowded, but since it's a piano bar, the conversation will be low and not boisterous."

"Another good thing is it's accessible only by elevator," Shooter said. "That way, if he sees us, he won't be able to get away very quickly 'cause he'll have to wait for the elevator to come."

Matt held up his glass. "A toast to our venture," he said. As they all clinked their glasses together, he said, "To success in our quest for a cure for TJ."

"And for all the other poor souls like Roger who want to become human again," TJ added solemnly.

Twenty-seven

Michael Morpheus opened the door to his home in Mettarie, a suburb of New Orleans, and invited his supporters from the Vampyre Council in. They'd arranged this private meeting following Carmilla's announcements at the last Council meeting.

Jean, Sarah, and Christina walked into his house and took seats in Michael's living room. On the coffee table, he'd arranged glasses and a bottle of vintage wine for them to drink while they discussed their strategy.

While Jean poured the wine, Michael paced in front of the group, too excited to sit. "I've asked you all to meet here to decide what we should do about the information Carmilla disclosed yesterday."

Sarah swirled the wine in her glass, staring into the sparkling red liquid before taking a sip. She smacked her lips in appreciation of the taste, and then she looked up at Michael. "I take it you don't agree with Carmilla's desire to assist the group of doctors in finding a cure for our disease?" she asked.

Michael glared at her. "Of course not!" he exclaimed. "Personally, I think it is the most dire threat to our existence since the pogrom against our kind in the Middle Ages."

"How so?" she asked.

"Think of what it would mean if we did find a way to reverse the changes of the Transformation," he said, waving his arms. "Soon we'd have ex-Vampyres appearing on talk shows like Oprah's, telling the world how they used to be monsters who sucked the life's blood out of innocent victims, but now they're cured. We'd have best-selling books detailing the lives we've led, and there'd be articles in the *Enquirer* like 'I Was a Teenage Vampyre.' Soon any of us who chose not to revert back to being a Normal would be treated as pariahs, hunted down and killed for our refusal to rejoin the human race."

Christina waved her glass in the air. "Oh, Michael, I think you're exaggerating."

"Am I?" he asked, turning to her. "I think not. In any event, it would soon turn those of our race who want to revert against those of us who believe, as we do, that we are the superior race. It would at the very least cause a civil war in our ranks that would sooner or later destroy us all and end our way of life forever." He stared at them through a zealot's eyes. "We would no longer be able to feed upon the Normals in secrecy. Every vicious murder committed would be blamed on us, whether we did it or not."

Jean emptied his glass and refilled it from the bottle on the table. "There may be something in what you say, Michael." He took another drink. "And I must say that I have much enjoyed the little meetings we've been having out at your place on the bayou." He grinned savagely. "I'd almost forgotten what a pleasure it is to hunt and feed like we did in the old days."

Michael took a seat in an easy chair across from the others and leaned forward, his elbows on his knees. "I, too, have enjoyed our little gatherings," he said. "How about you, Sarah? And you, Christina?"

Both of the women looked at each other and nodded. "Yes," Sarah said. "I, for one, would hate to give them up and go back to Carmilla's way of nonlethal feedings."

Christina licked a drop of scarlet wine from her lips. "I have not felt so alive in years," she said.

Michael leaned back and spread his arms. "Then our course is clear. We must do whatever it takes to prevent these interlopers from destroying our way of life."

"What do you have in mind?" Jean asked, holding his wineglass in both hands and peering over the rim at Michael.

"It is simple. We must somehow sabotage the work of the group that is trying to find a way to reverse the Transformation. If our fellow Vampyres have no choice about remaining Vampyres, I feel that sooner or later we can convince them that our way of feeding is superior."

"Do you mean, you think we should kill them?" Christina asked, her eyes glittering.

Michael pursed his lips, considering her suggestion. "No, I think that would only reveal our position to Carmilla and might give her the leverage with the other members of the Council to array them against us. I feel we should be more subtle than that."

"What do you suggest?" Sarah asked.

"First we need to try and gain allies among our fellow Vampyres. Perhaps if we approached them one by one and very cautiously sounded them out, we might find others who want to feed and hunt as we do."

Jean nodded. "If they show sufficient interest, we could invite them to join us on one of our hunts," he suggested.

"A capital idea, Jean," Michael agreed. "Also, we already know the one known as the Ripper feels as we do. We must do all in our power to find him and try to get him to join us before the others do."

"That won't be easy," Sarah said.

"None of this is going to be easy," Michael said, "but it must be done. The next step will be to stop the research into the cure."

"How can we do that except by killing the doctors?" Christina asked.

"The same way Roger Niemann attempted in Houston," Michael said.

"You mean, kidnap this TJ person and try to enlist her help?" Jean asked.

Michael shook his head. "No, that won't work. We already know that she is violently opposed to becoming one of us and is working as hard as she can to develop the cure. She would never agree to work with us, and since she has already gone through the Rite of Transformation, there is nothing we could hold over her head to force her cooperation."

"Then what do you have in mind?" Sarah asked.

"According to Carmilla, there are four people involved in the research. A policeman and three doctors: TJ O'Reilly, Matt Carter, and Samantha Scott. The policeman has no medical knowledge regarding the cure. We must focus on one of the doctors. TJ is of no use to us, so we must choose one of the other two. Either Matt or Samantha will have to be convinced to help us sabotage the search for a cure."

"But how can we do that?" Jean asked. "From what TJ told Carmilla, these people have dedicated themselves to finding this cure so they can reverse TJ's transformation."

"I suggest we kidnap Samantha Scott," Michael said, "and use her to force the others to stop their research."

"As you said," Jean reminded Michael, "killing one of the doctors would be very risky."

"I don't propose to kill her," Michael said with a sly grin, "merely to Transform her. Once she is one of us, she may feel different."

"And if not? If she still desires to reverse her Transformation, as TJ did?" Sarah asked.

"Then we raid her mind and find out all she knows about the research and how we might sabotage it," Michael said. "At the very least, we'll know exactly what we're up against."

"What if Carmilla finds out what we're doing?" Sarah asked.

Michael shrugged. "How will she find out? When we take Samantha, we'll let the others know if they go to the police or tell anyone about her abduction, she will immediately be killed. That should keep them from talking."

"It's a very risky plan," Jean said, shaking his head.

"All life is a risk, Jean," Michael replied. "But letting these Normals destroy our way of life is much riskier."

He held up his glass in a toast. "To victory over our adversaries," he said solemnly.

"To victory," they all chimed in, and downed their wine as one.

I finished adding the latest findings on plasmid research into my laptop and closed the computer.

There were some older papers on my ship I wanted to go over, so I dressed and got my car out of the garage. My research was coming along much faster than I'd dared hope and I was excited.

There was little traffic, so I made the five-mile trip in less than twenty minutes. I parked on the street in front of the *Moon Chaser* and walked toward the gangplank. As I approached the ship, I felt a familiar tingle on the back of my neck—it was as if I were being watched.

Stopping, I turned and slowly looked around. There was no one visible, and when I cast my mind out, I could sense no other presence nearby.

I shook my head, thinking I was becoming paranoid in my old age.

When I got to the gangplank and reached up to deactivate the alarm system, I noticed an envelope taped to the keyboard.

On full alert now, I checked the area again and still saw no one. I took the envelope and opened it. Inside was a sheet of paper with a handwritten message on it.

> Roger,
>   I need to see you. I will wait every night for the next week in the club at the Top of the Sheraton for you to come to me.
> TJ O'Reilly

My heart began to pound and my hand shook as I remembered the nights and days I'd stayed with TJ, taking her slowly through the Rite of Transformation, hoping she would be my mate forever.

Could this be a trap? I'd missed her terribly since that awful night on my ship in Houston, and several times had thought seriously about returning to

Houston to see if I could locate her. It had been long enough now that her Transformation must be complete; she was a Vampyre, like me.

I wondered briefly if she still hated me for what I'd done to her, or if she had come to accept her fate, as I had two hundred years ago.

Was it possible she missed me as I missed her? Could there still be a chance for us to go through life together and perhaps even work together to find a cure that would release us both from this curse of Vampyrism?

I gently folded the paper and put it back in the envelope. Trap or not, I had to find out. I put the envelope in my coat pocket and walked to my car.

After all, if this were a ruse to bring me out of hiding, why would she suggest we meet in a crowded place? The TJ I remembered would never allow innocent people to be put in jeopardy, even to get back at me.

As I got into my car, I felt a familiar heaviness in my loins, remembering the passion we'd shared so many months ago. I smiled, thinking I had not had another woman since TJ. If she were ready to forgive me, I would show her a night of passion like no other she'd ever known.

Twenty-eight

TJ sat at the table they'd picked for her rendezvous with Roger Niemann—if he showed up. She sipped a white wine and stared out the wall-to-wall windows of the nightclub that sat atop the Sheraton Plaza Hotel. The view was spectacular and encompassed the entire downtown area of New Orleans, but TJ she barely noticed the beautiful buildings on the horizon.

Matt and Sam were at a table in a far corner; they were close enough to intervene if it became necessary, but far enough away that Roger wouldn't be able to see them in the semidarkness of the club. A man in a tuxedo sat at a nearby piano and was playing soft-rock tunes intermixed with old show tunes from the forties and fifties. The crowd present was older and less boisterous than some of the other nightspots in the French Quarter. It would be easy to have a private conversation with Roger when the time came.

The plan was simple. She would meet and greet Roger, hopefully establishing some trust during the first few minutes of their conversation. She planned to tell him about her treatment to reverse the Transformation, and if he were still interested in his own reversal, she would try to get him to agree to work with them on perfecting the treatment that would accomplish it.

If he seemed agreeable, she would give Matt and Sam and Shooter a signal; then they would join her and Roger to work out the details of their collaboration.

Her hand shook and she almost spilled her wine when her cell phone rang. She flipped it open and Shooter spoke. "Hello, TJ?"

"Yes," she said, her heart pounding in excitement.

"A man just approached the boat and read your message," Shooter said.

"Was it Roger?" she asked, not knowing for sure if she hoped it was or wasn't.

"I couldn't tell," Shooter replied. "I was too far away, but he's in his car and seems to be headed for the hotel. I wanted to call and give you a heads-up that he was on the way."

"Shooter," she said in a low voice, "I'm scared."

"I know, babe, me too. But I'll be right behind him and we'll make sure nothing happens."

"OK. And Shooter," she said after a pause.

"Yeah?"

"I love you."

"I love you, too, sweetheart," he replied. "See ya soon."

TJ closed the phone and glanced toward Sam and Matt's table. They were watching her closely. She pointed at the phone and nodded her head, indicating Roger was on the way.

Sam smiled and gave her a thumbs-up signal, while Matt just looked worried.

TJ downed the rest of her wine and ordered another one, unable to keep her eyes off the doorway into the club.

She had almost finished her second glass of wine when she saw a tall, dark figure appear in the doorway. He stood there a moment as he let his eyes roam around the room, and TJ could feel a tickle in her mind as he let his mind search the room along with his eyes.

When his gaze stopped and fixed on her, TJ thought her heart was going to burst out of her chest. She swallowed to get rid of the lump in her throat and watched as he slowly made his way through the crowded tables to her.

He stood there, looking down at her, a small, quizzical smile on his lips. God, she thought, she'd forgotten how handsome he was.

"Hello, TJ," he said in a low, husky voice. "May I sit down?" He seemed to exude a musky smell, like an animal in rutting season, and she realized he wanted her desperately.

She nodded, unable to speak as his eyes bored into hers. Suddenly the unexpected happened. She felt a wave of passion and lust begin in her gut and travel downward, leaving her sex wet and throbbing. She had no idea the sight and smell of him would affect her so strongly.

He pulled a chair out and sat down, his back to Matt and Sam's table. As he raised his hand to order a drink from the waiter, TJ noticed Shooter ease his way into the room and join Matt and Sam at their table.

When the waiter appeared, Roger said, "Martell brandy, a double if you please."

The waiter glanced at TJ's glass and saw that it was almost empty. "Would the lady care for another wine?" he asked.

"Yes, please," TJ said, her voice a croak in her nervousness.

Roger leaned forward, and TJ saw his nostrils dilate as he took in her scent. "God, how I've missed you," he said, his obsidian eyes glittering in the candlelight of the room as he put his hand over hers.

It took every bit of willpower TJ had to pull her hand away, trying to ignore the hurt in his eyes as she did so.

"Roger, I didn't ask you here to renew old acquaintanceship," she said.

The waiter appeared and set their drinks on the table. Roger thanked him and took his brandy snifter in hand and leaned back, crossing his legs and swirling the dark fluid around in the glass as he inhaled its aroma.

He sighed. "Then why did you ask me here?" His voice sounded sorrowful.

"Because I need your help."

He raised his eyebrows. "Oh?"

"I need your help to reverse what you did to me," TJ said, unable to meet his gaze and staring into her wine.

His eyes narrowed and he took a deep swallow of his brandy. "I don't know if that's possible."

TJ's voice became more strident. "It must be!" she said forcefully. "You made me into this monster I'm becoming and you've got to help me stop it."

His face paled at the force of her reply. "Do you hate me so much?" he asked.

TJ took a deep breath and drank her wine, trying to get control of her emotions as she thought about his question. Strangely, she found she felt no animosity toward him. "No," she finally answered, looking into his eyes. "I can't blame you for what you did any more than I blame a wild animal for doing what his nature forces him to do."

Now Roger smiled, though with more sadness

than humor. "I see." He sipped his brandy, thinking about her reply. "You say you're still becoming a monster. Does that mean the Transformation is not yet complete?"

"It's a long story," she said, "but the short answer is that my friends were able to reverse the changes temporarily with medication. However, the symptoms have begun to recur recently."

"How far along are you in the Transformation?"

"I don't know," she replied, her face flushing with embarrassment.

"This is very important. Have you fed on human blood yet?"

She remembered the nights with Shooter and the feel and taste of his blood on her lips as they made love. "A little, I guess," she finally answered.

He leaned forward and put his hand on hers again. "TJ, will you open your mind to me so that I may see for myself?"

"Is that necessary?"

"Yes. If I'm to determine how advanced the changes in your body are, I must examine your mind without interference."

"Why do you need my permission?" she asked. "Can't you just do it?"

He shook his head. "No. With Normals, I can enter their minds at will. They have no defense against it, but with other Vampyres, it's a different matter. Vampyres have the ability to block their thoughts, even from members of their own race."

She leaned back in her chair and closed her eyes. "Go ahead then."

He stared at her and she felt him enter her mind. It was a pleasurable feeling, and her nipples became hard and her sex throbbed again at the feel of him inside her. It was everything she could do not to jump across the table and couple with him in wild abandon. She had never felt so close to anyone in her life.

After a moment, Roger smiled. She knew he could sense how she wanted him, and she could sense the same lust for her in him.

He glanced over his shoulder at the table where the others were sitting, staring at them. "You might as well ask your friends to join us," he said.

"You knew they were there?" she asked, astounded at his powers.

"From the very beginning," he answered. "But I could tell they meant no harm, so I decided to see why you'd asked me to join you after all these months."

TJ waved at Shooter and Matt and Sam, indicating they should come over.

When they got there, Roger stood up and stuck out his hand to Shooter.

Shooter took it. "Roger Niemann, I presume?" he asked.

"No, actually. Roger Niemann died that night you attacked me in Houston. Now I'm known as Albert Nachtman."

"I'm Shooter Kowolski, and this is Dr. Matt Carter and Dr. Samantha Scott."

Albert nodded and gestured for them all to take a seat. "TJ has been telling me she wishes my help in reversing her Transformation," Albert said. "Are you the ones who are working with her on this?"

"The doctors are," Shooter said. "My presence is more . . . personal."

"Ah, I see," Albert said. His eyes went to the small bandage on Shooter's neck and the other tiny healed wounds on the other side of his neck. His gaze turned to TJ and he asked, "Is this the one?"

TJ knew he was asking if Shooter was the one from whom she'd taken blood, and she nodded.

"The one what?" Shooter asked belligerently.

"Should I tell him, or will you?" Albert asked TJ, not unkindly.

"Roger—that is, Albert," TJ began, her face turning bright red, "needed to determine how far along my symptoms had gotten, so he asked me if I'd tasted human blood." She dropped her eyes. "I told him I had."

As she spoke, Shooter's eyes dilated and his hand went unconsciously to the bandage.

Matt and Sam just stared at TJ as if their worst suspicions had been confirmed.

While they were preoccupied, Albert raised his hand and signaled the waiter to bring them another round.

They sat there in embarrassed silence until the drinks were delivered.

He picked up his brandy snifter and swirled it as he gave them an ironic smile. "I take it, since you've agreed to meet with a monster such as I and put your lives in jeopardy, you all care very much for TJ."

Everyone at the table nodded. "Then I feel I must warn you that what you are attempting to help TJ do has never been done before, and it is very dangerous."

"I don't care!" TJ blurted. "I'd rather be dead than carry on like this."

Albert gave her a sad smile. "I wasn't only referring to danger to you, TJ. There are others of our species who consider the successful reversal of Transformation a danger to them and to their way of life. Working on such a process, if it comes to their attention, could put all of our lives in jeopardy."

"But why?" Sam asked. "I would think that having a choice of whether to remain a Vampyre would appeal to everyone, even those who wish to remain as they are."

Albert shrugged. "That is the logical way to think about it, Sam. And it is how I thought about it, until a Council of my own race in Houston attempted to kill me to prevent my work from succeeding."

"What have they got to lose by having such a choice?" Matt asked.

"It is my feeling, they are afraid that the Normals would somehow find out about the existence of our race if such a process was available," Albert said. He put his glass down and spoke earnestly. "You have to realize, even though we are very hard to kill, as you found out in Houston, Shooter, we are mortal. Our only protection from the Normals, who outnumber us a million to one, is the reluctance of your race to concede the existence of mine. Barely two hundred years have passed since people believed in us, and we were hunted then like wild animals. Hundreds of us were slaughtered before the Normals became too enlightened to believe in us." He shook his head. "There are those among my race who fear the return of those days and will do anything to prevent its recurrence."

"So you think we will all be in danger if we continue to work on reversing TJ's Transformation?" Sam asked.

"Only if other Vampyres find out about it."

"Oh, no," TJ said softly.

"What is it?" Albert asked.

She told him about her conversation with Carmilla. "But she seemed most supportive of our efforts," TJ added.

Albert nodded grimly. "She may be," he said, "but there is no telling how the others on her Council will feel."

He picked up his brandy and drank as he considered what she'd told him. Finally, he set the glass back down. "We have no choice," he said. "As far as I know, the other Vampyres here don't know where I live or work. If you elect to continue with this, you'll have to go underground and stay out of sight. Your very lives depend on it."

"Speaking of our lives," Shooter said grimly, "there's a question we have to ask you before we agree to work with you."

"Yes?" Albert asked.

"Are you the one the newspapers call the Ripper?"

Albert's face clouded. "No, I am not the Ripper. In fact, I almost succeeded in killing him the other night."

"That was you the police chased?" Matt asked. "The one with the sword and gasoline?"

"Yes, that was I. I've been tracking the Ripper for some weeks now and I almost ended his reign of terror the other night." He held up his hand. "Not out of any altruistic motives, but because his wanton killings bring danger to all of my race."

"So," TJ said hesitantly, "you haven't been . . ."

Albert stared into her eyes. "I give you my word, TJ. I have not hunted or taken a life since leaving Houston," he said, not mentioning the two boys he'd killed in self-defense. "In fact, I've found a way to feed that doesn't entail killing of any sort."

He added—mentally so only she could hear

him—"And I've not been with another woman since you, dear."

He turned to the others. "Now you must disappear. Unfortunately, my place is too small to accommodate all of you. However, there is a furnished two-bedroom apartment near mine that is for rent. I suggest you let me rent it, using cash so there will be no record of your names on the lease, and you can move in there tomorrow. Once you're settled in, we can begin to work on helping TJ."

They looked at each other, each wondering if they could trust this man who was an admitted killer of hundreds.

After a moment, TJ nodded and took Shooter's hand in hers.

Albert noticed the gesture, but didn't comment on it. "All right, then, it's settled." He wrote the address down on a napkin and handed it to TJ. "I'll make the arrangements first thing in the morning. You'll be able to move in after lunch."

Twenty-nine

The same night TJ and her friends were meeting with Albert Nachtman, Michael Morpheus set up a meeting at his bayou house with a couple of the Council members who'd proved receptive to his suggestion they try a new experience in hunting.

Sarah Kenyon's mate, Adeline Ducayne, who was at first very jealous at the thought her lover had hunted and fed without her, readily agreed to savor the thrill of a double hunt with her friend at Michael's house.

Louis Frene was also receptive, but the others Michael approached begged off, stating they agreed with Carmilla that nonlethal feedings were the best for their race. Michael did extract a promise from them not to notify Carmilla of his offer, though it was clear they were opposed to his intention to hunt and feed as it had been done in the past.

Michael, this time with Sarah and Jean's help, secured several suitable candidates for the evening's festivities from the nearby rural town of Liberty. Jean even laughed that they were doing something the police had been unable, or unwilling, to do: rid the town of most of its prostitutes and deadbeats.

As per his usual protocol for these gatherings, Michael provided wine for everyone to enjoy prior to their feeding. Louis appeared nervous as he helped himself to a generous portion of the wine. Red-tinged sweat was beaded on his brow, even though the evening was cool and there was a breeze blowing off the nearby bayou that smelled of dead fish and rotting vegetation. He glanced around at the others gathered in Michael's living room. "It's been so long; I don't know if I'll remember what to do," he said with a nervous chuckle.

"Oh," Sarah said with an evil laugh, "you'll remember all right."

"Yeah," Jean joined in, holding his glass up as if in a toast, "it's like riding a bicycle. Once you get back in the saddle, it'll all come back to you."

Michael, knowing how Sarah preferred innocent young girls, had stopped the previous day and picked up a teenage hitchhiker on her way to New Orleans from Baton Rouge. He held up a key with 1 on it. "Sarah, I understand you and Adeline wish to dine together tonight. Your feast awaits you behind door number one."

Sarah put her wineglass down and took the key. She put her arm around the diminutive Adeline's shoulders and they marched down the hall toward the first door.

As she opened the door and they stepped through, a young girl rushed at them with a wooden chair over her head. Adeline ducked and tried to cover her head with her arms as the girl swung with all her might.

The chair crashed down on Adeline, knocking her to the ground before Sarah could respond. The girl bent and picked up one of the chair legs lying on the floor; brandishing it like a baseball bat, she circled around the fallen Adeline toward the door.

Sarah grinned maliciously and crouched, her arms spread out before her as she moved to cut the girl off from escape. "Now, dear," she said in her husky voice, "why'd you go and do a nasty thing like that?"

The frightened prisoner turned her eyes to Adeline, who was shaking her head and getting to her feet, a large gash on her forehead already beginning to heal and knit together.

"All I know is a horrible man kidnapped me and has been holding me prisoner here for two days," the girl said in a scared, shaky voice. "I don't want to hurt you, but I want out of here now."

Sarah straightened up and smiled, holding her hands out palmside up. "But, my dear," she said in her most sugar-sweet voice, "that's what Adeline and I were coming to tell you. We've convinced the man who took you to let you go."

"Really?" the girl asked, lowering the chair leg and trying to smile.

Sarah nodded. "Yes, of course. It was all a mistake. He thought you were someone else."

"Oh, thank God!" The girl stepped back to sit on the edge of the bed.

Sarah stepped over to Adeline and smoothed her hair and kissed her on the cheek. "Are you all right, darling?" she asked.

When Adeline nodded, the girl on the bed asked, "Say, you two aren't dykes, are you?"

Sarah's smile turned into a frown. "We prefer the term life partner, dear."

The girl rolled her eyes. "Oh."

"What is your name, sweetie?" Adeline asked, moving slowly toward the girl.

"Lou Ann, Lou Ann Cargill," the girl replied, shrinking back at Adeline's approach.

When Adeline sat on the bed next to Lou Ann and reached over to comb her fingers through her hair, the hitchhiker jerked her head away. "Listen, you need to know. I don't swing that way. I prefer boys."

"Why, Lou Ann," Sarah asked, her voice again sweet and syrupy, "what makes you think we care what you prefer?"

"Huh?"

Sarah swung a backhand blow to Lou Ann's cheekbone, knocking her flat on her back on the bed. Adeline quickly leaned over and grasped Lou Ann's shirt in both her hands and ripped it off her body, pulling her bra with it.

Sarah, at almost the same time, bent over and grasped Lou Ann's blue jeans; with a tremendous tug, she jerked them down and off her legs.

As Lou Ann struggled to get up, Adeline placed her arm across her neck and pinned her to the bed while she reached down and stuck her left hand into Lou Ann's panties.

When Lou Ann tried to kick her away, Sarah stepped between her legs and wrapped her hands around her thighs, holding them apart.

Adeline's hand was busy. She inserted her middle finger into Lou Ann and began to waggle it around while she lowered her head to the girl's breast and sucked gently on her nipple.

"I want to see," Sarah growled in a husky voice.

"Certainly, darling," Adeline replied, and moved her hand forcefully enough to tear the panties off. When she began to fondle and rub Lou Ann's sex again, she asked, "There, is that better?"

Sarah, consumed now by lust, only grunted as she began to change, her eyes fixed on what Adeline's finger was doing to Lou Ann.

"Good," Adeline said, and resumed her sucking on Lou Ann's breast, though not so gently this time.

Lou Ann, after a moment, ceased struggling and began to moan softly under the ministrations of Adeline's hand and tongue. When Sarah saw her begin to move her pelvis against Adeline's hand in rhythm with her stroking, she let go of her legs and stepped back and quickly got out of her clothes.

Naked, with her hands becoming claws and fangs protruding from her lips, she got down on her knees between Lou Ann's legs and gently moved Adeline's hand, replacing it with her mouth.

Adeline stood up and got out of her clothes and then moved to the other side of the bed and stood straddling Lou Ann's face.

She slowly lowered herself until Lou Ann's lips were on her and then she leaned forward to grasp both her breasts and fasten her lips on Lou Ann's left nipple.

The two women worked on Lou Ann until she was writhing in pleasure on the bed, her pelvis bucking against Sarah's mouth while her lips and tongue moved hungrily on Adeline's groin.

Sarah looked up and caught Adeline's eyes as she moved one claw from Lou Ann's buttocks to grab and hold Adeline's breast.

Adeline moaned and grunted in pleasure as both Lou Ann and Sarah fondled her. Minutes later, she climaxed with a howl and grabbed Sarah's head in her hands and pulled her up to kiss her deeply.

While they were kissing, Sarah let her hand fall back down on Lou Ann's groin and continued to fondle and caress her there until she, too, screamed in final release.

Sarah pulled her head back and stared into Adeline's eyes. "Are you ready, my darling?"

"Oh, yes!" Adeline said, and her features began to melt and coalesce into a fearsome beast.

Sarah lay on Lou Ann's right while Adeline lay on her left. As their fangs ripped into Lou Ann's neck from both sides, their hands reached across her bucking, jumping body to continue to fondle each other as they fed.

In the living room, Michael and the others grinned at the sounds coming from room 1. He tossed a key with 2 on it to Louis. "Looks like you're up, Louis," he said.

Louis grabbed the key out of the air and entered room 2. He found a white woman dressed in a skimpy halter top and skintight jean cutoffs sitting on the edge of the bed smoking a cigarette. Her hair was tinted a garish orange color and she looked like a poster girl for trailer trash.

"Look, buster," she snapped as she angrily stubbed out her cigarette in an ashtray next to the bed. "I was brought here yesterday with the promise of earning some good money. What the hell's goin' on?"

Louis, who was short, pudgy, and pale, looked like a mild-mannered accountant; he began to undress. "I need you to do something special for me," he said in a meek voice, his eyes not meeting hers.

She raised her eyebrows and sneered. "Oh, yeah?"

"Yes," Louis replied, pulling a wide leather belt from his trousers and handing it to her as he stood naked before her.

"Oh," she said, nodding. "You're one of those, huh?"

"I need to be punished," Louis answered in a low, embarrassed voice, his head hanging down.

"Listen, sweetie, if you need me to beat you to get that"——her eyes dropped to his small penis hanging flaccidly between his legs——"worm to stand at attention, then I'll do it. But it's gonna cost you two hundred."

"I'll pay anything," Louis said.

The woman stood up and removed her clothes under Louis's watchful eyes. When she was nude, there was still no response from his penis.

She stepped up to him, raised her hand, and began to beat him fiercely about the shoulders and chest with the belt. He leaned his head back and grinned as red whelps appeared on his pasty flesh.

"Oh, yes, do it harder," he begged.

Her eyes widened and she whispered, "Jesus," but she continued to beat him over and over again with the belt.

After a moment, she saw his penis begin to stir, slowly becoming erect.

"Now we're getting somewhere," she said through clenched teeth, her body becoming covered with sweat with the exertion of whipping him.

Suddenly his fat, pale body began to grow and change; the prostitute stepped back, her mouth hanging open as his face melted and began to rearrange itself while his penis grew to an unbelievable size and width.

"Oh, my God!" she screamed as his fangs protruded, his eyes became red and bloodshot, and his claws began to flex.

"No . . . no . . . ," she begged, dropping the belt and inching backward until the back of her legs hit the bed.

Louis, now a towering monster, growled deep in his throat; he caressed his enormous penis with one claw as he moved toward her. Before she could cry out, he was on her, pressing her back onto the bed and spreading her legs with his knees until the head of his penis was directly in front of her groin.

With one lunge, he was embedded in her, split-
ting her wide open below as his fangs fastened themselves onto her neck. He bucked and pumped
frantically, sucking her life out of her until she was
limp as a rag doll.

Michael and Jean had stepped out on the porch
overlooking the bayou to finish their wine. As Michael leaned on the railing overlooking the slowly
swirling black waters of the stream, several shapes
moved from the banks to swim languidly toward the
house.

"I see my friends are eagerly awaiting their meal,"
he said with a chuckle.

Jean shuddered. "Don't they ever get their fill?"
he asked, taking a large drink of his wine.

"No more than we do, Jean. I'm afraid their hunger for meat matches ours for blood." He paused,
cocking his head to the side and listening to the
muted screams coming from the two bedrooms inside the house. "And I suppose they look forward
to a good hunt just as much as we do."

Michael finished his wine and set the glass down.
He looked at Jean Horla. "Jean, my friend, I'm
afraid pickings were slim in Liberty yesterday. I was
only able to get one more subject to accompany me
here tonight."

"Oh?" Jean asked, draining his wineglass, his eyes
locked on the reptiles swimming below them.

"Yes. I'm afraid we're going to have to share."

Jean smiled and shrugged. "Well, what are friends
for, if not to share in life's little bounties?" he asked
as they moved toward room 3.

Thirty

After their meeting with Albert Nachtman, the two couples returned to their hotel. They were all in a subdued mood, wondering if they were right to trust Nachtman and if it was wise to put their lives in his hands.

As they approached their rooms, Matt hesitated with his key in his hand. "You guys want to talk about this tonight?" he asked, looking at TJ and Shooter.

TJ shook her head. Her face was pale and she had an almost vacant expression in her eyes, as if she were somewhere far off. "No," she answered, finally coming out of her reverie and focusing on Matt. "Let's all sleep on it and go over our options in the morning over breakfast."

Matt shrugged. "All right. See y'all later."

Shooter opened the door and followed TJ into their room. He emptied his pockets onto the dresser and began to undress while TJ slipped out of her dress in front of the closet.

"You OK, babe?" he asked.

She turned to him, wearing only her bra and panties. "I don't know, Shooter. Somehow I feel dirty . . . unclean."

He nodded. "I know. Meeting with someone like Nachtman does that to you."

He moved to her and wrapped his arms around her. "Sometimes, after I've interrogated a suspect that I know has done terrible things, I have this urge to take a long, hot bath and get the filth off me."

She leaned her head back and smiled wanly at him. "Well, that sounds like a good idea to me."

He glanced toward the bathroom. "You think we'd both fit in that tub?"

She shrugged. "I think we can manage," she said, stepping back and unhooking her bra and letting it fall to the floor. She stepped out of her panties and moved back into Shooter's arms. "Come on, sweetheart, we need to talk."

By the time Shooter had the lights off in the bedroom and got into the bathroom, TJ had steaming hot water filling the tub and was pouring some bubble bath into the water. She glanced over her shoulder. "I picked this up yesterday in the gift shop downstairs. It's vanilla bean."

Shooter grinned, admiring his view of her bending over the tub. "I love the smell of vanilla."

She looked down at his naked body and what was happening to him. Laughing, she replied, "I notice it's having quite an effect on you."

"It's not the bubble bath that's doing this to me, babe—it's you."

She took his hand and they stepped into the steamy hot water. Shooter sat down and leaned back with TJ, between his legs, facing away and resting against his chest.

His arms automatically circled her and he cupped her breasts as they talked; fragrant bubbles rose to cover their legs.

After a moment, Shooter spoke softly. "TJ, I need to know how you feel about Nachtman. Is it going to be a problem being around him while we try to find a cure for you?"

She shook her head. "I truly don't know how to answer that, Shooter," she said, her voice equally soft.

"Matt and Sam, after they examined you in the hospital, said that . . . that there was evidence he'd assaulted you sexually. Do you remember any of that?"

She sighed deeply. "I don't know. It's all mixed up in my mind. I've had dreams and some fuzzy memories, but I'm not sure how much of what I remember actually happened."

"You want to tell me about it?" he asked.

"Are you sure you want to know?" she asked, twisting her head to look into his eyes.

"Yes. At least, I think I do."

"All right," she said, turning her face back around and shifting her hips to the side. She slipped her hand under the suds and grasped him, slowly stroking as she spoke. "Do you know what the Stockholm syndrome is?"

"Yeah. It's where people who are kidnapped and held against their will become sympathetic with their captors and tend to form strong bonds with them."

She nodded. "It was like that, only a thousand times stronger. Remember, these creatures are able to enter our minds and make us feel and do things against our nature. Only, while we're doing these awful things, it's as if we're on the outside watching us do them and knowing it's wrong."

Shooter felt himself respond to her touch. "What did he do?"

"At first, when he captured me, I hated him with all my strength. I'd seen what he did to his victims and I loathed the thought of him. He put me in a small room and took away all my clothes, leaving me naked and defenseless in the dark."

"Yeah, that's a typical maneuver used in brainwashing prisoners. When you take away their clothes and keep them in the dark, it makes them feel more vulnerable and alone and aids in breaking down their defenses," Shooter said bitterly.

"I lost all track of time, not knowing whether it was day or night or how long I'd been there," she said. "Soon, against my will, I found myself looking forward to his visits. Anything was preferable to the darkness and isolation."

"How did he treat you when he showed up?"

"He was very kind. There were no threats and no physical abuse. He just talked to me about his life and how lonely he'd been for two hundred years."

"Did he try to force himself on you sexually?" Shooter asked, pain evident in his voice.

TJ hesitated. She knew he wouldn't like what she was about to tell him, but she knew she had to be truthful. "No, not physically. After what must have been several days, I was a mess. I'd thrown up in my cell and was dirty and stinky. I felt terrible. He picked me up and carried me into the shower he had in the warehouse. He got undressed and put me under the water and began to wash me off."

"And then—"

"He entered my mind and I could feel his lust for me. It was as if I could see myself through his eyes, and his lust became my lust, too. Before I knew it, we were making love with the water cascading over us. It was as if I were someone else standing there watching. I hated my body and how he was making it respond to him, but I was powerless to stop it."

She shuddered and Shooter squeezed her tight, realizing how painful this was for her.

"Then he bent and bit my neck, and began taking my blood into his mouth while we made love." She shook her head at the memory. "It was the most erotic thing I'd ever experienced, and when he opened a vein on his own neck, I just couldn't help myself and I began to drink his blood at the same time."

"Jesus," Shooter whispered, disgusted, and yet aroused, by the mental picture she was painting.

TJ felt his penis swell in her hand and knew how she was affecting him. She half-turned and leaned against him in the hot water. "I'm sorry, Shooter," she said softly.

"Don't be," he said, stroking her hair with his hand. He bent down and kissed her softly on the lips.

"Let's go to bed," she said.

They got out of the tub and toweled each other off, then got into bed together.

As they lay there in each other's arms, Shooter said, "I want you to do it to me."

She looked at him in the semidarkness. "What?"

"Enter my mind."

"Are you sure?" she asked.

"Yes. I want to be one with you like he was. It's the only way to be certain you are over him and still belong fully to me."

"All right." She rolled on her side and stared deep into his eyes and concentrated.

Shooter felt her come inside his head and felt their beings merge into one. Through her eyes, he saw himself lying on his back on the bed, and felt her desire and love for him as she looked up and down his body. He was almost overwhelmed with lust; wanting her, he reached over to run his hands lightly over her breasts, which were swollen with desire for him.

When she rolled on top of him and slowly lowered her pelvis over his, he thought he was going to explode. As he entered her warm, soft wetness, he pulled her head down to his neck and offered himself to her.

She hesitated, and then as he began to move inside her, she opened her mouth and bit his neck gently. When his blood flowed into her mouth, he could taste it as she could; they came together in a rapturous climax.

The next morning, they showered together and made love in the shower again, with TJ in his mind and his body responding as it never had before.

Afterward, while they were getting dressed for breakfast, the phone rang. Shooter picked it up, thinking it was Matt saying they were ready.

"Howdy," Shooter said, his mood still high from their lovemaking.

"Well, howdy to you, cowboy," Chief Boudreaux said in his New Orleans accent.

"Oh, I'm sorry, Chief," Shooter said. "I thought you were someone else."

"That's all right, Shooter," Boudreaux said. "I just called to ask if you and your doctor friend could pay me a visit this mornin'."

"Has something happened?" Shooter asked.

"You might say that. We've got a little situation over in a nearby town that might have some bearing on the Ripper cases, and on the man you're lookin' for from Houston."

"We were just fixing to have breakfast . . . ," Shooter began.

"Oh, take your time and eat your meal,"

Boudreaux said. "There's no hurry. Anytime 'fore noon will be OK."

"We'll see you in an hour and a half, then," Shooter said.

"Lookin' forward to it," Boudreaux said, and hung up the phone.

When Shooter told Sam and Matt of the police chief's summons, they decided to put off their discussion of what they should do until they heard what the chief had to say.

Matt and Shooter decided to skip breakfast, grabbing a quick cup of coffee instead. They left the girls to discuss matters over a full meal while they hurried to meet with Boudreaux.

When they climbed into a cab and told the driver to take them to police headquarters, the cabbie laughed. "Don't get too many fares to the police station," he said, pronouncing it *Po-leece* station. "Usually, the cops, they provides they own transportation."

Matt and Shooter smiled politely at the joke, even though neither was in a joking mood. Things had been happening too fast and they were still trying to get a handle on what was going on.

When they got to the station, the desk sergeant gave them a crooked grin. "Go right on up, boys. The chief's waitin' on y'all."

The sergeant must've called ahead, because when they got to the top of the stairs, Boudreaux was standing in his door, waiting for them.

He waved them inside and again offered them chicory coffee, which they both accepted this time.

After they had their coffee in hand and took seats across from the chief's desk, he leaned back in his desk chair and crossed his arms over his belly.

"Guess you boys're wonderin' why I called you here."

Both Shooter and Matt nodded.

" 'Fore I get into that, let me tell you a story 'bout me. When I was seventeen, I applied for a job on the police force here in New Orleans. Since I wasn't eighteen yet, they wouldn't take me, so I moseyed on down to a small town east of here called Liberty. The sheriff there took me on as a deputy and I worked there for four or five years, getting experience 'fore I transferred up here to the big city."

He stopped his narrative long enough to take a toothpick out of his shirt pocket and stick it in the corner of his mouth. "Reason I'm tellin' you boys this, I still got a name in Liberty. Folks down there know they can trust me."

He leaned forward in his chair and pointed his chin out the window of his office toward a bench on an adjacent wall. Matt and Shooter turned to look.

A young black woman dressed in the provocative garb of a street prostitute was sitting there, chewing gum with her mouth open and filing long artificial nails with an emery board.

"Liza May there come all the way up here to ask me for some help," Boudreaux continued. He stared at Shooter and Matt as he went on. "Seems a whole lot of her friends have suddenly taken missing in the past couple of weeks."

"You think it's more than the usual moving around prostitutes do?" Shooter asked.

Boudreaux inclined his head. "Yeah, I do. Women workin' the streets in small towns are different than in big cities," he said. "If'n it was here in New Orleans an' several of the ladies of the night took off for better parts, I wouldn't think nothin' of it. But Liza says that ain't the case in Liberty. She knew all of these girls an' none of 'em, according to her, were thinkin' of leaving town."

"How many women are we talking about, Chief?" Matt asked.

"Six or seven at least," Boudreaux said, reaching for some papers on his desk and holding them up, "an' that's not counting another five or six young girls who their families say were headed up this way on buses or hitchhiking. Suddenly I got these here missin' persons reports comin' outta my ass."

"Since you called us about this," Shooter said, a speculative glint in his eye, "you must think this has something to do with the Ripper cases."

Boudreaux shrugged and leaned back. "Well, now, I do and I don't. These folks goin' missing don't fit with the usual profile of the Ripper, who tends to leave his bodies where they lie when he's finished with 'em. But I'm damned if I can explain such a glut of missing people any other way. I was wonderin' if you boys had any notions that might be of help to me?"

"Do you have any suspects in mind?" Shooter asked, changing the subject while he tried to decide what and how much to tell the chief.

Boudreaux glanced out the window at the girl on the bench. "Liza there says a tall man who wears his hair in a ponytail and has a gold stud in one ear, like some New York big shot, has been hanging around lately. She got me a license plate number off his big black car, but it's stolen and don't match the color or make of the vehicle she describes."

"That's not anyone we know or have seen, Chief," Shooter said, glancing at Matt with his eyebrows raised.

Boudreaux snorted through his nose. "Then that

don't sound like this Niemann guy you been lookin' for?"

"No, sir," Matt said. "Niemann is average height and wears his hair short, or at least he did last time we saw him."

Shooter cleared his throat. "Uh, Chief, we've made some contacts here in the city in the last few days. Contacts who wish to remain anonymous. How about if we ask them if they know of anyone who fits that description, or who might be causing some problems over in Liberty?"

For a moment, Boudreaux stared at Shooter as he flicked a pencil against his desk like a rock-and-roll drummer. "Shooter, I hope you're not blowin' smoke up my ass," he said. "I'm gonna go with that for now, since your chief back in Houston says you're a stand-up guy. But if any more girls go missin', I'm gonna want to know who these 'contacts' of yours are. Do we understand each other?"

"Yes, sir, Chief," Shooter said, getting quickly to his feet before Boudreaux could change his mind.

Thirty-one

As they got into a cab to return to their hotel, Matt said, "Well, that went well."

"You think so?" Shooter asked, turning to look over his shoulder as he entered the taxi.

Matt shrugged. "I think he bought our story."

"Bullshit," Shooter said. "Boudreaux has been around too long to let us get away with stalling him like this." He pointed out the back window. "Look."

Matt glanced out the rear window in time to see a man in a porkpie hat and a garish plaid sport coat two sizes too small climb into a nondescript Ford sedan and pull out into traffic behind them.

"The smart son of a bitch has put a tail on us," Shooter said, shaking his head. "Look at that dumb bastard. He's dressed up like Popeye Doyle in *The French Connection.*" He chuckled. "He's probably worn out his video of the movie trying to look like his favorite cop."

"What do we do now?" asked Matt.

"Not much we can do," Shooter replied. "It's only in the movies you can ask a cabbie to try and lose a cop who's following you. We just go on back to the hotel like we're supposed to and have a talk with the girls about what Boudreaux told us, only we don't do it in our rooms."

Matt raised his eyebrows. "You think he's bugged our rooms?"

"I wouldn't put it past him. Boudreaux's no fool. He knows we know more than we're telling him and he wants to find out what it is."

"But he hasn't had time to get a court order for a bug," Matt replied.

Shooter laughed. "This is New Orleans, Matt. Do you really think the chief cares about court orders and due process? Hell, we're lucky he didn't throw us in a cell until we spilled our guts."

"Why do you think he didn't?"

"Obviously because he thinks we'll lead him to our contacts."

Matt sat back in the seat, wondering what all this was leading to.

Shooter pulled a pack of cigarettes out of his coat pocket and lit one up. He smiled at Matt as he opened the window so the smoke wouldn't bother him. "I gotta think, and this helps. Just don't tell TJ, OK?"

Matt laughed. "Pussy whipped already, Shooter?"

"You know it, pal," Shooter replied as he drew smoke deep into his lungs with a satisfied look on his face.

When they got to the hotel, Shooter said, "You go collect the girls and I'll get us a table in the dining room. We need to talk and that's probably the safest place."

Shooter procured a table in a corner that was relatively private and had another cigarette while he waited for the others. When he finished, he stubbed it out in the ashtray provided, then switched the ashtray for an empty one on an adjoining table, and popped a stick of gum in his mouth to get rid of his smoker's breath.

He'd just managed this when Matt appeared at the dining-room entrance with Sam and TJ in tow.

After they'd ordered drinks and sandwiches, Matt and Shooter took turns recounting what the chief had said, including the fact they were being followed and that their rooms were most likely bugged.

"That son of a bitch," Sam said heatedly.

Shooter held up his hand. "Now, Sam, he's just doing his job. Hell, if this were my case back in Houston, I'd probably do the same thing."

"What do you think all this means?" TJ asked, her face pale at the thought of so many people being missing.

"I agree with Boudreaux," Shooter said. "It's probably not the Ripper's work. He doesn't give a damn if the bodies are found—so why would he suddenly go to all the trouble of hiding them somewhere?"

"There's another thing to consider," Matt said, his eyes thoughtful.

"Yeah? What's that?" Shooter asked.

"Remember the cases we had in Houston, when Roger was the killer? How often did he feed, as he put it?"

Shooter thought back. They'd found victims on an average of one a week, with sometimes two weeks going by between kills. He slowly nodded his head. "I see what you mean. Unless this Ripper has a hell of an appetite, this has to be the work of more than one Vampyre."

Matt counted on his fingers. "If all of the missing persons are, in fact, victims of Vampyres, there's got to be three or four involved, from the frequency of the murders."

Shooter glanced at TJ, who'd remained silent when the subject of Vampyre feedings came up. "Do you agree with that reasoning, sweetheart?" he asked gently.

"Yes," she said quietly. "From what I learned from Roger, or Albert as he calls himself now, the Vampyres only need to feed about once a week. Of course, some of them may just like the thrill of the hunt and may do it more often to get their kicks, but this many victims in so short a time indicates to me that there are several different ones involved."

"Didn't you say that woman you talked to, Carmilla, who was head of the local Vampyre Council, told you she strictly enforced a nonlethal feeding for all the members under her control?"

TJ agreed. "Yes, so either there are a number of Vampyres in town who are not members of her Council, or some of the Council members have gone renegade."

"She would probably know either way, wouldn't she?" Matt asked.

TJ nodded.

"Then it's imperative you go and talk to her," he said. "If members of her Council are rebelling against her edict of nonlethal feedings, she needs to know about it."

"Perhaps she can put a stop to it," Sam said.

"One way or another," Shooter said, "we've got to have something to give to Boudreaux to get him off our backs. Otherwise, we'll never be able to work on a cure for TJ in peace."

He glanced over his shoulder and saw the detective in the porkpie hat at a table across the room. He was trying his best to be inconspicuous and failing miserably.

As the waiter appeared with their food, Shooter leaned across the table and spoke in a low voice. "In a few minutes, you and TJ go to the rest room,

Sam. That way, TJ can slip out the back without our friend over there suspecting anything. By the time he realizes TJ's not coming back, it'll be too late for him to call for a backup tail."

"You want me to go and talk to Carmilla now?" TJ asked.

Shooter nodded. "Yes. We need to let her know what's going on, and also let her know that her friends are attracting the attention of the local police. That should shake her up enough to do her best to put a stop to whatever's going on in Liberty."

He leaned back in his chair. "We'll meet you later at the apartment Nachtman's arranged for us."

"How will you get there without that policeman following you?" TJ asked.

Shooter smiled grimly. "Leave that to me, sweetheart."

"But won't that piss Chief Boudreaux off if we lose his tail?" Matt asked.

Shooter shrugged. "Better to be pissed off than pissed on, I always say."

A few minutes later, while they were still eating their lunch, TJ motioned to Sam and they stood up. "We're going to the little girls' room," she said in a loud voice.

As they made their way toward the rest rooms off the lobby, Shooter noticed the cop get to his feet and follow them. When he saw them go into the ladies' room, he returned to his table and resumed his surveillance of the men.

Shooter shook his head. "Boudreaux made a bad mistake sending only one man to try and follow four."

"He probably thinks the girls are less important to follow than you and me," Matt observed, trying to keep his eyes off the officer.

A few minutes later, when Sam returned to the table alone, Shooter saw the man get a worried look on his face and pull out a cell phone and begin to speak into it.

"Uh-oh," Shooter said, "he realizes something's up."

"What do you think Boudreaux's going to do now?" Sam asked.

"He'll probably tell porkpie to stay with Matt and me, and arrange to send more men or even a female cop to follow you and TJ," Shooter said.

"What are we going to do?" Matt asked.

Shooter looked at Sam. "Did you and TJ finish packing up all our stuff in the rooms?"

"Yes. We're all ready to go."

"Good. Then, this is the plan. . . ."

When they finished eating, the three got up. "Sam, go on up to the room and wait for us," Matt said. "Shooter and I need to get some things from the gift shop."

Casually, Sam agreed and headed for the elevators while Shooter and Matt went directly to the gift shop in the lobby.

The cop, unable to trail all of them, elected to stay with Matt and Shooter. Looking over her shoulder just before she entered the elevator, Sam saw the policeman follow the boys and take up station just outside the gift shop. When she saw that he couldn't see her, she slipped out a side door and went around to the front of the hotel. She found the plain blue Ford sedan parked in a no-parking zone near the entrance to the hotel, just as Shooter had said she would.

Trying to appear nonchalant, she stepped into the street and bent down near the front left tire.

She took the small penknife Shooter had slipped her and stuck it in the front tire.

As the tire began to go flat, she hailed a cab and got in, giving an address a couple of blocks from the apartment they were going to be staying in. Shooter told her not to take the taxi to the exact address because Boudreaux, when he found they'd gotten away, would almost certainly question the cabs that worked the hotel to try and find out where they'd been taken.

After buying some shaving cream and toothpaste in the gift shop, Shooter and Matt went up to their rooms, the cop not far behind.

Once in their rooms, they used the television to do a fast checkout, making certain not to say anything out loud in case the rooms were bugged.

Ten minutes later, they met in the corridor with their suitcases in hand and went down the back stairs. "The cop will probably be stationed where he can watch all the elevators," Shooter said. "With any luck, he won't see us leaving until it's too late to stop us."

"Let's just hope there's a cab out front waiting," Matt said.

When they exited the stairway, the two men walked rapidly toward the front doors. Shooter saw the cop standing near a column across from the elevators smoking a cigarette and pretending to read a newspaper.

By the time he saw them, they were out the front door and climbing into a taxi. As the cab pulled away from the curb, Shooter looked out the back window and saw the policeman jump into his car and start to follow them.

The car lurched to the side and stalled as the flat front tire came completely off the rim. Shooter turned back around, laughing. "I'd sure hate to be that poor son of a bitch when Boudreaux finishes chewing his ass off."

"What do you think the chief will do?" Matt asked.

"Probably put out a BOL for us," Shooter said.

"A BOL?"

"Be on the lookout for," Shooter replied. "If we're spotted, he'll have us picked up."

"That's not good," Matt said.

"Well, I'm gonna try not to let it get that far," Shooter said. "As soon as we find out what that Carmilla dame says to TJ, I'm gonna call Boudreaux and give him whatever we can."

"How are you going to explain losing the tail he put on us?" Matt asked.

Shooter shrugged. "I'm going to act innocent and tell him we didn't know there was a tail on us, and if he sent some dumb son of a bitch who couldn't follow a couple of tourists, then it was his fault the guy lost us."

"Do you think he'll buy it?"

Shooter shook his head. "Not for a minute, but hopefully we'll have something to give him to take the heat off by then."

Thirty-two

TJ arrived at Carmilla's antique shop and found a sign on the door: CLOSED FOR LUNCH. She cupped her hands around her face and leaned close to the glass door, peering inside. The lights were on in a back room, so she knocked on the door loudly several times, hoping Carmilla was still there.

After a few moments, she saw a dark figure move from the back room toward the door. Carmilla looked out the window, saw it was TJ, and unlocked the door.

"I'm just having some tea and biscuits in the kitchen. Would you like some?"

"Yes, I could use some, thank you," TJ replied, and followed Carmilla as she wound her way through the antiques and into the room where they'd talked before.

While Carmilla poured a cup of tea for TJ, she spoke over her shoulder. "I was just thinking of calling you, dear." She handed the cup to TJ. "Sugar and lemon, right?"

TJ nodded and took a sip of the delicious brew.

Carmilla sat down at the table across from TJ so they could talk face to face. "I've spoken with my friends on the Council. They agree with me that Roger is in town, as you suspect. He probably is the creature known locally as the Ripper, and they have agreed to keep a sharp lookout for him and to let me know if they locate him."

Carmilla paused, as if thinking about how to say something. Finally, she looked up, a frown on her face. "I must tell you, however, there is some disagreement among my colleagues about the wisdom of going ahead with your research on finding a way to reverse the process of Transformation."

"And have you changed your mind?" TJ asked, wondering if Carmilla was still an ally, or had she switched sides since their last meeting.

"Oh, my dear, I couldn't agree with you more. In fact, if such a treatment is discovered, I will be one of the first to avail myself of it, as will many of my friends." She hesitated again. "However, there are a few—how shall I put it—traditionalists on the Council who are against it, and we might have a difficult job convincing them it is in everyone's best interests to proceed."

TJ ran her finger around the rim of her cup, trying to decide how to tell Carmilla what Chief Boudreaux had discovered. "Carmilla, you told me before that you and your friends on the Council all practice nonlethal feedings. Are you sure of that?"

Carmilla looked surprised at the question. "Of course. Why do you ask?"

"When my friends and I first came to town, two of us approached chief of detectives, William Boudreaux, and explained how we suspected a serial killer from Houston, named Roger Niemann, was in town and could be responsible for the Ripper killings.

"Well, Chief Boudreaux called us yesterday and told us some very disturbing news."

"About the Ripper?" Carmilla asked.

"No. He said he had information that there have

been more murders, as many as fifteen or so, that have occurred in a small town east of here named Liberty. Young men and women have been disappearing at an alarming rate over there, and the chief is convinced they've all been killed."

"Has he found any bodies?" Carmilla asked, a worried frown on her face.

"No," TJ answered, "and that's why he doesn't think they're being done by the Ripper, who leaves his bodies in plain sight when he's done with them."

Carmilla stared at TJ for a moment, and then she got up to fuss with the teapot, fixing herself another cup of tea. She asked over her shoulder, "Are you telling me this because you feel either I or one of my council members is responsible for these murders?"

TJ shook her head as Carmilla returned to sit at the table. "Not one of your members, Carmilla. Several."

"What?"

"There are simply too many people missing for it to be the work of just one person. I know from my association with Roger that you—that is, we—only need to feed once every week or so. These people have all disappeared over the course of just a couple of weeks. That is far too many to be the work of just one Vampyre. There must be more involved."

Carmilla had a stricken look on her face.

TJ put out her hand and touched Carmilla's. "Of course, it could be the work of Vampyres not associated with your Council. Perhaps there are some living here who aren't known to you and your friends."

Carmilla considered this for a moment, and then she slowly shook her head. "No . . . no, that's not possible. There might be one, or even two wild ones in the area, but I doubt even that many could be here and be actively hunting without one of us on the Council knowing about it."

"Wild ones?" TJ asked, not being familiar with the term.

"That's what we call renegades, Vampyres who are not associated with our organizations across the country," Carmilla explained. "They do occur, but invariably, because of our mental connections with one another, they are known about. That is how my aunt's Council in Houston found Roger, who was a renegade there."

"Then, if several Vampyres are hunting and killing people in the area, they must be from your Council?" TJ asked.

Carmilla remembered the strange looks that passed between Michael Morpheus and some others on her Council and slowly nodded. "I'm afraid so." She looked up at TJ. "I might even have an idea who it could be."

"The police have a description of a man who was seen in the area of the missing people," TJ said, watching Carmilla's eyes closely as she spoke. "He is tall and thin, with black hair he wears back in a ponytail, and he has a gold stud in his left ear."

Carmilla's lips turned white and TJ knew she recognized the description. "You know who this is, don't you?" TJ asked.

"Yes, I do," Carmilla answered in a tight voice. "And I think I know who his accomplices are."

"You must stop them, Carmilla," TJ said.

"Oh, I will, TJ. But if the one I suspect is behind this, I must be very careful. He is immensely powerful and must have the support of some of my Council members to be acting so openly in defiance of my orders concerning nonlethal feedings."

Carmilla got to her feet, a distracted look on her face. "Now I must get to work. I've got to think about this and decide how best to handle it. Can you show yourself out, my dear?" Her mind was clearly elsewhere.

"Of course," TJ said. She walked to the front door and looked back as she opened it. Carmilla was sitting once more at the table, staring off as if deep in thought.

TJ left the antique shop and walked along the street, looking for a taxi to take her to the apartment Roger had arranged for them.

Across and down the street, Sarah Kenyon and Adeline Ducayne were sitting by the window of a small café. Sarah touched Adeline's arm to get her attention and pointed. "There's the half-breed bitch now," she said, indicating TJ as she exited Carmilla's shop.

Adeline put some money on the table and they hurriedly left the café. They got into Sarah's car parked outside.

"But she's not the one Michael wants," Adeline said.

"No, but we'll follow her and perhaps she'll lead us to where they're staying," Sarah said grimly. "Once we know that, it'll be a simple matter to watch and wait until the other one shows up."

TJ finally hailed a cab and got in. As it took off, Sarah pulled out into the street behind it.

Adeline looked over at her, excitement in her eyes. "Do you think Michael will let us perform the Rite of Transformation?"

"Does the thought of sinking your fangs into her friend excite you so much, darling?" Sarah asked, an edge of jealousy in her voice.

"Only if you're there to share her with me, my

angel," Adeline answered, reaching across to run her hand along Sarah's leg.

Sarah smiled and moved her thigh under Adeline's touch. "Then I'll be sure and ask Michael when the time comes."

Thirty-three

When TJ got to the apartment, she found Albert and her friends already at work. Albert was just hanging up the phone, and the others had pleased looks on their faces.

"What's going on?" TJ asked as she entered, shutting the door behind her.

Shooter came over and put his arms around her. "Good news, babe," he said, looking into her eyes. "Albert just finished talking with the professor at McGill University."

She glanced from Shooter to Albert, who was busily arranging some papers and fitting them into a fax machine.

"Oh?"

Albert looked up after dialing a number on the machine and pressing the transmit button. "Last week," he said, "I finally made a breakthrough in my research. I used a DNA sequencer to identify the family of plasmids that cause the infection leading to Vampyrism. They belong to a group called the F-like plasmids. I believe, and Dr. Wingate agrees with me, that they're related to the prototypic fertility factor, F."

TJ shook her head. "You're losing me, Albert. I know a little about plasmids, but this is all way over my head."

He grinned. "That's understandable. Probably not more than five or six men in the world understand exactly how plasmids replicate, and even less than that are working on plasmid infections in humans. The important thing to know is Dr. Wingate has worked with the F-like plasmids before. He has on hand a supply of a compound he calls Fin-P, which when he combines it with a protein called FinO, he believes will repress the plasmids' ability to conjugate, or reproduce themselves."

"And if the plasmids can no longer reproduce themselves," Sam added excitedly, "sooner or later the ones causing your infection will die off, leaving you cured."

Albert held up his hand. "Wait a minute, Sam. Don't get her hopes up too much." He looked over at TJ, still in Shooter's arms. "We, that is Dr. Wingate and myself, *think* that's what will happen. But, since infections in humans are so rare, we don't know for certain."

TJ took Shooter by the arm and led him over to where Albert and Sam were standing. "So what's the next step?" she asked, her face flushed with excitement.

"I've just faxed the professor copies of my work, including the exact DNA sequence I worked out last week. If it is the same family as the ones he's been working with, he already has on hand enough conjugation-repressing serum for us to get started. Once he makes sure it's the same plasmids, he said he'd overnight us the serum he's got and get to work making some more."

"When does he think he'll know?" TJ asked.

"By tomorrow," Sam said, a wide grin on her face.

"So if it is the same, we could have the serum by day after tomorrow?"

Albert nodded. "As soon as we get it, along with the instructions from Wingate about appropriate dosages, we can begin injecting you with it."

"How long until I'm cured?" TJ asked, cutting right to the bottom line.

Albert glanced at Matt and Sam. "We don't know exactly, but Wingate says the plasmids normally live only about thirty to forty days in the bloodstream. He seems to feel once you start the injections, you should be free of symptoms within six or eight weeks."

"Oh, thank God," TJ said, sitting in a chair and putting her hands over her face.

Shooter caressed her hair. "It looks like it won't be long now, sweetheart."

Albert, watching them, noticed the twin scabs on Shooter's neck. He cleared his throat. "Uh, TJ, there's one more thing."

"Yes?" she asked, glancing up at him.

"In order to weaken the plasmids in your system as much as possible, you should refrain from . . . uh—"

"Go on, Albert. What?" she asked impatiently.

"Well, you shouldn't drink any more blood . . . from any source," he finished, looking significantly at Shooter. "The plasmids already in your system feed on, and are aided in their conjugation and replication, by sources of extraneous blood."

TJ took Shooter's hand in hers. "Don't worry, Albert. Those days are behind me forever."

Matt clapped his hands together. "Well, since all we can do now is wait, I have a suggestion," he said, smiling broadly.

"What's that?" Sam asked.

"Let's go celebrate. I feel a need for some champagne and some real New Orleans cuisine."

Albert got to his feet. "That's a great idea. I know a place that makes a mean shrimp Creole, and it's not too far from here."

"Champagne and shrimp, now that's a great combination," Shooter said, laughing.

As the group left the apartment, Sarah and Adeline, parked down the street in Sarah's car, watched them walk down the street.

Sarah took a cell phone from her purse and dialed Michael Morpheus's number. When he answered, she said shortly, "Michael, we've found them."

"Are they all there?" he asked.

"Yes. The half-breed, two men, another woman, and a big man who's got to be Roger Niemann." She shuddered. "I can feel the power emanating from him from a block away."

"Keep your mind shielded," Michael warned. "We don't want to warn him that he's under observation."

"Right. They're walking down the street like they're going somewhere," Sarah said.

"Follow them and call me back when they get to wherever they're going. I'll meet you there."

After walking four blocks, Albert showed them into a restaurant named Marie's. It didn't look like much from the street, but once they were inside, the smell of Cajun cooking made their mouths water.

"Jeez," Shooter said, "I could gain weight just smelling this food."

A large woman wearing an apron greeted them at the door. "Come in, come in," she said in a good-natured voice.

"Marie," Albert said, "I've brought some friends

of mine to dine with me tonight. They want some authentic New Orleans food."

"Then you've all come to the right place," Marie said with a laugh. "I'll put you at my best table."

She picked up a stack of menus and led them across the room to a corner table set for six. "Pierre will be your waiter tonight," she said, placing menus around the table and picking up the extra place setting. "Can I get you some wine?"

"Two bottles of your best champagne," Albert said, taking a seat between Sam and TJ.

"You got it, Dr. Nachtman," she said, and hurried off toward the bar.

"You must eat here often," TJ said.

Albert nodded. "Yes. I like to eat at a place where they know your name and greet you like family when you arrive." He looked at TJ with a strange stare. "It gets lonely living as I have. Not able to have any friends or loved ones to be with."

Shooter opened his mouth to say something, but TJ squeezed his thigh under the table. "I know, Albert. But, hopefully, after we're cured, you won't have to live like that any longer."

Marie arrived with two silver buckets with champagne in them. Albert took one out of its bucket and popped the cork. "I'll drink to that," he said with feeling.

Shooter leaned over and kissed TJ on the cheek. "So will I," he said.

While the group was enjoying their meal and champagne, Sarah called Michael from outside the restaurant and gave him their location.

He arrived twenty minutes later and pulled up next to Sarah's car. "Are they still in there?" he asked through the window.

"Yes," Sarah said. "They're in a corner table in the back."

"Good. You can leave it with me now."

Adeline glanced at Sarah, then turned to Michael. "Are you going to take her tonight?"

Michael stared at the restaurant. "No. The place is too crowded. I'll follow them home and wait for my chance at the female doctor when they're not all together."

"When you take her, can Sarah and I have her?" Adeline asked, licking her lips in anticipation at having a chance at Sam.

Michael gave her a severe look. "That will be decided later. For now, go on home and leave them to me."

Adeline started to reply, but Sarah grabbed her arm. "Yes, sir," she said to Michael, and hurriedly drove off before Adeline could make him angry.

As they drove toward home, Adeline pouted, her arms crossed in front of her chest. After a few miles, she glanced over at Sarah. "Why did you cut me off when I was talking to Michael?" she asked.

Sarah sighed and shook her head. "Honey, I love you, but you can be dumb as dirt sometimes." She looked sideways at her lover. "If you piss Michael off, he'd just as soon rip your head off and shit down your neck."

"Are you *that* afraid of him?" Adeline asked sarcastically.

Sarah nodded emphatically. "You'd better believe it!"

Thirty-four

The next morning, Sam woke early, too excited to sleep. She looked at Matt, still sleeping soundly next to her. She eased out of bed and went into the kitchen, intending to make some coffee.

She opened the cupboard and realized they hadn't stocked it with food or staples yet. They'd been too anxious the previous day to get to work on Albert's research papers and get them sent off to Dr. Wingate.

"Damn," she uttered softly. She wasn't worth spit in the mornings until she'd had her first cup of coffee.

She went into the bathroom and brushed her teeth and combed her hair. Then she slipped out of her nightgown and into a pair of jeans, throwing on a sweatshirt and tennis shoes.

Just as she was getting ready to leave, she heard Matt call out her name. She stuck her head back in the bedroom door. "Yes, sweetie?" she asked.

He mumbled, "What are you doing up? Jesus. It's still dark out."

She walked over to sit on the edge of the bed. Leaning down, she kissed him softly on the lips. "I'm in dire need of caffeine, darling, and since the cupboard is bare, I'm gonna run down to the local store and get some."

He shook his head, trying to come awake. "Hey, while you're at it, pick up some cinnamon rolls or something, will you?"

"Sure thing," she answered, kissed him again, and said, "Be back in a jiffy."

She went out the door and stood on the stoop for a moment, trying to remember which direction the nearest supermarket was in. Finally, she decided to just start walking. It couldn't be too far.

As she walked down the sidewalk, a large black car behind her started up, made a U-turn in the street, and pulled to a stop fifteen yards in front of her. It was a Lincoln Navigator with windshields tinted so dark she couldn't see the occupants.

When she pulled abreast of it, the passenger door swung open and a tall, thin man with black hair pulled back in a ponytail jumped out in front of her.

She gasped and took a step back, startled. He looked familiar, as if she should know him. As he started toward her, she suddenly realized he matched the man Chief Boudreaux had described as being at the scene of the murders in Liberty. Sam took a quick step to the side, intending to run past him. He grinned and, without a word, moving faster than she had ever seen anyone move, swung his hand in a sweeping slap and hit her square on the jaw. Blackness opened up and swallowed Sam.

Before she could fall, he swept her up in his arms and deposited her in the passenger seat like a load of groceries. He shut the door. After looking around to make sure no one had observed his actions, he quickly ran the few yards back to their apartment door and took a small notebook out of his jacket pocket. He scribbled a couple of lines on a page, tore it out, and stuck it in the doorjamb.

Walking nonchalantly now, as if he hadn't a care in the world, he went back to his car and got in. He drove off, the entire episode only taking three minutes from start to finish.

Thirty minutes later, Matt crawled out of bed, holding his head and cursing champagne for the hangover it left. He peeked out the bedroom door and looked in the kitchen. Sam wasn't back yet, so he decided to take a quick shower.

When he got out, TJ and Shooter were both sitting at the kitchen table, talking softly.

"Hey, pal," Shooter said. "We thought you two were still asleep, so we were trying not to wake you."

Matt joined them at the table. "Where's Sam?" he asked, looking around the apartment.

TJ and Shooter stared at him. "What do you mean?"

Matt glanced at his watch. "She left over thirty minutes ago to go and get some coffee and sweet rolls for breakfast."

"Thirty minutes?" TJ asked, frowning. "She must've taken the long way round. I noticed the store's only a couple of blocks away."

Matt shook his head, beginning to get a sinking feeling in his stomach. "I don't like this. I'm going after her."

He went to the door and opened it as Shooter called, "Wait a minute. I'll go with you."

As the door swung open, a note drifted to the floor. Matt bent and picked it up, his face going pale as he read, "We have your friend. Do nothing until you hear from me." It was unsigned.

"Oh, shit!" Matt cried, running out onto the porch steps and looking both ways up and down the street before coming back into the apartment.

"What is it, Matt?" TJ asked.

He slowly sat at the table and handed Shooter the note. "They've got Sam," he said in a low voice, tears forming in his eyes.

"Who?" TJ asked, looking at Shooter as he read the note.

Matt shook his head. "They didn't say, but I'm betting it's the Vampyres who are against us developing a cure."

Shooter looked up, his face grim. "How in the world did they find us?" he asked.

Matt shrugged. "Somehow they must have followed us when we came here."

TJ put her hands to her mouth. "Oh, no. I'll bet it was me they followed after I left Carmilla's place. They must have known I'd go see her eventually, and I led them right to us."

Matt patted her arm. "It's all right, TJ. You couldn't have known."

Shooter got to his feet and went into their bedroom. He emerged moments later, checking the loads in his pistol.

"What are you going to do?" Matt asked.

"I'm gonna go over to that Carmilla's place and make her tell me who has Sam, and then I'm gonna find them and blow their goddamn heads off."

TJ jumped up and ran to him. She put both her hands on his arms. "Shooter, you can't do that."

"Why not?" he asked heatedly.

"TJ's right, buddy," Matt said sadly. "You forget who you're dealing with. Any one of these creatures is more than a match for that peashooter of yours. Remember how you put a full clip into Roger and he *still* was able to survive?"

"But we can't just sit here and do nothing," Shooter said. "There's no telling what those bastards will do to Sam."

When he saw Matt's face fall at his words, he went to put his hand on his shoulder. "Hey, Matt, I'm sorry. I shouldn't have said that."

"No, you're right, Shooter," TJ said, moving next to him. "We don't have a minute to waste."

"What do you have in mind?" Matt said. "It won't do any good to go to the police."

She shook her head. "It's not the police I had in mind. Albert is our only chance."

"What can he do?" Shooter asked, jealousy in his voice.

TJ looked at him, her face serious. "Maybe he can force Carmilla to tell us who the renegade Vampyres are and how we can find them."

"She's right," Matt said. "He is our only hope."

TJ picked up the telephone and dialed Albert's number.

Michael drove well within the speed limit as he headed for the freeway and his lair on the bayou near Liberty. He didn't want to have to explain an unconscious woman on the front seat of his car to an inquisitive traffic cop.

When he was almost at his cabin, Sam began to stir on the seat next to him, moaning and holding her jaw. He reached across and ran his hand over her forehead, mentally instructing her to go back to sleep. She immediately calmed and leaned her head against the window, drifting off again.

Michael parked his car behind the house so it couldn't be seen from the drive. He opened the door and took Sam in his arms and carried her into the house.

He gently laid her on the bed in room 1. It, like all the other captive rooms, was equipped with a lock on the door that couldn't be opened from the inside.

Now he would begin the process of breaking this Normal down and extracting everything she knew about the process used to cure Vampyrism. First, while she was still unconscious, he stripped off her sweatshirt, jeans, and her underwear, until she was lying completely naked on the bed.

Michael stepped back and looked at her. She was uncommonly beautiful, he thought. Her hair was a deep auburn, almost a red color, and her skin as pale and creamy as one of the Vampyre women he dated. Her breasts were firm, covered with a light dusting of freckles. Her nipples were a light pink and were erect due to the chilliness of the room. He felt a stirring in his groin, unusual for him since he had never mated with Normals, preferring Vampyre women when he needed sexual release.

He forced himself to turn and leave the room. There would be plenty of time for that later, if he so chose. Now it was time to begin his campaign to break her mind. He would keep her naked, to add to her feelings of helplessness and defenselessness, while treating her alternately with compassion and cruelty. He'd read several books on brainwashing techniques used by the Vietcong against captured American airmen, and he thought these methods, along with judicious use of his mental powers, would be sufficient to learn everything she knew.

Moving into the kitchen, he began to cook scrambled eggs, bacon, and toast for their breakfast. While the skillet was warming, he prepared a pot of his favorite chicory coffee. First, the kindness, he thought, and then the steel fist later, when she least expected it.

* * *

Albert arrived at the apartment less than thirty minutes after they called him. "Let me see the note," he said.

He read it, shaking his head. "The bastards! It's Houston all over again."

"What do you mean?" Matt asked.

"The Vampyre Council in Houston tried to get me to stop my research," he explained. "I had to kill several of them in order to get them off my back." He looked at TJ. "The leader was Carmilla's aunt."

"Oh, shit!" Matt said. "Then she'll never agree to help us."

Albert's face turned grim. "Oh, she'll help us all right. I'll see to that."

He got to his feet. "TJ, you'll have to take me to her, right now. We don't have a minute to waste."

"We'll come, too," Shooter said.

Albert turned to him. "No, that wouldn't be wise. Carmilla will only speak to a Vampyre about this. If you two are there, it will complicate matters."

"But we can't just sit here and do nothing," Matt pleaded.

"That's exactly what you have to do," Albert explained. "Whoever left this note may call with instructions. They must not know what we're doing." He turned the note over and wrote a number on the back of it. "This is my cell phone number. Call me immediately if you hear from them."

"But what if they hurt Sam?" Matt asked.

Albert shook his head. "I don't think they'll do that, at least not yet. They want our cooperation in stopping our research. If they harm Sam, they've lost their bargaining chip. That should give us some time to locate them, but we've got to get going."

TJ grabbed Shooter's face in her hands and kissed him on the lips. "I've got to go, Shooter, for Sam's sake."

He stared into her eyes, and then he glanced up at Albert. "Don't let anything happen to TJ, Albert," he commanded.

"Don't worry, Shooter. Carmilla is not where the danger lies, it's with the people whose names we're going to get from her."

As they left the apartment, TJ looked over her shoulder. "We'll call as soon as we know anything."

Thirty-five

When TJ and Albert arrived at Carmilla's shop, it wasn't open for business yet. Albert stepped back into the street and looked upward.

"What are you doing?" TJ asked.

"A lot of these old shops in the French Quarter have living quarters over them." He pointed up at the second-story, where there were two windows and a small balcony with ornate wrought-iron railings surrounding it. "See. I'll bet she lives above her shop."

He went back to the front door and began pounding on it with his fist, the force of his blows denting the ancient wooden frame. After a few minutes, a light came on in the shop and Carmilla peered out from behind the shade. She looked from Albert to TJ, and finally unlatched the door.

When she opened the door, she was still in her robe. "Hello, TJ," she said suspiciously, turning her eyes to Albert. "It is awfully early for a visit."

"We've got to speak with you, Carmilla," TJ said urgently. "Someone has kidnapped my friend Sam."

Carmilla's eyes widened slightly before she opened the door wide and stepped to the side. "Come in, I'll fix us some tea."

As they followed her into the back room of the shop, where she put some water on to boil, she turned and stared at Albert. "Would you introduce me to your friend?"

"This is Albert Nachtman, Carmilla," TJ said.

"Perhaps you know me by my previous name, Roger Niemann," Albert said, inclining his head in greeting.

Carmilla's eyes narrowed with hate and her hand made a fist. "Yes," she said through gritted teeth. "My aunt Jacqueline mentioned it to me, just before she was murdered."

"An unfortunate occurrence," Albert said gravely, "but one that couldn't be helped. It was either she or I, and I preferred it be she."

"You bastard!" Carmilla said, and moved toward him, her hands outstretched, fingers clawed.

Albert held up his hands. "Hold on for a moment, Carmilla. We can settle our differences later, but for now, there is something more important to discuss."

Carmilla took a deep breath and seemed to force herself to relax. "And what could be more important than the vicious murder of my aunt?"

"The possible extinction of all that you have worked for over the years," Albert said. "Someone in your group has embarked on a course of events that will surely lead to the discovery of your group of Vampyres here in New Orleans. If these people are not stopped, you will all have to move, or you will be systematically hunted down and exterminated."

"What are you talking about?" she asked, turning as the kettle began to whistle. She poured the boiling water over the tea bags she'd set in three cups. She handed two to TJ and Albert as she took one for herself, then sat at the large conference table in the corner of the room.

Albert and TJ sat across from her. Albert took a sip of the tea and continued talking in a reasonable voice. "As TJ told you yesterday, some members of your Council have disregarded your edict forbidding lethal feedings. They have kidnapped and presumably killed over fifteen people in the last two weeks."

Carmilla nodded. "Yes, and I told TJ I was going to investigate her charges. Unfortunately, several of my Council members are out of town and I haven't been able to speak to them yet."

"It's gone far beyond that now, Carmilla," Albert said, glancing at TJ. "This morning, Samantha Scott, one of the doctors working with us to perfect a cure for Vampyrism, was abducted."

"How do you know it was one of my friends?" Carmilla asked, peering at him over the rim of her cup as she drank.

"A note was left indicating we should cease working on the formula until we hear from them, or Sam would be harmed."

Carmilla's face fell. "He must be out of his mind," she muttered, as if speaking her thoughts out loud.

"Who is doing this, Carmilla?" TJ asked, leaning forward, her voice pleading. "We must know so we can save Sam."

Carmilla looked up at her, biting her lip as she decided whether to confide in them or not. "It must be Michael, Michael Morpheus," she finally said. "He has been against my policy of nonlethal feeding from the start, but I never thought he'd go so far as to—"

"Well, he has," Albert interrupted. "But he can't be acting alone. There have been too many murders for it to be the work of one Vampyre. He must have co-opted others on your Council to feed with him."

Carmilla slowly nodded. "Yes, I've had my suspicions," she said in a low voice. "Sarah and Jean have both been acting nervous and anxious around me the last couple of days."

"Where can we find this Michael Morpheus?" TJ asked.

Carmilla's face paled and she held up her hand. "No, that is impossible. He would never speak to you."

"We plan to do more than speak to him," Albert said in a menacing voice.

Carmilla gave a weak grin, looking at Albert with appraising eyes. "He is a very powerful man, quite old," she said. "He might be more than a match even for you, Albert."

She noticed her teacup was empty and got up to refill it. "No, I think it much better if I give Michael a call and try to reason with him. It will be safer for all of us."

"I think he is beyond reason," Albert said. "To risk the safety of all of you in such a cavalier manner does not bespeak reason."

She turned and leaned back against the counter as she sipped her tea. "Nevertheless, I must try. Give me until this afternoon to see what I can do." She glanced at an antique grandfather clock standing in a corner. "Call on me at four this afternoon. I should know by then if I can persuade him to leave this dangerous course he is on."

Albert got to his feet. "All right, Carmilla, but be careful. Morpheus has risked much to do this. I am afraid he will not be willing to give it up so easily."

Carmilla smiled. "He would not dare act openly against the leader of our Council. There are too many of us for him to fight and succeed. I think I can make him see the light."

"Thank you, Carmilla," TJ said, taking her hand. "We're counting on you to save our friend's life."

"I'll see you at four, dear," Carmilla said, and showed them to the door.

As soon as they were gone, she went up the back stairs to her room and looked in her address book for Michael's cell phone number. She knew he wouldn't have the girl at his house. That would be too dangerous, as he had neighbors.

She dialed his number and waited for him to answer.

"Morpheus," he said shortly into the phone.

"Michael, this is Carmilla," she said. "You must stop this madness!"

"Why, Carmilla. Whatever are you talking about?" Michael answered in a silky smooth voice.

"You know what I mean, Michael. This abduction and killing of Normals, and the kidnapping of that lady doctor."

There was silence on the phone for several seconds, and then Michael asked, "Have you discussed these accusations with the Council?"

"Not yet," Carmilla answered, "but that's my next step if you don't cease this craziness immediately."

"Carmilla, I was just about to have breakfast. How about if I come by your place about noon and we'll discuss it further?"

"All right, until noon then."

Michael put the phone down and picked up the breakfast tray he'd prepared for Sam. He went to room 1 and knocked on the door before unlocking it and entering.

He found Sam sitting on the bare mattress, leaning back against the headboard with her legs crossed and her arms covering her bare breasts. He thought he'd find a frightened, scared woman, but the person staring back at him showed only defiance and hatred, not fear.

"Good morning, Sam," he said jovially, as if greeting an old acquaintance. "I hope I may call you Sam instead of Doctor."

In a calm, level voice, Sam replied, "You can call me anything you want, as long as you give me back my clothes and let me out of here."

Ignoring her words, Michael placed the breakfast tray on the bed at her feet. He brought a straight-backed chair from the corner of the room and sat down next to the bed. "I've brought you some food. I thought you might be hungry."

She made no move to uncover herself, but merely stared at him. "Are you going to return my clothes?" she asked.

He smiled sadly and shook his head. "I'm afraid not, my dear."

She gave him one more look, and then sighed. Without any signs of self-consciousness, she picked up the tray and set it on her lap and began to eat, ignoring him completely.

This woman has spirit, he thought. *She knows she needs to keep up her strength, but resistance at this point is useless. She's just waiting for a chance to escape. She's very brave.*

"Aren't you going to ask why you're here?" Michael asked.

"I know why I'm here," she answered, still not looking at him, and making no effort to hide her nakedness.

"Oh?"

"Yes. You think by kidnapping me and holding me against my will, you'll force my friends to give up on their search for a cure for your sickness."

Michael sat up in his chair, offended. "I don't

believe being a member of a superior race is a sickness, as you call it."

She gave him a scornful look. "Oh, and do members of a superior race get their kicks staring at naked women, women who wouldn't give them the time of day unless they were forced to?"

Stung, and a little embarrassed by her accusations, Michael bristled. "What do you know about it?" he asked heatedly. "You Normals with your mayfly lives. I've seen the rise and fall of countries, and I've taken thousands of you as my rightful prey."

Sam, unimpressed, glanced around the shabby room. "And what do you have to show for all those years?" she asked, her voice dripping with sarcasm. "Wisdom? Understanding? No, all you have is some dump in the woods where you can take someone weaker than you and keep her prisoner." She shook her head. "Doesn't sound like much of a bargain to me, this sickness you have."

"You bitch!" he screamed, and jumped to his feet. Sweeping the breakfast tray off the bed, he grabbed her by her shoulders and lifted her in the air.

Instead of cowering back, Sam doubled up her fist and hit him as hard as she could in the face, flattening his nose and causing it to spurt blood. As his eyes filled with tears and he let go to put his hand to his face, she ran from the room, making for the front door.

He was on her in a flash, tackling her and rolling on the floor with her in his arms until he was on top of her.

She glared up at him, her chest heaving, her hands clawing at his face and leaving deep furrows on his cheeks.

He cursed and finally managed to grab her arms

and pin her underneath him where she couldn't move.

Taking a few deep breaths, he stared down at her, his blood dripping down onto her breasts. *Jesus,* he thought, *I've never seen a Normal with such fire and spirit.* He looked at her breasts, glistening with sweat, stained scarlet with his own blood; he felt a heaviness in his groin.

Grinning evilly, he leaned down and licked the blood from her breasts, causing the nipples to spring erect. Sam whipped her head from side to side, still fighting him and trying to get away.

He laid himself out on her body, pushing the hardness of his penis against her loins, and whispered in her ear. "I could take you right now and you'd be powerless to stop me." He chuckled. "In fact, I think you'd like it."

She pulled her face away from him and spit in his eye. "Then you'd be wrong!" she shouted.

"Oh, then let's see," he challenged with a growl. He pulled her arms over her head and held her wrists in one of his hands; with the other, he pulled his pants down. He rubbed his penis against her while he explored her groin with his hand and bent his head down to kiss her, moving his tongue into her mouth as he used his mind to impress his lust on her.

Unlike most Normals he'd attacked in the past, she didn't immediately respond to his mental commands, but fought him tooth and nail. She shut her eyes and resisted him as no one ever had.

However, after a few minutes, the inevitable happened and he gained at least partial control of her mind. She stopped resisting him and lay beneath him, unmoving and limp.

As his hand continued its probing and caressing,

he felt her sex become wet and saw her nipples become erect in the first throes of passion.

Instead of fighting, she returned his kiss, pushing her tongue into his mouth and moving her hips against him as he pushed against her.

She moaned deep in her throat and put her arms around him, pulling him tighter against her. As he became more excited, he felt his body begin to change. His fingers became claws and his face began to melt and reshape.

He pulled his fingers out of her sex, lest the claws injure her, and moved his body over her, ready to couple.

Suddenly she bared her teeth and bit down hard on his tongue, almost severing it.

When Michael screamed and jerked back, Sam kneed him in the groin and pushed him off with her legs.

She crawled and scrabbled on hands and knees until she was out from under him, then ran out the door next to the kitchen. Unfortunately, the door led onto the balcony. She was trapped.

Michael stumbled to his feet and followed her out onto the balcony, where she stood with her back against the railing.

He wiped the blood off his mouth and waited for his tongue to heal itself enough for him to speak. They stood there, staring at each other for four or five minutes, with Sam glancing back over her shoulder at the bayou below.

Finally, when his tongue had knit itself back together, Michael growled. "That was very good, Sam. My congratulations. No Normal has ever been able to resist me mentally before, and certainly none has had the strength of will to pretend to be under my control when she wasn't."

As she looked over her shoulder again, Michael said, "You can jump if you want to, but before you do, look at that bank over there."

Sam looked across the bayou to the far bank and saw several six-foot-long alligators slide into the water and make their way through the black liquid toward the balcony.

"My friends are used to being fed when someone appears on the balcony. Are you going to disappoint them?" he asked.

She seemed to wilt when she found there was no escape. "Come, my dear," Michael said in a reasonable voice. "Let's forget all this unpleasantness and return to your room."

Sam moved past him, shrinking back as she passed so their bodies wouldn't touch, and walked toward her room. Her back was straight and her movements dignified in spite of her nakedness.

As Michael shut the door, he said, "I have a luncheon engagement, but I will be back for supper."

Sam took her place on the bed, crossing her legs and covering her breasts as she stared at him in contempt.

Thirty-six

On the way to meet with Carmilla, Morpheus reflected on the woman he had abducted. He'd never met a Normal with such fire and spirit, or one with the mental strength to fight his domination. He laughed to himself, something extremely rare for Michael, who was by nature a somber man. It would be a shame to destroy such a person, even to achieve the defeat of their plan to reverse the Transformation. He decided whatever the outcome of his meeting with Carmilla, he would release the lady doctor and find another way to halt their research. Such a spirit deserved to be left unchanged.

Now all he had to decide before arriving at Carmilla's shop was whether the time was ripe for him to challenge her for leadership of the Vampyre Council. He'd stayed in the background far too long. His friends among the other Vampyres deserved his style of leadership, he decided. Yes, he would give Carmilla a choice: defer to his superior ideas voluntarily, or he would force her.

Upon his arrival, Morpheus entered Carmilla's shop without knocking, to show her his contempt for her position as leader. He put the Closed sign on the door and proceeded into the shop. When he walked into the back room, he found her waiting for him, drinking her damned tea as usual.

"Hello, Morpheus," she said, not at all surprised by his entering without being invited.

"Good afternoon, Carmilla."

"Would you care for some tea?" she asked, having the gall to treat this as just another social gathering.

He shook his head. "No, this calls for something stronger." He stepped to the bar next to the kitchen counter and poured himself a brandy from a crystal decanter she'd kept from colonial days.

He swirled the amber liquid in the snifter and took a seat across the table from her. "Now, what is all this nonsense you called me about?" he asked, leaning back in his chair and crossing his legs, straightening the seam on his trousers so the razor-sharp crease wouldn't be wrinkled.

Carmilla cut right to the chase. "Do you have any idea of the risks you are taking?"

He took a drink and let the fiery liquid caress his tongue. "No, dear Carmilla. Why don't you tell me?"

"Michael, we have followed the nonlethal-feeding rule for many years for a very good reason. I know you are aware of the pogroms in the Middle Ages when people realized we walked among them. Do you want to return to those days by letting the authorities know of our existence?"

He sighed, slowly shaking his head. "Oh, Carmilla. You give the Normals too much credit for logical thinking. All the mortals think about nowadays are their movies, television shows, and computer games. They are no more ready to believe in the fact of our existence than they are of alien abductions. If the authorities do become aware of my friends' and my hunting, which I have taken pains to avoid, they will simply put it down to some depraved serial killer going about his business. Without the bodies of our victims, there is no way they can ascertain the cause of death, let alone who is responsible."

She stared at him as if he were beneath contempt. "You are wrong, Michael." She hesitated. "What if I told you the police have a very good description of you and know that you were in the area where the people went missing?"

He started, unaware that he'd been seen and noticed on his scouting expeditions. Before he could respond, she went on. "And furthermore, they know that all of the disappearances are related and probably due to the actions of several persons working together."

"I don't believe you," he said stubbornly.

"You better believe it, my friend," she said forcefully. "These days are far different from the years in the past when we could hunt and feed in one area and move on, without fear of being tracked or traced. Those computers you speak so disdainfully about allow the police in every area of the country to trace murders done in similar manners."

She got up and went to refill her teacup, speaking over her shoulder. "If you and Sarah and Jean, and whoever else has been corrupted by your ideas, continue on this path, it will only be a short time until we are once again hunted down like dogs."

He was startled to realize she knew who his accomplices were. He thought he'd managed to keep it a secret from her.

"So what if a few do come to believe in our race and recognize what we're doing?" he asked, furious at her for not being able to see the natural superiority of their race. "If they dare to try and go public with what they know, they'll be branded as fools, or worse."

He decided to try and reason with her one more time. "Carmilla, Vampyres are the future. We are far superior to the Normals in every way, and I am tired of having to skulk around, sipping a little blood from this one and taking a small snack from another one. It is far past the time we should assume our rightful place in the world as predators no mortal can stand against."

She leaned back against the counter and stared at him with wide eyes. "Why, you really are as crazy as the one called the Ripper," she said in a wondering voice, as if she were just now coming to understand the depth of his insanity. "You would bring us all down to satisfy your pathetic ego."

He finished the brandy in a deep swallow and threw the glass against a far wall. "Enough of this useless chatter, Carmilla." He nearly screamed. "I can see you haven't the vision necessary to lead us any longer."

She smiled grimly and shook her head, a deeply sad look in her eyes. "Oh, so you think the Council members will follow you now?" she asked. "Well, we'll see about that after I call them and tell them what you've done, including the fact that you kidnapped one of the doctors working to find a cure for this dreadful disease you are so proud to suffer from."

He stood up and flexed his muscles, letting himself begin to change. "I can't let you do that, Carmilla. Not until I'm ready," he answered, rasping through a throat already becoming thicker and more massive as he assumed the Vampyre form.

Carmilla's face blanched and she bolted for the stairs at the other end of the shop. She tried desperately to change, too, so she could fight him, but he was minutes ahead of her in the process.

He caught her halfway up the staircase when she was only partially Transformed. His claws sank into her shoulders and he whirled her around, picking her bodily up off the steps and holding her above him, her feet dangling off the ground.

She swiped at him with a claw-hand, laying his cheek open to the bone. He growled deep in his throat and threw her against the wall like a rag doll, grinning through fangs stained with crimson drool. Her head bounced off the wall with a resounding cracking sound, leaving a trail of blood on the wall.

Growling deep in his throat, he entwined his claws in her hair and dragged her up the stairs to her bedroom while she moaned and tried to finish her Transformation.

He picked her up and tossed her limp body onto the bed. As she lay there, moving feebly, trying desperately to regain her senses, he stripped off his clothes.

Reaching down, he stroked himself into full tumescence and approached her. "Carmilla, I once asked you to mate with me as equals, as Vampyres should, and you refused me."

He grabbed the front of her dress and ripped it from her body, baring her heaving breasts and blood-soaked groin to his view. "Now I'm going to take you like one of my victims, and I will enjoy every second of your torment."

Her Transformation finally complete, she bared her fangs at him and growled as she tried to claw his face again. He brushed her weak attempt aside and straddled her on the bed, letting his engorged penis rest between her legs while he took her head in his claws. With a vicious thrust, he impaled her, causing her to thrust upward in pain as he lowered his head and kissed her roughly on the lips while he held her face steady.

Thrusting his tongue between her lips, he began to pump into her, kneading her breast with his right claw, while he pulled her face against his in a wild animal-like coupling.

After a moment, in spite of her pain and humiliation, Carmilla began to respond to him. She spread her legs and pushed her pelvis against his in an obscene parody of lovemaking.

Soon, against her will, the pounding of his penis in her caused her to climax with a sound, deep in her throat, between a shriek and a groan. As he felt himself begin to come inside her, Michael lowered his face to her neck and began to rend and tear until her blood flowed and spurted into his open mouth. He drank her life's blood as fast as he could, continuing his wild coupling until she lay depleted beneath him.

To finish the act, as his penis grew flaccid within her, he grasped her head in both his hands and, with a mighty wrench, ripped it from her body, holding it aloft and staring into her open, dead eyes.

His blood lust satiated, he rolled to the side and tossed her head to the foot of the bed, then calmly walked into her bathroom and stepped into the shower. He leaned against the wall of the stall, exhausted, as the steaming water washed all traces of Carmilla de la Fontaine from his body.

Once he was dressed, he took her corpse and head and rolled them up in a priceless antique Persian rug. "It wouldn't do for the police to find you like this, my dear," he said softly to the form in the rug as he carried it down the stairs. He peeked out the door to ensure that the street was clear before he carried the rolled-up rug to his car and placed it in the trunk.

Only one more thing to do, he told himself as he reentered her shop. He went to the cash register and opened it, taking all the money out of it and scattering a few dollars around on the floor. The police must think this was a routine burglary and robbery, he thought, and since they'll never find your body, Carmilla, it will go down as just another instance of inner-city crime.

As he drove toward his lair, he chuckled. *My little bayou friends are going to get a special treat for lunch,* he thought, *and the sight of what happens to people who disobey me will be a good lesson for the lady doctor before I send her back to her friends. This will be a warning that they face the same fate if they continue in their research.*

Thirty-seven

After leaving Carmilla with the promise to return at four o'clock, Albert and TJ went back to the apartment.

They walked in and found Shooter and Matt anxiously awaiting their return. "Did you find out anything?" Matt asked, jumping to his feet as soon as they walked through the door.

Albert shrugged. "A little. The name of the Vampyre behind Sam's kidnapping is probably Michael Morpheus, and Carmilla let slip a couple of other names of ones who are probably in it with him: Sarah and Jean, although she didn't give us their last names."

"Does she have any idea where to find him?" Shooter asked, his jaw set tight.

"No," TJ explained. "She says he almost certainly isn't at his home, but most likely has a hiding place, where he's taken Sam."

"So what do we do now?" Matt asked, plainly agitated.

Albert held out his hands. "We wait. Carmilla is going to have a noon meeting with Michael and see if she can't talk some sense into him."

"She's going to threaten retaliation by the rest of the Council if he doesn't release Sam and stop his hunting and feeding on innocent people," TJ added.

Matt nodded, though he clearly wasn't happy with sitting around and waiting for something to happen.

"Hey, Matt," Shooter said, "tell them about the call from Wingate."

"Oh, yeah. I almost forgot. He called and said with Albert's data, he felt sure the serum he had on hand would stop the reproduction of the plasmid family causing the symptoms you and TJ are having."

Albert sighed and looked at TJ, giving her a somber thumbs-up sign. "At least that's something."

"When will he get the serum to us?" TJ asked.

Shooter walked over and hugged her tight. "By this time tomorrow, sweetheart. He's FedExing it for overnight delivery."

"And," Matt added, though it was clear his heart wasn't in it, "he said he'd have enough more made to treat five or six people by the end of the week, Albert."

"That's good," Albert said, a tight smile on his face, "but first things first. We've got to find Sam and prevent this Morpheus creature from doing her any harm."

Matt glanced at his watch. "They should be meeting about now. You think we should go over there and confront Morpheus in person?"

Albert shook his head. "Carmilla knows him the best and said that would be the worst thing we could do."

TJ walked to Matt and hugged him. "Carmilla felt sure she could reason with him, Matt. I'm sure Sam will be all right."

Matt returned her hug, tears of relief in his eyes.

To break the somber mood, Albert got to his feet. "How about I go out and get us some muflattas?"

"What the hell is a muflatta?" Shooter asked.

Albert smiled and shrugged. "About the closest I can come to describing it is to say it's a type of Italian sub. Two pieces of pita bread with ham and cheese and salami and tomatoes and olives and onions—all swimming in olive oil inside."

When Matt didn't say anything, Shooter clapped him on the back. "We've got to eat something and keep our strength up, pal, so it might as well be something delicious."

Matt laughed. "Of course, you're right. Let's eat and, meanwhile, wait and hope for the best."

"Come on, Albert, I'll help you bring the grub back," Shooter said, thinking he'd leave TJ and Matt alone for a while to get their feelings under control.

They were back in less than twenty minutes, and as Albert promised, the muflattas were delicious. They were each wrapped in butcher paper and were so rich in olive oil that it had soaked right through the paper. Shooter also had a large bag of potato chips and a six-pack of Orange Slice soda water.

The mood, either because of the food or the passage of time, was considerably lighter, and the four easily discussed the possible timetable of TJ's treatment with Wingate's serum.

Before they knew it, three hours had passed; it was time for Albert and TJ to return to Carmilla's shop.

"You sure we shouldn't go with you . . . just for backup?" Shooter asked. He wasn't used to standing on the sidelines and letting someone else do the dirty work.

TJ shook her head and gave him a light kiss on the lips. "No, lover. Carmilla made it plain she would only talk to us 'creatures of the night.' " She said this with a Bela Lugosi accent to show she was kidding.

"All right," he said, trying without success to hide a smile, glad she was taking things so much better after the promise of a possible cure. "But"—he pointed a finger at her—"you are to call us on your cell phone as soon as you know anything. Got it?"

"Yes, sir," she said, with only a little sarcasm in her voice, and followed Albert out the door.

When TJ and Albert arrived at Carmilla's shop, they found the door locked and the Closed sign in the window. TJ glanced at her watch. "That's odd," she said, a puzzled frown decorating her face. "It's five after four. She should be here waiting for us."

Albert knocked loudly on the door several times and received no answer. He looked at TJ. "I don't like this," he muttered. He looked over his shoulder and waited a moment until there were no passersby on the sidewalk, then stepped close to the door, turned the knob, and punched the wood hard with the palm of his hand just over the dead bolt.

The wood splintered with a sharp crack and the door eased open. With another look to make sure the sound hadn't aroused any attention, Albert opened the door wide enough so he and TJ could squeeze in, then shut it behind them.

His nostrils dilated and TJ noticed his features coarsen slightly, as if he were about to change into his Vampyre form.

"What's wrong?" she asked, not liking the feral expression on his face.

"I smell blood, lots of it," he whispered, his fingernails lengthening into claws. "Something is terribly wrong here."

In spite of herself, TJ felt similar changes begin to take place in her body. Her muscles seemed to bunch and quiver as they got ready for action, and her fingernails lengthened slightly.

"Follow me, but be ready to fight," Albert said in a low voice. Assuming somewhat of a crouch, he moved across the room toward the stairway leading up to Carmilla's bedroom.

He paused, then snorted through his nose, pointing up the stairs. TJ stared upward and they both saw a large splatter of blood on the wall that had trailed down almost to the stairway.

Without taking his eyes off the stairs, Albert said, "Check the back room. Make sure no one's hiding in there."

TJ whirled and slowly crept into the back room. She saw a shattered brandy snifter near the wall and a used teacup on the table. She sniffed, and recognized the acrid scent of alcohol on the air. Returning to Albert, she whispered, "Some one was here. He drank brandy and Carmilla had her usual tea. Then something must have happened and he threw the glass against the wall."

Albert expelled his breath. "They must have had a disagreement." He looked over his shoulder at TJ. "You want to go up with me, or would you rather wait outside?"

"I'll stay with you."

"It's probably not going to be very pretty up there."

"I know," she said, and gave him a slight nudge up the stairs.

When he got to the door of Carmilla's bedroom, his nostrils dilated again and TJ could hear him sniffing. She followed suit and detected the odor of sex permeating the room, mixed with a coppery scent of old blood and the stronger smell of urine and feces.

"Wow," she uttered, almost gagging. "That's strong."

Albert glanced at her. "Your sense of smell is hundreds of times more acute than a Normal's," he said, making her blanch when she realized he meant she was no longer quite human.

He moved into the room, checking behind the door and in the bathroom to make sure they were alone before he relaxed and began to examine the room more closely.

He pointed to a bloodstain on the mattress and some other smaller stains nearby. "Blood and semen and urine," he said after bending his head to take a close smell of the area.

"Michael must have mated with her and then killed her," she said, "and her bladder emptied when she died."

"That would be my guess," Albert said.

He knelt down next to the bed and pointed at the wooden floor. "Look here," he said, "the floor is darker in a rectangle, about four feet by six feet, with a dark bloodstain in the center."

"What could that mean?" TJ asked.

"I think Carmilla had a rug over the floor here, and Morpheus used it to wrap her body in so he could take it someplace and dispose of it. He wouldn't want the police to find it in the shape he left it in."

"But with all this blood, they're gonna know someone was killed here," TJ said.

"Yeah, but they won't know *how.* They won't connect it to the type of killing a Vampyre does, and they'll probably just put it down to a burglary and rape gone bad."

TJ shuddered. "Albert, let's get out of here."

"Not yet," he said, getting to his feet. He went over to the dresser and began pulling out drawers and throwing things out of the way as he searched.

"What are you looking for?" TJ asked.

He glanced at her. "I've never known a Vampyre yet who didn't keep some kind of journal. When you live several lifetimes, it's hard to keep track of people and places and times, so most of us use a journal to refer back to in order to refresh our memories when needed. I'm hoping Carmilla left something in writing that will help us identify the Sarah and Jean she mentioned as being in league with Morpheus. Otherwise, we're dead in the water."

TJ nodded. "I see what you mean." She went to the closet and began to search through Carmilla's things, checking the hatboxes and shoe boxes she found behind the hanging clothes.

Suddenly she heard a whoop of joy from Albert and turned to find him holding up a leather journal, not unlike his own.

He opened it and scanned a few pages. "Let's go," he said. "This is what we need. It's got all the members of the Council in here and where they live and work."

"Should we call the police?" she asked, following him down the stairs.

"No. It won't help Carmilla, and we may need to come back here and search the place further. Better not to get the police involved just yet."

They peeked out the door to make sure they could make it to his car without being observed. When no one was about, they eased out the door and pulled it shut behind them. Once in Albert's car, heading for the apartment, TJ hurriedly scanned the journal for clues to the whereabouts of Sam or the people who took her.

Thirty-eight

After Morpheus left Sam, locking the door behind him, she jumped off the bed and searched the room for anything that might allow her to escape. The room was like a prison cell—absolutely nothing in it that might be used to force the door lock. Even the sheets had been removed to prevent her from fashioning a rope to lower herself out the window.

Finally, she went to the window and looked out again, trying to decide whether she could dive into the bayou and make it to shore before the alligators had her for lunch. The ancient forms could be seen slowly gliding back and forth beneath the porch. Morpheus must have been feeding them for some time for them to hang around so close. She shuddered and shut the window, refusing to think about what he'd been throwing to them.

Sam lay on the bed, figuring to get a few hours' sleep and charge her batteries so she'd be able to cope with him better on his return. She was so exhausted from their earlier confrontation and the energy she'd expended trying to fight his mental commands, she fell asleep almost instantly.

Waking up two hours later, shivering and shaking, she was covered in sweat. Her eyes burned and her mouth was dry and cottony. She stumbled out of bed, nearly falling from weakness. Putting the back of her wrist to her forehead, Sam realized she was burning up with fever. Almost fainting, she steadied herself on the dresser and finally gained the strength to wobble on unsteady feet back to the bed. Flopping down, she breathed heavily with the exertion. *Hell, it's not even flu season,* she thought. *What the hell's the matter with me?* And then she passed out and lay sprawled, soaking the bed with her sweat as she shivered in her sleep.

Michael pulled his car around to the back of his cabin and retrieved Carmilla's body parts from the trunk. He slung the rug over his shoulder and entered the house, moving straight to the porch and dumping it there. He didn't immediately throw Carmilla to the gators because he wanted the lady doctor to see what happened to people who crossed him.

He pulled a key from his pocket and opened the door, surprised at the gamy, stale odor of the room. When he saw Sam lying on the bed, shivering and shaking, covered with sweat, he felt his heart jump.

"Oh, shit!" he exclaimed, moving to sit on the edge of the bed. He gently reached down and shook her shoulder, trying to wake her without startling her too badly.

She moaned and turned; her red-rimmed, bloodshot eyes stared up at him for a moment without recognition. "What . . . Where am I?" she croaked through dry, chapped lips, her eyes blank and staring.

He got up and went to the kitchen and filled a glass with ice and water. Returning, he held her head up and let her drink greedily of the cool liquid.

"Sam," he said, "it's Michael Morpheus."

Her eyes flickered once, and then they seemed

to clear as she shrank back from his touch and scrambled up against the headboard. Crossing her arms to cover her nakedness, she stared at him with hatred.

"Oh, now I remember," she said, her voice sounding as if she'd swallowed razor blades.

He simply nodded and didn't reply.

She wiped sweat off her brow with the back of her arm and frowned when it came away soaking wet. "What is going on?" she asked. "What's wrong with me?"

He took a deep breath. "It appears, Sam, as if you are in the first stages of Transformation."

"Transformation?" she asked weakly. "What do you mean? How could that be? I haven't drunk of your blood . . ." Then it hit her. "Oh, God, no!"

"I'm afraid so, Sam. When you bit my tongue as I kissed you, you must have swallowed enough of my blood to begin the Transformation."

"Well, make it stop!" she demanded with as much strength as she could manage.

He shook his head. "That is impossible. Once begun, the process and end result are inevitable."

She covered her face with her hands. "You bastard!"

He reached out to touch her shoulder gently. "Sam, for what it's worth, I came back here to let you go."

She peeked up at him, her face swollen and pale.

"Yes. I so admired your spirit in resisting me, I was determined to find another way to stop your friends without harming you."

"Bullshit!" she exclaimed.

"No, it is true." He sighed. "I am as sorry about this as you are."

"I seriously doubt that," she said with some exasperation, and then she doubled over in pain, wrapping her arms around her stomach and moaning. "Jesus, it hurts so bad!"

"It will only get worse, I'm afraid," Michael said.

"Christ, you're just full of good news."

He smiled, intrigued that even in extreme pain, she could still joke and try to make light of her situation.

"I can help you a little, if you'll let me," he said, gently stroking her arm as he talked.

"How?" she groaned, her face a mask of pain.

"The fewer of the organisms in my blood you ingest, the slower and more painful the process of Transformation. If you take in a larger quantity, the process will proceed much more quickly and there will be almost no pain."

She looked at him in amazement. "You don't seriously think I'd consent to drink more of your blood, do you?"

He shrugged. "Of course, that is entirely up to you. But, in the long run, it will make no difference. You will transform with or without taking additional blood, but you will be in intense pain for a considerable amount of time if you do not agree to . . . additional feedings."

"Fuck you, Morpheus," she almost screamed, pushing his hand away. "I'd rather die than do that."

"Oh, you won't die, my dear. You will wish you had many times over because the pain will be excruciating and it will go on and on for weeks."

She looked at him, then narrowed her eyes and sniffed loudly. "What is that god awful smell?" She sniffed again and then looked down at her sweat-covered body. "Oh, Christ, it's me, isn't it?"

He nodded. "Will you let me assist you? I can help you get clean."

She smirked and spread her arms, revealing her breasts, shiny with a film of perspiration. "What the hell? You've already seen all there is to see."

"I'll be right back," he said, and got up and went into the bathroom. Seconds later, she heard water running and he returned.

He bent over and picked her up and carried her like a baby in his arms into the bathroom. The tub was filling with warm water and she noted he'd added some sort of good-smelling bubble bath.

He gently lowered her into the suds and laid her head back against the rear of the tub. Then he took a washcloth and soap and began to wash her body, scrubbing softly with the cloth around her face and neck, and then down over her breasts and stomach. Finally, he washed her legs and thighs, moving them to the side so he could do her genitals and buttocks under the water.

She was too weak to resist, so she lay there, her eyes closed, enjoying the softness of his touch and the refreshing feeling of the warm, fragrant bubbles as they caressed her body.

While she was submerged in the warm liquid, the pain seemed to abate a bit. But when he stood her up and began to towel her off, her joints felt as if someone had lit a fire in them, and her muscles contracted in spasms and cramps so bad she could barely stand unaided.

Once she was dry, he again picked her up and carried her to the bed, laying her down on some pillows and bed linens he'd brought from another room. As she shivered, he covered her with a sheet and sat on the side of the bed, watching her.

After two hours of unrelenting agony, with the

pain not having let up for a second, Sam finally turned her face to him. "I think I'm ready for another dose of blood, if it'll make this go away for a while."

Michael inclined his head. He stood up and began removing his clothes.

"Wait a minute," Sam asked, her face clouding. "Is that necessary?"

"Yes. I do not want blood on my clothes," he replied as he removed the last of his clothing.

Against her will, her eyes dropped to his penis, which was rapidly growing larger as he stared down at her nakedness. It was the largest she had ever seen; she shuddered at the thought of what it would feel like to have it inside her.

He lay on the bed next to her, stretching out with his lower body against hers. He used a fingernail to open a small vein in his neck and raised his chin so she could get to it.

Hesitantly, a look of extreme distaste on her face, she put her lips against his pale, cold skin and began to suck the blood as it trickled into her mouth.

At first, it tasted coppery and salty, and then it slowly began to taste sweet; she thought it the best thing she'd ever tasted. Almost without realizing it, her arms went around his shoulders and she pulled him to her, enjoying the feel of her breasts flattening against his chest.

He put his hand behind her head and stroked her neck as she suckled him, drawing his blood into her mouth faster and faster.

She finally pulled her head back, a wondering look in her eyes. "What's happening?" she asked in a small voice as her nipples sprang erect. She felt herself becoming wet with a desire so overpowering she couldn't breathe.

He leaned away from her and moved his hand to cover her breast, which swelled and throbbed with his touch as he caressed her. "The act of feeding is essentially a sexual one for a Vampyre," he said in a husky voice. "Though I've never had sex with a Normal I've fed on, I invariably seek out a female of my species immediately afterward and couple with her; otherwise, the lust is overwhelming."

She shook her head. "No, I don't want this!" she said heatedly. "I'm in love with Matt Carter."

He continued to move his hand in small circles over her breast, pinching the engorged nipple gently, and then moving his hand lower on her abdomen until his fingers were entwined in her pubic hair. "Love has nothing to do with it," he explained. "The act of feeding releases hormones into my bloodstream in such an amount, they act as an irresistible aphrodisiac, both to me and to you."

Sam moaned deep in her throat as her vagina pulsed and throbbed under the influence of her blood meal. She thought her breasts were going to explode—they hurt so much and her nipples still tingled from his touch.

As his fingers gently spread the lips of her sex and entered her wetness, she groaned and pushed against his hand, even though she fought it with every fiber of her being.

Michael reached over and pulled her lips back down to his neck and she began to suck and swallow again. As he caressed her, she continued to feed and let her body slide down in the bed, opening her legs to his touch, moving her pelvis against him harder and harder.

As she drank his blood, Michael leaned his head down and began to kiss her ear and cheek, flicking his tongue against her soft skin and reveling in the taste of her sweat.

Her hand moved to him as if it had a mind of its own, her fingers wrapping themselves around his hardness and squeezing while she continued to drink and suck his blood.

Between swallows, she gasped in pleasure at the feel of him inside her, and when his penis throbbed and jumped under her touch, she began to move her hand up and down as her pelvis pumped against his hand between her legs.

Finally, Michael could stand it no longer. He pushed her onto her back and straddled her, his penis erect between her legs and resting against the entrance to her sex.

He leaned down and kissed her, feeling her mouth open under his lips and her tongue reach into his mouth, teasing and flicking against his in a dance of love.

He grasped her breast and squeezed as they kissed, and he slowly moved his hips forward until he was just inside her.

Suddenly, with a gasp and a small cry, she pulled her head back and looked into his eyes. "Please, I know I can't stop you, Michael, and God knows right now I don't want to, but if you have any regard for me, don't do this."

Michael gritted his teeth and took a deep breath, staring down into her eyes. His penis, the head of it just inside her, throbbed and moved.

With a growl of frustration, Michael forced his hips back and rolled off her, breathing heavily and fighting a desire to take her with every bit of his strength.

After a moment, Sam rolled on her side against him, her left breast resting on his chest and her arm across him with her hand on his cheek. "Thank you, Michael, for being so strong . . . stronger than me."

She moved her hand down his stomach until her fingers brushed against his hardness. "Would you like me to . . . help you another way?" she asked in a quiet voice.

"Oh, God, yes!" Growling, almost out of control, as he pushed himself against her hand.

Thirty-nine

On the way back to the apartment after leaving Carmilla's shop, Albert suddenly pulled over to the side of the road and parked the car.

"What is it?" TJ asked, looking up from Carmilla's journal.

"We need to talk," Albert said, shutting off the engine and turning sideways so he could look directly at TJ.

TJ shut the journal and laid it in her lap, her hands folded over it. "All right."

"It's time we decided what we're going to do about Sam, and about curing you of this curse I inflicted on you."

"Albert, my first priority is to find Sam and to make sure nothing happens to her," TJ said firmly. "It's great that we finally have a way to reverse the changes that have occurred in me, but my first loyalty is to Sam."

"I thought that's how you'd feel," Albert said. "So all we have to do is find out where Morpheus has taken her, then go and take her away from him."

"That's right."

He smiled, his eyes sad. "However, that is not going to be easy. From the looks of things, even Carmilla, who knew him well, underestimated his determination to keep the cure from ever being used, and even underestimated his strength and power."

TJ closed her eyes, trying to put the picture of Carmilla's bloodstained shop out of her mind. "I know."

"I don't want to make the same mistake, TJ," Albert said softly.

"What do you mean?" she asked, her eyes boring into his.

"If I go up against Morpheus by myself, and lose, it will be the end of all of us. There will be nothing to stop him from coming after you and Shooter and Matt, after he kills Sam." He hesitated. "And that is just what he'd have to do to make sure the cure stays a secret."

"What are you saying?"

"I'm going to need some help, some backup when I go after him. I thought I could count on Carmilla and would be able to leave you out of it, but"—he shrugged—"obviously things have changed."

Her eyes narrowed. "But of course you'll have my help, and Shooter's and Matt's, too."

He shook his head. "Having Normals with me will be of no help at all, TJ. In fact, it'd probably be a hindrance because then I'd have to spend time and energy looking after you all instead of concentrating on taking Morpheus down."

"So what do you want?"

"I need you to complete the Transformation. I need you to be a full-fledged Vampyre, to stand beside me and help me in the fight against Morpheus."

Her face paled. "But I am—"

"No. No, you're not," he interrupted. "You're still only halfway there, caught somewhere in limbo between being human and being one of us. And if you're seriously considering undertaking the destruction of one as powerful as this Morpheus appears to be, then I'm going to need you at full strength."

She dropped her gaze to her hands. "What must I do to finish Transforming?"

"You must again start to feed on blood, and you must take in as much as you can in the next couple of days. That will cause the plasmids to conjugate and reproduce in large numbers, completing the changes in your DNA."

Her eyes rose to fix on him. "You mean I should take more of your blood?"

He shook his head. "As far as Transformation goes, that would be best, but I think it would be a grave mistake for us to share blood again."

"Why?" she asked, wondering what his objections were.

He sighed and leaned back against the door. "TJ, you must be aware of the changes that take place when we feed. Our hormones go into overdrive and the act is always a mixture of sexual desire and fulfillment as well as nourishment."

She blushed, remembering the times she'd taken his blood and the wild coupling that invariably occurred, as well as what had happened on the few occasions she'd drank of Shooter's blood.

"Yes, I know."

He leaned across the seat and put his hand on hers. "You know what would happen if you and I—"

"Yes," she said, squeezing his hand in hers.

"TJ, I still love you, and I would give anything to have you as my mate, but you love Shooter. It wouldn't be fair to him or to you to let our emotions get carried away in a feeding frenzy and spoil what you two have together."

A solitary tear formed in her eye and dropped onto her cheek. "I agree. So," she said, brushing the tear away, "I'll just have to take what I need from Shooter."

He shook his head again. "No, that won't be possible, at least not all of it. You're going to need a lot of blood, and taking that much from one person would probably kill him."

"But what can I do?" she asked. "I'm not about to feed on some poor innocent person, even if it means saving Sam."

He cleared his throat. "I thought, well, perhaps Matt will volunteer to give you some of his blood, in order to save Sam."

"Jesus, Albert," she said, her face aghast. "I couldn't do that. I'd be too ashamed."

He shrugged. "TJ, it's the only way. That's why I stopped here to talk to you without Shooter and Matt being present. You are going to have to decide which is more important: your pride or saving Sam."

"That's not fair," she protested, turning to stare out the window.

"Life's not fair, TJ. It's not fair that you're in this predicament, or that Sam has been kidnapped. But that's the way it is. The choice is up to you."

He turned forward, started the car, and began to drive toward the apartment.

By the time they arrived, TJ had made up her mind. Albert was right. She was ready to do whatever it took to rescue Sam, even if it meant debasing herself by feeding on Matt and Shooter.

The men were both pacing nervously when they entered. Matt rushed up to TJ. "Well, what happened?" he asked. "Was Carmilla able to talk Morpheus into releasing Sam?"

"You'd better both sit down," Albert said, motion-

ing them to the couch in the living room. TJ sat
next to Shooter and took his hand in hers, with
Matt at the other end of the sofa.

Albert sat across from them in an easy chair and
told them exactly what they'd found in Carmilla's
shop.

"Oh, Jesus," Matt said, his eyes losing all hope.

Albert went on to explain about the journal
they'd found, and how they hoped it would lead
either to Morpheus or to the others in league with
him.

"One way or another, we're going to find the bastard and get Sam back," he said.

"Then let's get on with it," Matt said.

Albert looked at TJ. She cleared her throat and
went over the arguments Albert had presented
about needing her to finish her Transformation in
order to help him in his fight against the Vampyres
of New Orleans.

"No way!" Shooter protested, his face red and
flushed. He turned to TJ. "Baby, we'll have the serum tomorrow. You'll be able to begin your cure,"
he said persuasively.

She shook her head. "No, Shooter. Albert is right.
Unless we defeat this Morpheus and those working
with him, none of us will live to enjoy the cure. It
has to be this way," she said, her eyes staring into
his sadly.

"But, Albert," Shooter said, "if she completes the
Transformation, won't that make it harder to cure
her?"

He shrugged. "Theoretically, yes."

"Then I'm against it!" Shooter said firmly.

TJ looked at Matt. "Matt, what do you think?"
she asked.

He stared at the floor. "I'm with Shooter." He

took a deep breath. "As much as I love Sam and want her back, I know she'd never agree to let you sacrifice yourself to save her. That's not the answer. We'll just have to find some other way—"

"There is no other way," Albert interjected. "Either we find and kill Morpheus, or he will find and kill us all. He cannot allow us to live as long as we have a cure for Vampyrism in our possession."

"But—" Shooter began.

"No, Albert's right," TJ said. "Besides, if the cure works, I'll still be able to become normal once again after all this is over."

"But what if it doesn't?" Shooter argued.

"Then nothing has changed," TJ said. "As it is, I'm still Transforming. If the cure is worthless, I'll eventually change anyway; all this will do is speed up the process."

"So what you need to do is to take some blood from Matt and me so you'll be strong enough to go up against this Morpheus, is that the plan?" Shooter asked.

"That's correct."

Shooter looked at Matt and saw the pain in his eyes. "Then let's get on with it," he said.

TJ blushed and looked around the room. "I can't—I just can't do it in front of everyone," she said, her embarrassment evident.

"Matt, why don't you go into your room, and, Shooter, you go into yours? While TJ does what she has to do, I'll stay out here and go through the journal to find some clues. I'll probably bunk here."

Matt and Shooter looked at each other, shrugged, and went into their separate rooms, leaving TJ and Albert alone.

She glanced at him, apprehension on her face.

"Albert, remember what you said about feeding releasing our hormones?"

"Yes."

"What if . . . what if I can't control myself and something happens with Matt?"

"You must feel no shame, TJ. It is all part of the process we must go through to save Sam, and it will be out of your control."

"But I could never face Matt again," she protested.

"Then, if bad does come to worse, use your mental powers to cause him to forget. It is what we do when we engage in nonlethal feedings with others."

TJ got to her feet, straightened her back, and walked into the room Matt and Sam shared.

She found Matt pacing, obviously frightened and apprehensive. He looked at her with fear in his eyes. "Will it be very painful?" he asked.

She smiled and shook her head. "No, Matt. In fact, I'm going to use some psychic commands to make you relax."

He gave a weak grin. "Like mental Xanax?" he asked, referring to a popular tranquilizer.

"Why don't you take off your shirt and lie on the bed?" she asked.

He unbuttoned his shirt and removed it, laying it on a chair before he lay on the bed on his back and closed his eyes. TJ stood next to the bed and concentrated her mind, commanding him to relax and feel no fear.

His face became soft and peaceful and he smiled slightly. "Um, this is nice," he mumbled. "Kinda like the gas the dentist gives."

TJ eased down on the bed next to him and turned his face away slightly so she could get to his neck.

She felt herself begin to change as she lowered her face and gently bared her growing fangs.

When she bit into his skin over his jugular vein, he moaned softly once and stiffened slightly, then went limp as her mental commands caused him to relax once again.

As his warm, salty blood flowed into her mouth, TJ drank, feeling her face coarsen and begin to coalesce into her Vampyre persona.

Within minutes, her skin began to feel hot, then burned and itched under the influence of the hormones the feeding released into her bloodstream. Her breasts swelled and her nipples became hard; she felt her sex become wet and start to throb.

She fought the feelings, resisting the urges she was experiencing, and tried to think of Sam.

As the hormones in TJ's saliva went into Matt's body, he groaned and began to breathe heavily under their influence. His chest heaved and he moved his head back and forth, his hands moving over his chest.

Matt's eyes opened and he moved his head to look at TJ's body, pressing against him as she sucked his blood. He shifted his body slightly to the side and reached down to put his hand on her left breast, feeling the nipple press into his palm.

TJ, in spite of all her resistance, pressed her breast against his hand as her arms went around his shoulders and she pulled his neck tighter against her mouth.

They were lying on their sides now, facing each other as she fed, the length of their bodies touching. She felt him become hard as he pushed his pelvis against hers, his eyes blank and staring as he panted in desire.

When his hand slipped inside her blouse and under her bra to cup her breast, she couldn't help herself. She slid her hand down Matt's stomach and under his belt to grasp his hardness, never taking her lips off his neck.

Unaware of what he was doing, Matt released her breast and grabbed her pants, undoing the button and pushing them down onto her thighs along with her panties.

His fingers moved into her pubic hair and they both groaned as he felt her warm wetness.

She was on fire, fighting with all her might not to go any further, gasping as her hormones grew stronger.

Before she knew it, she had his pants open and his manhood exposed to her view. She held it out and was pushing her groin toward it when she finally realized what she was about to do.

With every bit of her willpower, she took her mouth off his neck and moved away from him on the bed, breathing heavily as she fought to regain control.

Matt sighed and his eyes closed when she released his neck. She gently moved his hand from inside her and placed it on his chest. With a final glance, she pulled his pants up and rearranged his clothing back to normal, trying to ignore the bulge in the front of his trousers.

Commanding him to sleep and not to remember, she refastened her bra and fixed her clothes. Then she sat on the edge of the bed and tried to get her breathing under control. As she slowly changed back into her human form, the lust for sex abated somewhat as his blood was assimilated into hers.

She stood up and sighed, stretching her arms out and smiling. She felt wonderful, refreshed and rejuvenated, as if she'd just partaken of the elixir of life itself. *Jesus,* she thought, *no wonder Morpheus and the others don't want this to end. This could become very addictive!*

She glanced at the wall between the two bedrooms, knowing Shooter was in there waiting for her. *Thank God I won't have to resist my lust with him,* she thought as she moved toward the door.

Shooter, she mused as she entered their bedroom and saw him lying on the bed, *you are in for one hell of a night!*

Forty

Jacques Chatdenuit was hungrier than he'd been in months. He'd been trying to be careful since the attempt on his life by the other Vampyre, and he'd been so careful he hadn't been able to find any suitable prey in his last three outings. Each time, just as he was about to pick someone, he'd sensed the presence of another of his kind nearby. It was almost as if they were looking for him, and he'd left without satisfying his Hunger.

Now he could feel the Hunger gnawing at him like a rat in his stomach, making him think crazy thoughts about just going up to the first woman he saw on the street and taking her right there in front of everyone.

He had to find prey and he had to find it quick. He dressed in his dark clothes and left his apartment, heading for the first nightclub he could find.

He sat at the bar, as usual, and scanned the crowd. There were several possible victims and he was about to go over to a table and try to get one to leave with him when he again thought he felt someone in his mind. Damn, he thought, not again. He was about to leave the club when two of the girls he'd been watching got up to leave.

Good, he thought. He'd just follow them out, and if the Vampyres who were trying to get into his mind followed and tried to interfere with his feeding, he'd just have to kill them, too.

He trailed the two girls for six blocks through the dark streets and was just about to make his move when they came to a parking lot. He stood in the shadows and watched as the two girls hugged each other and said good-bye.

When one of them got in her car and left, he eased toward the other one, who was sitting in her car, pawing through her purse. He leaned down and looked in.

She looked up and saw him through the window and screamed, punching the lock on the door, as if that could keep him out.

He grinned, already beginning to change, and smashed the window with his fist. He wrapped his claw around her hair, jerked her through the window, and threw her on the ground, pouncing on her like a jungle cat.

His Hunger out of control now, he slobbered, drool dripping off his fangs as he lowered his face toward the yelling girl.

Unable to stop and enjoy his conquest, he ripped her throat open and almost fainted at the delicious taste of her blood. He sucked and gulped and swallowed as it pumped in a stream into his mouth.

She was still moving feebly as he grabbed the front of her dress and prepared to rip it off and take her sexually, when he got the feeling of being watched. He felt a prickle in the back of his mind and knew there was another of his kind nearby.

"Shit," he mumbled, desire for sex momentarily replacing his Hunger for blood. He looked around, scanning the darkness, but could see no one. Still, he could feel their presence in his brain.

The girl beneath him sighed, blood bubbling

from her lips as she died, going limp in his arms. Coupling with a dead body wasn't nearly as satisfying as when they were alive and terrified. He released her and let her fall to the cement as he jumped to his feet and ran into the darkness.

Forty-one

Sam awoke with the early-morning sun shining in the window to find herself lying in Michael Morpheus's arms. They were both naked.

Her mouth had a vile aftertaste and she blushed with disgust at what she'd done the night before under the influence of feeding lust, as Morpheus called it.

He was still asleep, lying on his side with one arm under her neck and the other draped across her with his hand cupping her breast. He was softly snoring through an open mouth.

Moving as slowly as she could, she moved his hand off her breast and gently disengaged herself from his arm. She eased off the bed and tiptoed across the room to the pile of his clothes still lying on the floor where he'd thrown them.

She squatted and felt in his pockets until she found his car keys. Slipping them out of his pocket, she stood up and moved silently toward the door.

Just as she reached it, a hand with a grip like steel closed on her shoulder, making her jump and drop the keys.

"Going somewhere, Sam?" Michael asked, covering a wide yawn with his other hand.

"Uh, no," she stammered, her face flushing as she turned and found him standing right behind her, still naked. "I was just going out to the kitchen to fix us something to eat. I'm famished."

He smiled and shook his head, showing he didn't believe her for an instant. He glanced down at his car keys on the floor. "And, of course, you needed my keys for that?"

"I thought I might have to unlock the door," she said unconvincingly, for Sam was never a good liar.

"Yeah, right," he said as he brushed by her toward the kitchen. "Well, feeding like you did last night does work up an appetite. That is a good sign that your Transformation is proceeding as it should."

"Uh, aren't you going to get dressed?" she asked, unconsciously covering her breasts with her arms.

"Why, Sam?" he asked with a wide grin. "I think we've both seen everything already, haven't we?"

She blushed again at his reference to the previous night's activities.

As he prepared the coffee, he turned and asked, "How is the pain, by the way? Better this morning?"

She followed him into the kitchen, flexing her arms. "Yes, now that you mention it. Just a slight ache in my muscles, but nothing like yesterday," she answered, not quite believing she was able to carry on a normal conversation with both of them naked as jaybirds.

He turned back to the counter and got them both coffee cups out of the cupboard. "It'll come back. By this afternoon, you'll be hurting almost as bad as yesterday. You'll need to feed again tonight."

She grimaced. "Will the side effects be the same?"

He looked at her, his eyes traveling up and down her body, and she could see the conversation was having an effect on him, for he was starting to become hard. "Oh, yes, I'm afraid so, Sam. That will happen every time you feed."

She groaned. "And how long will I have to endure this torture?"

"Only a few more days, perhaps a week. The Transformation should be complete by then."

"But TJ was in a coma for weeks during her Transformation."

He nodded. "Yes, but according to the story I got from Carmilla, you and your friends rescued her after only a couple of feedings with her mate."

"Yes," Sam said, "that's true."

"Well, if he had been allowed to let her feed on him nightly, as you are going to do, the entire process would have taken only a week or slightly more."

She could see by the way his body was responding, that all of this talk of feeding was making Michael more and more excited. She looked away, trying to think of a way to change the subject, when she saw an object lying outside on the balcony. "What's that?" she asked, pointing and walking toward the sliding glass door.

He put the coffee cups down and frowned, his face becoming severe. "That, my dear, is an object lesson for you."

"Oh?" she asked.

"Yes." He opened the door to the balcony and walked outside, with her following him.

Using his foot, he pushed at the rug and it began to unroll, revealing the dead body with its head between its thighs.

"Oh, Jesus," Sam said, gagging slightly and almost throwing up at the grisly sight. "Who is that?"

"That, my dear Sam, is Carmilla de la Fontaine," Michael answered. "And now I'll show you what will happen to you if you try to escape or go against my wishes ever again."

He bent and effortlessly picked up the body, casually tossing it over the rail into the bayou below. Before the splash had died down, several ominous-looking shapes glided off the far bank and made their way toward the body. Within seconds, three alligators were tearing at the corpse, ripping it into bite-size chunks, and disappearing under the water with them in their mouths.

What was left of Carmilla slowly sank beneath the scum-covered ripples the gators had caused. Michael stepped over and kicked the head off the balcony to land next to the body. It floated there for a few moments, its sightless eyes staring up at eternity before it, too, sank out of sight.

"Christ," Sam said, even more disgusted with Michael than she was before. "Did you have to do that? Couldn't you have buried her someplace where no one would find her?"

"And you think that would be a kindness, Sam?" he asked, leaning back against the rail and folding his arms across his chest.

"Certainly better than this," she replied hotly, and stormed back into the kitchen to fix a cup of coffee to ease the taste of bile in her mouth.

He stepped in beside her. "No, you're wrong, Sam. You see, there is only one way we can be killed. That is for our head to be severed from our body, and then the body destroyed completely."

She looked at him, her eyes wide.

"It's true. If the head is merely cut off and the body left alone, it will not die and decay but will go on in some sort of weird suspended animation for decades." He reached across her and took the cup of coffee she'd just poured. "In fact, I heard of one case many years ago where just such a thing happened. A Vampyre cut off the head of one of his mate's lovers and buried the poor man in a coffin with his head under his arm. His mate snuck back and dug up the body fifteen years later and it was still lying as it had been, although I'm told the clothes were not in the best of shape."

"What happened?" Sam asked, fascinated.

He shrugged. "The story goes, the head was put back on the neck and the poor creature soon revived and was as good as new, except his mind was never quite right after that. It seems he regained some semblance of consciousness the entire fifteen years and lay there in the dark with nothing to do but dream and think."

"I don't believe it," Sam said, shaking her head.

He smiled. "I don't know if I do, either, quite, but that's the way it was told to me."

When Sam turned to fix her coffee, his smile vanished. "In any case, Sam, I meant what I said. No more escape attempts or you'll follow Carmilla into the bayou."

"Yes, sir," Sam said sarcastically through tight lips as she raised the cup and took a drink.

When the phone rang, and Michael went into the living room to answer it, Sam took another quick peek at the bayou below. Two more alligators had arrived and were fighting over the scraps left by the first three. It was a nauseating sight and she turned away and walked back into her bedroom.

Michael picked up the phone. "Yeah?" he said.

"Michael, this is Sarah. Adeline and I got lucky."

"Oh?" Michael asked.

"Yeah. Last night we were at this club, just fooling around, when I got the feeling someone was scanning the room mentally. Being real careful, I scanned back and picked up on this guy who was checking out all the ladies in the place."

"Was it the Ripper?" Michael asked, beginning to get excited.

"Oh, yeah," Sandra answered. "Finally, this guy follows these two girls out of the club and I can sense his blood lust from across the room. He was definitely on the trail, all right."

"What happened then?"

"He follows these two chicks until they get to where they parked their cars. They must've met up to go clubbing and came in separate cars. One of the girls gets in her car and takes off, and just as the other one is fixing to leave, the guy smashes his hand through the window and pulls her right out, without bothering to open the door."

"No one else was around?" Michael asked.

"Naw, it was early yet and the parking lot was deserted."

"What did he do?"

Sarah laughed. "What do you think he did? He took her right there on the cement. He must've been awfully hungry 'cause he didn't bother to play with her at all, just ripped her open and drank his fill. Hell, he didn't even stop to fuck her, just ripped, drank, and left."

"Did you follow him?"

"Of course. That's what you told us to do, wasn't it?"

"Yeah. So you found out where he lives?"

"Yes. Matter of fact, I'm parked right down the street from his place now. I took Adeline home to get some sleep and I came back here. What do you want me to do?"

"Go get him and bring him to me at the bayou house."

"What if he doesn't want to come?"

Michael thought for a moment. "Don't force it, but let him know he's in no danger from us and that we have a proposition for him that he'll want to hear about."

"You got it. We'll be there shortly."

Chief William P. Boudreaux picked up his phone and told Sergeant Bo Deveraux to come into his office.

Moments later, a man wearing a porkpie hat and a checked coat too small for him appeared in the doorway.

"Yeah, Chief?" Deveraux asked as he entered and took a seat in front of Boudreaux's desk.

Boudreaux stared at Deveraux's clothes for a moment, wondering if the man had any color sense at all. "Bo, you been able to find those folks I had you tailin' the other day?"

Deveraux's face colored and he cleared his throat, his eyes shifting around the room, looking everywhere but at his boss. "Uh, no, sir. Like I told you yesterday, they checked outta their hotel, an' none of the other hotels in town have them listed."

"Any word yet on the BOL?"

"Uh-uh," Deveraux answered. "It's like they just dropped outta sight. None of the officers on the street have spotted 'em."

"And you think they ditched you on purpose?" Boudreaux asked, chewing on the end of a pencil.

"Yeah, Chief. One minute they're all eatin' lunch and the next they've split up, goin' in all different directions. So I stationed myself by the elevator to wait for them to come down. Like I told you, when the two men came out an' got in a cab, I found somebody had stuck a knife in my tire so's I couldn't go after 'em."

Boudreaux snorted in disgust. "Deveraux, I swear you're useless as tits on a boar hog!"

"I tell ya, it wasn't my fault, Chief," Deveraux whined. "They musta known I was on their tail an' flattened my tire."

"And just how did they know you were following them?" Boudreaux asked pointedly.

"Jeez, I dunno."

"It couldn't be those fucking clothes you're wearing, could it, Bo? Jesus Christ, when you tail someone you're supposed to fit in with the crowd so they won't see you."

Deveraux looked down at his jacket. "What do you mean?"

"The only crowd you'd fit in with would be at a circus, Bo," Boudreaux said disgustedly. "Until we hear from our friends or someone finds them, I want you to go on over to that elementary school on Franklin Avenue. I want you to pick out a couple of first graders and see if you can manage to follow them home. It'll be good practice for you."

"Uh, any particular kids you want followed?" Deveraux asked.

Boudreaux shook his head, his face turning red. "I was just kidding, to make a point, Bo. Now get the fuck out of my office and try to stay out of my sight until we find our visiting tourists! There's been another Ripper killing and I want to talk to them about those contacts they supposedly have."

Forty-two

TJ woke up feeling better than she had in months. She had none of the minor aches and pains she'd gotten used to since her partial Transformation, and her mind seemed to be clearer and more focused than it had in ages.

In fact, all of her senses seemed to be stronger and more acute. Her nose wrinkled at the smell of stale sweat, and the odor of their lovemaking the previous night hung in the air like a fog.

She bounced out of bed and went into the bathroom to shower and get dressed.

Shooter, awakened by her movements, sat up in bed and held his head. He felt tired, drained, and listless. His mouth was dry and cottony and tasted as if the entire Chinese army had washed its tennis shoes out in it.

He stumbled out of bed and walked slowly into the bathroom. He could see TJ's naked body through the glass shower door, a sight that usually filled him with desire. But not this morning. Not after their marathon lovemaking last night. He was sore and achy, and all he wanted was to brush his teeth and get some coffee down him. Maybe that would perk him up.

The sounds of stirring in the adjacent bedroom brought Albert fully awake on the couch in the living room. He hadn't slept well. The sounds of TJ and Shooter's raucous sexual exploits brought back too many painful memories of when he'd been the recipient of her desire.

He got to his feet and went into the kitchen to make some coffee and try to erase the images of TJ's face when they'd made love in his Houston lair.

Within half an hour, all four of them were gathered around the kitchen table drinking coffee and eating stale doughnuts from the pantry.

Matt and Shooter looked wan and weak. Albert hoped TJ hadn't taken too much of their blood in her excitement at feeding after so long a time of abstinence.

"I had some success going through Carmilla's journal last night," he told them while they ate.

"Did you get an address for Morpheus?" Shooter asked in a tired voice.

"Better than that," Albert replied. "Her journal is made like a day-planner notebook. There's a journal part in the front for making notes, and an address book in the back. I was able to find the full names for Sarah and Jean, and all of their addresses. She even had their home and cell phone numbers listed."

"That's good," Matt said sarcastically, his voice weak and thready. "Now we can just call them up and ask them to please bring Sam home."

Albert looked at him and decided to ignore the sarcasm after what Matt had been through last night.

"Only as a last resort," Albert said. "If they're not in their homes and we can't find them, we may have to use your police contacts to trace their cell phones. That will at least tell us which part of the city to search."

Shooter shook his head. "I doubt that the police will want to help us out, not after we ditched their tail and didn't report back to Boudreaux like we said we would."

"That brings up a point," TJ said. "Do you think we should let the police know about Sam? Maybe they can locate this Morpheus faster than we can."

Albert shook his head. "Not a good idea, TJ. If they did manage to find his hideout and went in with guns blazing, they wouldn't stand a chance of getting Morpheus and they might get Sam in the cross fire."

"So I guess it's just us," Matt said.

Albert agreed. "That's right. However, if TJ and I fail and Morpheus and his friends somehow beat us, then you and Shooter will have no choice but to go to the police and try to get them to believe your story."

Shooter snorted. "Hah. Fat chance!" he said. "I can see it now, us talking to Boudreaux. 'Hey, Chief. There's this band of renegade Vampyres running around your city sucking the blood out of your citizens and, by the way, they've kidnapped our friend. Would you help us get her back?'"

Albert shrugged. "You're right, Shooter, it won't be easy. That's why TJ and I won't fail. We'll get Sam back, I promise."

"And what are Shooter and I supposed to do while you two go off to find her? Sit here on our thumbs?" Matt asked.

"No," Albert replied. "We'll keep in touch with you by cell phone and let you know every step of the way what we find out. Once we've located Morpheus's hideout, we'll tell you exactly where it is."

"I still think I ought to go with you," Shooter protested, sulking.

TJ put her hand on his shoulder. "No, sweetheart. Like Albert says, we need you here where you can call in the cavalry if we aren't able to rescue Sam. Her life will be in your hands if we don't succeed."

Albert pushed a piece of paper across the table to Shooter. "Here are the names and addresses I got from Carmilla's journal. The Sarah she referred to is Sarah Kenyon, and the Jean must be Jean Horla. According to her journal, Sarah lives with another female, Adeline Ducayne. That should give you all you need to get the police going if it becomes necessary."

"OK," Shooter said, reading the paper, "but I still don't like it."

TJ and Albert got to their feet. "We'll keep in touch, babe," she said to him. "So keep your cell phone handy."

When they got in Albert's car, he turned to TJ. "How do you feel after your feeding last night?"

"Wonderful!" she said. "I feel so alive. It's as if I'm ten years younger and full of pep and energy."

He smiled, looking at her. She looked great, with a slight flush on her face and her skin radiant and glowing. "That's good, because we're going to need you at full strength when we go up against the others."

"What are we going to do first?" she asked.

"I've got to stop by my place and pick up a few things we're going to need, and I need to get some nourishment, too. I haven't fed for almost a week and I'm starting to show signs of weakness and hunger."

Her brow knitted. "Uh, how exactly do you plan to feed?"

He grinned. "Don't worry. I don't have some young female waiting to let me suck her blood. I have a supply of test tubes full of samples I've taken from patients over the last few months. I'll use that to get up to speed."

"Oh," she said, relieved.

When they got to his apartment, he took her into the spare bedroom where he had a small refrigerator in a closet. He opened it and took out a rack of test tubes. One by one, he opened them and drank their contents until the rack was empty.

She noticed his face becoming flushed and his body beginning to change slightly into his Vampyre form as he drank. She was also able to pick up the emotional changes the feeding caused, including his increasing sexual desire.

She noticed him glancing at her, lust building in his eyes as he examined her body, staring at her breasts and legs as he drank.

"Are you going to be all right?" she asked, blushing under his ardent gaze.

He took a deep breath. "I'm sorry, TJ, but as you can see, even this sterile form of feeding makes the hormones flow. I'll be OK in a minute, just let me get it under control."

Evidently, their strong mental bond caused TJ to respond to Albert's desire, for she felt herself becoming increasingly lustful, too. She cleared her throat and turned away, walking out of the bedroom and into his living room. "I'll, uh, I'll wait for you out here, Albert," she said, fighting the feelings and trying to think of the job ahead.

After a few minutes, Albert followed and seemed to have his emotions under control. He led her into his bedroom and opened his closet. He took out a pair of long swords in scabbards and handed them to her. "Here," he said as he rummaged deeper in the closet.

"What are these?" she asked, examining the swords.

"Those are called *katana,* Japanese long swords," he replied as he pulled a couple of one-gallon cans of gasoline from the closet.

"They're razor sharp and are excellent for removing heads." He pointed at the cans. "The gasoline is for after, to make sure the bodies stay dead."

"Do you really think it'll come to this?" she asked, a look of distaste on her face.

He nodded, his face serious. "Absolutely. Just remember Carmilla's room when you get to thinking we can reason with these creatures. This has gone far beyond the talking stage. We have to consider we are at war with these people, and we can't afford to think we can reason with them or take prisoners. This will be a fight to the death: ours . . . or theirs."

They loaded the equipment in the car, putting the gasoline in the trunk but keeping the swords in the backseat within easy reach.

Once they were ready, Albert drove to the address listed for Michael Morpheus in Carmilla's journal. He parked the car in front of the house and looked. The yard had several newspapers piled on the front porch and appeared deserted.

"It looks like he hasn't been here for several days," TJ said.

Albert agreed. "Looks like the next stop is Sarah and Adeline's place." He looked at her. "Let's hope they're home."

Sarah and Adeline lived in a small house in a suburb of New Orleans called Oak Forest. It was a typical middle-class community, with small homes, sidewalks, and not an oak tree in sight.

Albert pulled the car a couple of houses down

and parked it. He took one of the swords and handed another to TJ.

"Remember, keep your thoughts locked down tight. Vampyres can read your intentions as well as emotions, and that's a definite disadvantage in a confrontation."

TJ nodded and held the sword tight against her leg as they approached the house. "You ring the doorbell to get their attention and I'll enter through the rear while you keep them occupied at the door," he told her.

She walked up to the porch and he disappeared around the side of the house. She rang the bell and waited, trying to keep her mind blank.

The door opened a little and a young woman with tousled hair and a face puffy with sleep peered through the crack. "Yeah, what do you want?" she asked, covering a yawn with the back of her hand.

"Are you Sarah Kenyon?" TJ asked, holding the *katana* out of sight.

"No," the woman answered, her expression becoming suspicious as she looked TJ up and down. "What do you want with Sarah?"

"Then you must be Adeline," TJ said, stalling for time.

"Hey, don't I know you?" Adeline asked harshly.

Before TJ could answer, Adeline was jerked out of sight. She uttered a soft scream as Albert grabbed her and threw her bodily up against a wall.

TJ quickly entered the house, shutting and locking the door behind her.

Albert was holding Adeline by the hair, her feet dangling a foot off the floor, the sword in his other hand with the blade against her neck. "Check the rest of the house," he ordered TJ without taking his eyes off Adeline.

TJ slipped the sword out of its scabbard and held it in front of her as she quickly looked in all the other rooms.

"It's clear," she called, returning to the living room.

Adeline, her face screwed up in pain and her hands on Albert's trying to get loose, began to Transform.

"Stop," Albert commanded in a harsh voice, "or I'll take your head off now!"

Staring at Albert through hate-filled eyes, Adeline stopped her Transformation.

"What do you want?" she asked, her voice now whining. "Sarah's not here."

"We don't want Sarah," Albert said, squeezing her neck until her face started to turn blue. "We're looking for Michael Morpheus."

"I don't know any Michael . . . ," Adeline began, until Albert reversed the sword and hit her between the eyes with the metal hilt.

Her head bounced back off the wall and an ugly blue bruise began to appear on her forehead.

Adeline's eyes crossed momentarily and she almost passed out from the pain.

Albert jerked her downward and threw her flat on her back on the hardwood floor, bouncing her head again.

"He—he'll kill me," she wailed, no longer resisting his hold on her as her eyes flitted back and forth between TJ and Albert.

"Don't worry about Michael," Albert said in a nasty, cruel voice. "Worry about what I'm going to do to you if you don't tell us where he is."

"He's at his bayou house," she said, going limp and giving up. "Sarah went there to meet him."

"How many of you are there with him?" Albert

said, slightly relaxing his hold on her neck so she could talk.

"Sarah called and said she was taking the Ripper there to meet with him, so I guess there's just the three of them," Adeline croaked, her voice hoarse from the stranglehold Albert had on her.

Albert glanced over his shoulder at TJ at the mention of the Ripper. This greatly increased the odds against them. "How do you know the Ripper?" he asked.

"We followed him last night after one of his kills," Adeline said.

"Where does he live?" Albert asked.

Adeline gave them an address in the French Quarter. *Jesus*, Albert thought with astonishment, *that's only a couple of blocks from my house.*

"How do we get to this bayou house?" he asked.

Adeline hesitated and Albert squeezed again, making her gag with pain. "You go out the interstate toward Liberty. Take the first right after the city limits sign. It's a dirt road and it'll take you right to his house."

He put the blade against her throat. "If you're lying to me, I'll come back here and kill you," he said.

"I'm not lying . . . I swear it!" she pleaded, her eyes wide with fright.

"Open your mind to me now!" Albert commanded, leaning so close his lips were almost on hers.

She closed her eyes and her face relaxed as she did as he ordered. After a moment, Albert leaned back. He glanced at TJ. "She's telling the truth."

"Good," TJ said, "let's go."

Albert grinned and TJ saw him begin to change. "Not just yet," he growled, looking up at her.

"There are three of them there, TJ. We need an edge."

"What do you mean?" she asked.

He turned his attention back to Adeline, who was staring at him through fear-widened eyes. With a lightning-fast motion, he grabbed the front of her nightgown and ripped it from her body, exposing her sweating, heaving breasts.

Now fully into Transformation, Albert buried his face in Adeline's neck and chewed through the skin, beginning to feed on her as she writhed beneath him, again attempting her own Transformation.

The sight of him feeding caused TJ to change, too. She dropped the sword she was holding and dropped to her knees beside Adeline as her fangs grew and her face melted into her Vampyre form.

With a growl deep in her throat, TJ fastened her fangs on the other side of Adeline's neck and began to drink.

While she held Adeline down with her claws on the girl's shoulders, Albert moved back and quickly shed his clothes. TJ could see out of the corner of her eye that he was fully erect. He stroked himself with his hand as he got between Adeline's thighs and pushed them aside.

TJ stopped feeding and looked at him in astonishment.

"I'm sorry, TJ," Albert growled in an almost unrecognizable voice. "It has been so long. . . ."

TJ understood. She nodded as he rammed his penis into Adeline, making her raise her hips off the floor as she screamed in pain. Albert fastened one claw on her breast as he pumped into her and lowered his head to feed again.

His excitement was transmitted to TJ, whose own feeding was arousing her, too. She bent her head down next to Albert's and also fed. After a moment, while he was still moving inside Adeline, he raised his face and moved it across Adeline's chest toward TJ. She looked up and saw him staring at her, and then she kissed him, their tongues touching and her arm went around him, pulling him toward her.

Adeline, almost drained of her entire blood supply, fainted and went limp beneath Albert.

TJ released Albert's lips, took a final drink of Adeline, and then pulled her clothes off. She lay back on the floor, her nipples erect and her sex throbbing.

Albert pulled himself out of Adeline and moved over to lie next to TJ, his hand caressing her breast as he kissed her again.

"Are you sure?" he asked, his voice hoarse with desire.

TJ pulled him on top of her. "I'm sure," she said in an equally husky voice.

When he entered her, they both howled in pleasure, her claws drawing blood from his back.

Later, satiated, they got dressed and stood over the unconscious Adeline. Albert took the sword and handed it to TJ.

She hesitated; then with a vicious swipe, she cut off Adeline's head.

Albert went to the car and brought back one of the cans of gasoline. He poured it over the body, dropped a match on it, and they walked to the car as flames began to lick at the windows of the house.

As he started the car, he took TJ's hand. "That was the edge we needed," he explained. "A fresh feeding will give us the strength we need to take them all out and save Sam."

Forty-three

Sam was dozing on her bed, depressed and dispirited at the way things were going. She knew Matt and the others would be looking for her, but with Carmilla dead and eaten by the alligators, she realized they would have no way of finding her.

Tears of frustration were rolling down her cheeks when she heard a knocking at the front door. She quickly wiped her eyes and eased her door open, peering through the crack. After the gruesome Carmilla show-and-tell, Michael felt she could be trusted to stay put.

She saw a husky, tough-looking woman enter, followed by one of the most handsome men she'd ever seen. Even from across the room, Sam could see his startlingly blue eyes as they surveyed the house and finally fixed on Morpheus.

Michael, dressed now, stretched his hand out and smiled. "You must be this Ripper we've all been hearing so much about," he said.

After a slight hesitation, and with some wariness, the man took Michael's hand and shook it. "I prefer my own name, Jacques Chatdenuit," he said in a soft, mellow voice.

Morpheus inclined his head at the woman. "Obviously, you've already met Sarah. My name is Michael Morpheus."

Chatdenuit let go of Morpheus's hand and walked around the room, looking it over. After a moment, he walked out on the balcony, his eyebrows rising when the alligators, seeing him, glided off the far bank and swam out into the middle of the bayou, obviously expecting another feeding.

He smiled, and his face went from being handsome to something far more evil. "Quite a place you have here. Very isolated."

Michael chuckled as he joined him on the balcony. He waved his hands wide, indicating the circling gators below. "And it even comes with its own garbage disposal."

Chatdenuit glanced below, and Michael added, "Quite handy to get rid of leftovers, if you know what I mean."

Chatdenuit actually laughed, while Sam, watching and listening now through her window, shuddered.

Chatdenuit stiffened and raised his nose to the air, sniffing. He glared at Morpheus, suspicion on his face. "I sense another presence, one that is not one of us."

Morpheus waved a hand in dismissal. "That's only my mate. She is in the middle of the Rite of Transformation. She is of no concern to you at the present."

Sam almost gagged at the mention of the word "mate." Did Morpheus actually think she would consider being his mate, no matter what he did to her or what she became? She was sickened by the very idea.

"OK," Chatdenuit said, moving back into the house, "you've shown me your little getaway in the woods and we've had a nice chat." He took a seat at the kitchen table, leaned back, and crossed his arms, looking from Sarah to Michael. "Now, why did you bring me out here?"

Michael pulled out a chair for Sarah, and after she took a seat, he sat across the table from Chatdenuit. "To make you an offer I hope you won't refuse."

Chatdenuit snorted, a smile of amusement on his face. "An offer?" he asked. "What kind of offer?"

"First let me give you some background on the situation here, Jacques," Michael said. "Are you aware there are quite a few of our kind living in and around New Orleans?"

Chatdenuit shrugged. "I've run across a few of our race occasionally, but I'm a loner, Michael. I prefer to go my own way." He gave a short laugh. "Besides, from what I've gathered from the few Vampyres I've met locally, they're all namby-pamby types who don't believe in killing Normals." His lips curled in a snide smirk. "And that's something I've grown quite fond of recently."

Michael returned the smile. "You are right in your assessment of the local members of our race, at least that used to be the case." He leaned forward. "I've just taken over leadership of our Council and the rules are about to change. I, like you, have always felt Normals are our legitimate prey, put on earth to serve as food and enjoyment for us, the superior race."

Chatdenuit pursed his lips, a thoughtful gleam in his eyes. "So the rest of you are going to start feeding in earnest, as I've been doing?"

Michael nodded. "Yes, and that brings up an interesting problem."

"What problem?" Chatdenuit asked, grinning. "There must be a million people in New Orleans. Plenty to go around, I'd say."

"The problem is, when Normals start dropping like flies, with their throats ripped out and drained of all their blood, sooner or later the local authorities are going to realize they're not dealing with common serial killers and the hunt will be on for us."

"Yes," Chatdenuit agreed, "that can be a problem. I've always solved it by moving on when the heat got too high."

"That's no longer a practical solution, what with the computers and instantaneous communication between law enforcement agencies," Michael said.

"So what's your solution?" Chatdenuit asked.

"Two things," Michael answered. "First, we feed only on the lower strata of society: prostitutes, pimps, criminals, homeless people. Persons the police don't spend a lot of time over if they turn up missing." He hesitated. "And we stay strictly away from tourists and regular citizens like you've been targeting."

"But they're the most fun to track," Chatdenuit argued.

"They're also the ones the police get most excited about when they disappear," Michael shot back.

"OK, point taken," Chatdenuit agreed. "What's the second thing?"

Michael waved his hand, pointing out the window. "New Orleans is surrounded by over a million acres of swamp land that contains thousands of hungry garbage disposals like I have out my back door. My proposal is simple: We feed on the dregs of society, taking all we want. When we're done, we make sure the bodies are never found. Either by dumping them here, or finding other places of a similar nature to use."

Chatdenuit laughed, glancing out the back door

to the balcony. "Jesus, if we do that, your scaly friends out there are going to get mighty fat."

"That's the beauty of it," Michael said. "We get fat, the gators get fat, and the cops get zip for evidence."

"And what's this offer you were speaking of?" Chatdenuit asked, still grinning.

"I want you to join our Council and become an active member, abiding by the rules I've just set out."

Chatdenuit frowned. "Why should I do that, Michael? I've already told you I'm not much of a joiner."

"Because if you don't, we can't allow you to stay here and feed in our territory," Michael explained, his face going hard. "You're a wild card, Jacques, and by your irresponsible actions, you're bringing down too much attention on us."

"What, so you're giving me until sundown to get out of town, like some old Western?" Chatdenuit asked, smirking.

Michael shrugged. "That's about the size of it."

"And if I don't agree to this offer?"

"Then we will kill you," Michael said, smiling back at Chatdenuit without any humor in his eyes.

Chatdenuit laughed. "What makes you think you can kill me?"

Michael's smile died and his eyes grew cold as ice. "We found you once, Jacques, and we can find you again. Even Vampyres have to sleep, my friend. And if you don't agree to join us, or if you break the rules, one night you'll go to sleep and you'll wake up swimming with my friends down there, minus your head."

As Chatdenuit stared at him, Michael leaned back and smiled, spreading his arms. "But then again—

why can't we just all be friends, to paraphrase Rod-
ney King. You'll be giving up nothing by joining us,
Jacques, and the benefits you'll get will be many.
What have you got to lose?"

Chatdenuit pursed his lips, considering what Michael said. After a moment, he nodded. "You're
right. What have I got to lose?"

"Great," Michael said, reaching across the table
to shake Chatdenuit's hand. "Welcome aboard."

As Chatdenuit took Michael's hand, Michael said,
"Why don't we take a little nap, and later we'll head
on out and see if we can't round up a couple of
interesting guests for a little party tonight?"

"That sounds good," Chatdenuit said. "I didn't
get much sleep last night."

"So I heard," Michael said with a laugh. He
looked at Sarah. "Sarah, why don't you show Jacques to a bedroom and I'll go see to my guest."

When Michael went into Sam's room, he found
her doubled up in pain on her bed, her arms
crossed around her abdomen and her knees pulled
up to her chest.

He lay on the bed next to her and wrapped his
arms around her. "Has the pain returned?" he
asked, gently nuzzling the back of her neck with his
lips.

She nodded, unable to speak through her gritted
teeth.

"Would you like to feed again?" he asked. "It'll
help ease the pain."

She shook her head violently and turned to face
him. "I can't believe what I just heard," she said
through dry, cracked lips.

"What do you mean?"

"You sat there, calmly talking about treating people like cattle to be used as food for you and your friends."

Michael seemed surprised at her statement. "But, Sam, that's exactly what the Normals are. The Vampyres are the dominant species and it is only right for us to feed upon lesser beings."

"Yesterday, you were so kind to me, I thought maybe you'd changed," she said bitterly.

He reached a hand up and stroked her cheek. "I have changed, Sam. I've fallen in love with you. Otherwise, why would I make you my mate?"

She jerked her head back and turned over, putting her back to him. "I'll never be your mate, Michael. I'd rather die first."

He sighed. "You'll change your mind, Sam. You'll be one of us shortly and things will look different to you then."

"Never!" she said, and closed her eyes, groaning as the pain intensified.

Michael smiled. He knew it wouldn't be long until she was his, forever.

Forty-four

While Albert drove, TJ got on the cell phone and called Shooter.

"Hello," Shooter said, his voice betraying his anxiety.

"Shooter, it's TJ."

"What's going on, babe?" he asked. "Are you all right?"

"Yes. We found Adeline Ducayne at her house and she told us where Michael Morpheus is staying." She went on to give him the directions to Morpheus's bayou house. "We're on our way there now. We also found out the Ripper's address," she added, giving him that one, too. "Albert suggested you call the police and give them a heads-up on the Ripper. If they go there, they might find some evidence to link him to the killings."

"Is he there now?" Shooter asked.

"No, we think he's at Morpheus's place, along with the woman named Sarah."

"Damn!" Shooter said, alarm in his voice. "That makes it three to two. Maybe Matt and I should come with you to help out."

"No, Albert thinks we can handle it. We'll have the element of surprise, and this is the safest way for Sam."

"All right, but be careful, darling."

"I will. If you don't hear from us within a couple of hours, call the police and give them the address."

"OK."

"And, Shooter . . ."

"Yeah, babe?"

"I love you."

"Me too, sweetheart. I love you."

Dusk was falling when they pulled into the dirt road leading to Morpheus's house. Albert stopped the car well down the road so they wouldn't hear the engine. He took the two swords from the rear seat, handed one to TJ, and got out of the car. "We'll leave the gasoline and come back for it later."

"How should we handle it?" TJ asked. "Sneak in or go for broke?"

"Let's get a little closer to the house and I'll try and scan the premises with my mind. With any luck, they won't be expecting an attack and their minds will be open."

Crouching and moving slowly as the air around them darkened with coming night, they crept toward the house, holding their swords ready before them.

When they were twenty yards from the house, Albert held up his hand and stopped; he was concentrating his mind on the occupants within the cabin. TJ tried, too, but she was too new to get much more than garbled thought patterns.

After a moment, Albert turned to her and whispered. "I sense the thoughts of three Vampyres, and another, different one who must be Sam. Two of them are in the front of the house, off to the right of the door, and the other is in the rear of the house."

"What do you want to do?" she asked.

He grinned and she could see him turning into his Vampyre form. "We go in like gangbusters! As soon as I hit the door, you follow me in, sword ready, and turn to the right. We'll try and take out the first two before the third can join them."

TJ nodded.

"And TJ," he added as his face melted into a grotesque parody of a human, "show no mercy. If you hesitate, even for a second, we're dead!"

"Don't worry," she said, breathing hard as she began her Transformation. "I've seen what these bastards can do."

When she was finished changing into a Vampyre, Albert nodded and ran toward the house. He took the steps in a single bound and lowered his shoulder as he hit the wooden door, tearing it off its hinges as it shattered.

TJ was right behind him and moved to his right just as a woman came running from a bedroom down the hall. She was screaming and Transforming, her hands held clawlike in front of her, her fangs bared and dripping red drool.

TJ moved like lightning. Holding the sword in front of her, she took two quick steps toward the shrieking woman and ran her through, the *katana* entering just beneath her rib cage and exiting beneath her right shoulder blade.

Albert, who'd stumbled as he smashed the door, glanced up in time to see another Vampyre, this one completely Transformed, leap high into the air to come down on top of him, knocking the sword from his hands.

As Albert and Chatdenuit rolled on the floor, snapping and clawing at each other like two pit bulls in a dogfight, TJ tried to pull the sword out of the writhing, screeching female. The sword was imbedded in her breastbone, and the Vampyre had her claws wrapped around the blade so tight her fingers were almost severed by the razor-sharp edge of the sword.

Seconds later, Morpheus sprinted from the back bedroom, changing as he ran, his wolflike face a mask of hate and fury. Sam was right behind him, her eyes wide with terror as she ran into the living room.

Morpheus slowed enough to take in the situation, and then he quickly moved toward where Albert and Chatdenuit were struggling on the floor. He saw the sword off to the side and bent to pick it up, his savage grin exposing two-inch-long fangs.

Sam, just able to recognize Albert and TJ in their Vampyre forms, looked around for a weapon, anything she could use to help her friends. She saw a wooden block containing a set of knives on the kitchen counter and quickly jerked out the one with the thickest handle.

As Morpheus stood over Albert and Chatdenuit, the sword raised above his head for a killing blow, Sam screamed and ran up to him. She plunged the butcher knife up to its hilt between his shoulder blades.

Morpheus yelled and dropped the sword as he turned, his eyes wide at Sam's betrayal, his claws scrabbling behind his back as he tried to pull the knife out.

TJ finally put her right foot on the woman's chest and pushed, pulling the sword free. In one deft movement, she swung it like a baseball bat and grimaced as blood spurted onto her face when the blade severed the head from the body.

TJ whirled and took a step toward the straining Morpheus, the sword held high. When he saw her coming at him, death in her hands, he whirled and ran, crashing through the sliding-glass door of the balcony and diving over the rail toward the bayou below.

Albert finally managed to get his teeth into Chatdenuit's neck. He bit down on his windpipe and whipped his head back and forth, tearing the Vampyre's neck out.

When Chatdenuit rolled off Albert, his hands grabbing at his ruined neck, TJ calmly stepped over and finished the job, chopping downward with the sword like a hatchet and cutting his head off clean.

Sam knelt by Albert, holding him and trying to stop the bleeding from the many wounds Chatdenuit's claws and fangs had inflicted on his face and arms.

TJ, still breathing hard, walked to the balcony and saw the gators gliding toward Morpheus, who was trying to swim to the shore, the knife still sticking out of his back.

When Morpheus saw the gators coming toward him, he took a deep breath and dived beneath the surface . . . and was gone, leaving only a blood-tinged ripple behind.

Once Sam and TJ got bandages wrapped around the worst of Albert's wounds, Sam found a robe in Michael's closet and slipped it on, covering her nakedness.

The three friends sat on the couch and tried to regain their breath, watching the two bodies on the floor to make sure they didn't move.

TJ turned to Sam. "Are you all right?" she asked, smiling grimly.

Sam nodded, the skin of her face stretched tight against the pain she was still feeling. "I am now," she said, though her eyes were clouded with agony.

Albert, one hand still holding together the edges of the gash in his right cheek, croaked, "TJ, after you call Shooter, would you get the gasoline from my car, please?"

Forty-five

A week later, after Sam, TJ, and Albert had started their treatments with the serum Dr. Wingate had sent, Shooter and Matt were called to Chief Boudreaux's office for a conference.

They took seats across from his desk while he leaned back in his chair, staring at them through narrowed eyes. "Shooter," he said, a slight grin on his lips, "I don't know whether to kiss you or arrest you."

Shooter looked at Matt and laughed. "Chief, I hope those aren't my only two choices."

"I wanted to give you both a follow-up on the situation, since what you're going to read in the papers ain't exactly the whole truth."

"It never is in cases like this, Chief," Shooter said.

"After you called and told us the story your source told you, we went to check out the addresses you gave us. The house in Oak Forest had burned to the ground, but we did find a female body inside, one that had its head cut off."

Shooter didn't reply, but just continued staring at Boudreaux.

"We also checked out the antique shop in the French Quarter, the one where you said your source, Carmilla de la Fontaine, lived. We found evidence of a murder, lots of blood but no body."

Shooter looked at Matt. "Oh, no. The cult must have gotten to her," he said, a look of sadness on his face.

"Speaking of this so-called cult, we did go to that cabin out on Bayou Road, and guess what we found?"

Both Shooter and Matt shook their heads. "I have no idea, Chief," Shooter said. Matt remained quiet.

We found two more bodies, a male and a female, both burned beyond recognition and both with their heads cut off."

"Jesus," Shooter said, his face a mask of astonishment.

"Also, when our crime-scene guys checked out the bayou and surrounding area, we found piles of human bones and skulls around. They'd been chewed on by the gators in the area."

"Gosh, Chief," Shooter said. "Maybe that's where all those missing people ended up."

Boudreaux shook his head in disbelief. "As if you didn't know!"

Shooter put on his most sincere face. "Chief, I told you before. Our contact, Carmilla de la Fontaine, told us that she was a member of a secret cult who believed they were vampires, and that they were responsible for all the killings and missing persons you've had lately. As soon as she told us this, we gave you all the information we had."

"Yeah," Boudreaux said. "I'll bet."

"What about the other guy whose name and address we gave you?" Matt asked. "Jean Horla?"

"That's as strange as all the other bullshit you've been feeding me. When we went to pick him up, he did a rabbit on us; one of the SWAT guys swears he put a full clip into him at point-blank range. He says the guy never slowed down."

"So you didn't get him?" Shooter asked.

"No, and the computers tell us there is not, and *never* has been, anyone with that name anywhere in the county."

"Jeez," Shooter said, "imagine that."

"The good news is," Boudreaux added, "when we searched that house in the French Quarter where the man known as Jacques Chatdenuit lived, we found enough evidence from various victims stashed there to identify him as the Ripper."

Shooter smiled and spread his hands. "Then I take it the case is closed?"

Boudreaux leaned forward, a half smile on his face. "Yeah, the case is closed. But, Shooter, the next time you and Matt want to take your girlfriends on a vacation, please pick another town!"

Six weeks later, they were all back at work in Houston. Sam and TJ were still undergoing treatments with the serum, and so far their blood remained clear of the Vampyre bug. Albert had written to say he seemed to be doing OK, too, and he hadn't had a drop of human blood since the treatments began. He wrote further that it was worth giving up virtual immortality in order to be human once again.

One Saturday night, Matt was awakened by a phone call. He switched on the bedside lamp and picked up the phone. "Yes, Dr. Carter here," he said, stifling a yawn.

Heavy breathing for a moment, and then a deep voice said, "Tell Sam I forgive her for betraying me. But it is not over. She is still my mate and one night I will come for her. Tell her to be ready!"

Matt slammed the phone down and looked over

at Sam. She was smiling slightly in her sleep, and he noticed a trace of scarlet on her lips. Without thinking, he put his fingers to his neck. When he pulled them away, they were covered with blood.

Sam stirred beside him. When she opened her eyes, there was a glint of amusement; smiling up at him, she slowly licked his blood off her lips.

He opened his mouth to scream. . . .

Look for
James M. Thompson's
next vampire novel

Coming in July 2003
from Pinnacle Books!

Feel the Seduction of Pinnacle Horror

When Darkness Falls
Grab One of These
Pinnacle Horrors